THE TREES HAVE GOATS

THE TREES HAVE GOATS

A Story of Arab Women's Struggle for Love

JOHN BARBER

Editor:

Cheryl A. Ricker

RESOURCE *Publications* · Eugene, Oregon

THE TREES HAVE GOATS
A Story of Arab Women's Struggle for Love

Wipf & Stock
An Imprint of Wipf and Stock Publishers
199 W. 8th Ave., Suite 3
Eugene, OR 97401

www.wipfandstock.com

PAPERBACK ISBN: 978-1-6667-3058-6
HARDCOVER ISBN: 978-1-6667-2228-4
EBOOK ISBN: 978-1-6667-2229-1

To the women

≈ ≈ ≈

"...for it is the fate of a woman
Long to be patient and silent, to wait like a ghost that is speechless,
Till some questioning "voice dissolves the spell of its silence.
Hence is the inner life of so many suffering women
Sunless and silent and deep, like subterranean rivers
Running through caverns of darkness..."

— Henry Wadsworth Longfellow

Preface

My path toward writing this novel has been incremental. Gender-based violence and assault against women in the American home where it is found was something of which I had only cursory knowledge. It was when I went on the mission field in Kenya and Uganda that I became more aware of higher rates of abuse. I became even more aware of the problem of domestic violence while in India. When my travels took me to Rwanda and the Democratic Republic of Congo, the path of abuse many women trod in cultures largely indebted to tribal ways of life stunned me. It was when I began traveling several Arab nations that my eyes were fully opened to the severity of gendered violence.

Much of the Middle East and North Africa, or MENA, which this novel is limited to in its observations, maintains a repository of values and ways of life effecting women that would shock most westerners. The travails of women vary from place to place: Tunisia, where liberties have seen some advance to Libya and Saudi Arabia, where severe subjugation is practiced.

But awareness, even acute awareness, is not always a catalyst to action. What made me write a novel on the mistreatment of women in the MENA region? I wrote it because I believe the gospel. Whereas the first man, Adam, failed to stand in the gap for his bride, Jesus Christ loved and died for his bride—the church. Central to the gospel message is this tender and enduring love between God and his people. And so, to see and to hear the cries of the women under the duress of unloving subordination, which has been my intensive study now for several years, was not something I could keep tucked away in my consciousness any longer.

Even though this is a work of literary fiction, it contains many interviews I did with women in Morocco, Tunisia, and Algeria, about the maltreatment they have suffered. Except for light editing, the interviews you will read are untouched. These are the voices of real Arab women. The names and places are changed. I only wish I could have included all of the over two dozen women, some of which spoke to me in tears.

I'll never forget the plea of one woman after I asked if she would sit for questions. "Can you help us?" That is my question for the reader. Can you help us? This novel is a call to action. I am a writer, teacher, academic, and missionary. That is where my expertise ends. Many of you have other sets of skills and vision, which you can bring to help us end gendered violence against women wherever it is found.

It is to this end that this book is committed.

John Barber

Chapter 1

A clickity-clack pierced the dry, coolish air. When I stretched my neck to see what was happening, the sound became distinguishable as bites and scuffs along the walkway. The jangle then reverberated against the terminal wall and into the air above the olive-green canopies and palm trees.

I probably would have paid more attention to the distraction were it not for the fact that the minutes leading up to it had caused my mind to gulp in great gusts of frustration.

Mansour had promised to pick me up in front of arrivals at 8:00 a.m. sharp. But he was twenty-five minutes late. And I had a feeling he would be. That meant my least favorite experience when traveling internationally. The continual "Taxi?" from driver after driver, all of whom I suspected wanted to charge me more than the metered price. And I had to wonder if each successive driver hadn't seen me wave off the one before him. No merci.

At first, I toggled back and forth between hanging back by the terminal building and walking out to check for my ride, and had to admit, the demarcation between shade and sun at the sunline felt eerily fresh. October weather in Casablanca, I'd read before coming, was volatile. Either a visible radiation, like a green flash across the eyes when days are high and clear, making the pale arms of Germanic types like me come alive with goosebumps; or it could be a bonnet of a day: cloud-flecked to overcast. But the locals knew not for long. It wasn't Ireland.

Eventually, I decided to linger near the terminal wall. But cinching the strap of my laptop case to my shirt only ever ended with the machine sliding halfway down my developed trapezius muscle. And try hard though I did, every time I bent my knees and sprung upwards to generate enough force to hike up the strap to the top of my shoulder, it just slid back down, irritating my brachial plexus.

I'd put the computer down so many times to rub my shoulder and neck, I just decided to sit it down and lean it against my leg. But then it would fall over. I was so dead tired from my long trip from Florida, I gave up and sat on the walkway, my back leaning up against the wall, suitcase and comp at my feet.

That's when I heard the clickity-clacking. Fortunately, right after that, I heard a voice cry out, "Dr. Jack!"

Certain it was Mansour coming up from my left, I stood quickly and scanned the rush and muddle, but wasn't able to see him. His average size, rounded face, neutral undertone, wavy black hair—traits markedly similar to scores of men at the airport that day—made spotting him difficult. Then our eyes fixed, and I slackened to a sense of relief.

Laptop slung over my shoulder, suitcase in tow, I moved in Mansour's direction and again noticed the weird clattering. Instinctively, my eyes shifted slightly right. Scissoring through the crowd was a young woman in high-heeled shoes. Undeterred by the large pavement cracks filled with soldier-like ant platoons and inland gullies of spider grasses, she approached me, threw her arms around my neck, and with a sprightliness in her voice, said. "Welcome to Morocco!"

My torso pressed against hers in stiffened reserve, her scent of white flowers invigorated my senses. To look at Mansour, I backed away from her, my eyes stalling fleetingly before her breezy charm.

"Sorry we're late," Mansour said. "Traffic was heavy just outside Rabat."

"Oh, no problem," I replied.

"Dr. Jack," Mansour said. "This is Indela. Indela, this is Dr. Jack Lockhart."

"Hello, Dr. Jack," said Indela. "I'm so glad to finally meet you. We're both ready to go with you wherever you want."

Indela was twenty-four years old the morning we met. Her face was slim and nose retroussé. Her eyes were big, brown, and animated. She was five seven, I guessed. Only because when she spoke in those blue pumps of hers, we stood almost eye to eye. When I told her, I could carry my laptop, she replied with a mother's tenderness. "Dr. Jack, we're here to help you."

As we headed to the car, her pant legs tightened toward the bottom, showing off her turned up calf as she walked. Her light jacket with zippers on the arms was wrinkled just enough to suggest it had spent much of its life in a travel backpack. Her comfortable shirt matched the color of her jacket perfectly, but was a tad too long and could be seen from the back. The finishing touch, her scarf, draped artfully down her well-toned shoulders. Her makeup was perfect. She was a modern-day Catherine Deneuve.

"We're just up here," Indela said, pointing. "Isn't that right, Mansour?"

"Yeah. Just over there," he said.

I smiled. "I need the walk, no problem."

We made our way through the parking lot, and I couldn't help but notice Indela's shoes wobbling precariously on the uneven pavement. She walked as much sideways as forwards. My stuff in the trunk, and the three of us in the car, I addressed Mansour. "I didn't know you could rent an older car like this."

"We can't afford a new one," he replied, "but it's got everything."

The trac of Mansour's gaze led me to the center console and front dash. The clunker did have everything, sort of: coffee cup holders full of change for the tolls, his driver's license, and his Tic Tacs. It had a newly installed technicolor radio and an out-of-date air freshener hung from the rearview mirror.

I rechecked my seatbelt.

We departed the airport southward, and a mild breeze pushed ahead of a line of low-lying clouds surveying the fertile, northern coastal areas and cities. The uneven tread of the tatty front tires slapped the road, making dust plump up my passenger side window, triggering my recurrent asthma. The wabbly window knob took more strength to turn than I'd anticipated. And by the time I managed to roll up the window, shrieking with each push or pull of the knob, my all-too-familiar husky caw had started up. I took a drag of my inhaler and, angling my eyes over my left shoulder, asked weakly, "Getting enough air back there?" No reply. Earbuds in and head bobbing rhythmically, Indela's eyes were already a mystic glaze above the checkered pasturelands of verdant and beige.

Hardly had I turned around before my seat rocked back from Indela pulling herself forward. Her face snugged grinningly in the slit between the front seats, she said, "Dr. Jack. How long are you away from home?"

"Oh, I thought you were listening to music."

"I was, but I'd rather talk with you."

"I'm here two weeks. And I've been looking forward to my leave of absence from the university for a long time."

"You're here to study the trees, right?"

"Yes. I'm here to do morphological studies on some of the argan tree populations."

"But this is your first time here?"

"It is. I made arrangements with an associate at the university who's been to Morocco twice for me to work with an established group." I started to wipe my glasses. "And Mansour. You look good. I remember when you studied with us maybe—six years ago?"

"It's been that long?" Mansour said. "Time flies."

"Dr. Jack," Indela spoke up. "Mansour says you don't want to see Casablanca."

"We can still do it, Dr. Jack," Mansour said.

"Can I ask why you don't want to see it?" asked Indela.

"Casablanca would be interesting if I had more time. But I understand it's kind of a concrete jungle, and we have enough of that in America. Of course, with cooler climates maybe there's fewer tourists, so I don't know. I just think Marrakech would be more interesting, and it's in the direction I want to do my studies. Around Taroudant."

Conversation tailed off and my eyes floated the earth-lined banks and berms, and I recalled what others had told me about Casablanca. In the roads where the people rode dilapidated buses and pressed hard through overcrowded sidewalks, the natural beauty yearned and the urban heat islands formed. Old men in the cafés still talked of the veils and mirrors created by the nighttime, winter fogs of years earlier, as if that's all there was. Creatures great and small teamed in the Atlantic, and its hegemony normed the metropolis. The atoll of the Bouskoura forest, cool and green, wasn't of interest to one who had spent his life in the study of forests.

A sudden trouncing of vitamin D through my window broke my concentration and made me grab for my sunblock just as I was reconsidering a quick visit to the dominant, Hassan II Mosque and its 690-foot minaret that joins earth and sky.

"Mansour," I said. "Have we driven too far from Casablanca?"

"Yeah, by now, I think so. But we can still go back if you want."

"Oh, no problem. It's okay. Then do you think we can stop somewhere? I slept through breakfast on the plane." Not only did I need some coffee, but I had swallowed a pain pill after the flight service had ended, and a sloe aftertaste was causing me to taste and retaste the backflow.

"There's a place not far," Mansour assured. "And you can try something new. Ever try fried, Moroccan Doughnuts?"

"Oh, how about Ghriba?" Indela added.

"I don't know what that is," I told them, "but I'm okay for a stop. And maybe we can review our plans there and then go to Marrakech?"

"It's a plan, Dr. Jack," Mansour said.

Second gear mashed as Mansour's hand searched hard for third using what I suspected to be little more than intuition. He found it and the transmission popped out of gear, suggestive to Mansour, a self-taught mechanic, that the clutch master cylinder may not be entirely up to the task. "Dr. Jack," he said. "I think we need to have the car looked at. We can do it at the same place."

We pulled over at La Croissanterie on the southern side of Berrechid, and my niched suspicions about the older rental were proving true. Mansour got out and motioned a man preparing to leave in a light truck, rust having digested its discolored exterior like a brown radiator. Mansour insisted the man knew all about cars. I had my doubts. The repose gave Indela a chance to rush me inside, her arm locked in mine.

"Now please give the Ghriba a chance, okay?" she asked, opening the door to the store and entering first.

"What is it?" I asked.

"It's a special cookie with an almond in the middle."

"I've never met a cookie I didn't like."

"Huh?" she hesitated. And then, after a long bat of her eyes, stared at me in the most delightful manner. "Come with me," she insisted. Her arm still laced in mine, she helmed me directly to the counter and, navigating les patisseries, exclaimed dejectedly, "Oh, I don't think they have it!" She kicked her heel on the floor. "Wait," she added, "they have Ghriba Bahla." And she clamped my arm extra firm the way a pair of locking pliers do, almost dragging me over to the opposite end of the cookie case.

"These are a little different, Dr. Jack. But you'll love them."

"I'm sure. Can I have some coffee too?"

"Of course."

"Indela?"

"Yes?"

"Can I have my arm?"

"Oh, I'm sorry."

We sat at a little round table and had our delights and on cue truffled our mouths together and in friendship new all the world seemed lost.

"I'm not familiar with the name Indela. Is it Moroccan?" I asked.

She slid her tongue along the side of her cookie as if her mouth were full of marbles. "It's an Arabic name," she said, chewing a little more with her hand to her mouth in girlish embarrassment. "But I changed it a little." She swallowed hard. "Actually, my real name is Fatima. But it's used so much in Morocco, I use Indela as a nickname. I think it means, like a nightingale. I got it from a famous singer. Sorry, my mouth was full."

"My fault," I replied. "I should have waited. So, how'd you learn English so well?"

"All my friends speak it; in fact, it's all we speak when we're together." I was trying to listen to her, but the perk was as thick as ink and bitter all the way down to my bones. It made my expression prickle even more than the pain pill, and my head shuttered in a chilly-blue freeze.

"Oh, did I say something wrong?" she jumped.

"No, no. It's this coffee." Indela had, from what I could tell, misinterpreted my acidic grimace as a criticism of her.

"You want me to get you another? I'm so sorry," she said, this time apologizing for the bog.

Trying to allay the possibility of an endless looping of propitiations for errors not her own, I spoke earnestly. "Dear, wait. I absolutely assure you. You haven't said or done anything wrong."

She looked at me as if to say, nice try, and with that, took my cup to the counter and her air was verve and her walk cool and unbound.

Indela had really impressed me. I sensed in her a genuine care for others, and a gentle manner like the misting droplets after a light shower. Since I had only expected to see Mansour at the airport, and he hadn't said a great deal about her, questions began to form in me. Who was she to Mansour? Was she along for the whole trip? The sun still stippling its rising dominance on the new day, and with much travel yet ahead, I thought it best to defer my curiosities.

Mansour reentered the side door, having spoken with his mechanic friend. He walked toward me, his arms wooden straight and fists clenched. Indela followed behind him with my replacement coffee in her hand.

"Dr. Jack," Mansour said, "the car just needed a heavyweight manual transmission oil."

"Here is your new coffee, Dr. Jack," Indela said, her pitch modulating sweetly. "I hope it's good now. I told her the first one wasn't good."

"Can you wait, please?" Mansour said to Indela, his tone sharp. "I'm talking to Dr. Jack."

"Sorry." Indela stood still. She looked disconnected now, her eyes down and mouth flat in the middle and the corners turned up.

To ease the sudden change of mood, I spoke energetically. "Say, if we got the oil, why don't we get our little entourage underway? And thanks for the coffee." She handed it to me and walked to the car with Mansour right behind her. A gray mood came over me then, looking for a thought to decipher it. But a white slash of sun down my face intercepted the mood and I walked partially blinded, exchanging my glasses for my sunglasses.

My passenger door had developed a new whine as I got back in. We took off down the expressway, and no one was speaking, so I reached for some chit-chat. "Mansour, you remember Takwa and Ghofrane at school? I think they live near Casablanca? In fact, I communicated with Ghofrane on social media and told her I might be in the area."

"Those two are dirty girls," Mansour bellowed. "They're a couple of chasers. I had some run-ins with them too. They told lies about me. They're watery." Mansour's pitch fevered higher and higher, and a heightened sensitivity filled the air. "I know you were their teacher, Dr. Jack," his volume and cadence intensifying, "but you really don't know those girls."

"Mansour," I interrupted. Please keep your eyes on the road. You're swerving." The car bladed along the edge of the pavement unobtrusively to Mansour who appeared lost in an angered soliloquy.

"They wanted to do things I didn't appreciate," he blurted. "A friend from Tunisia and I met them here, and—"

"Okay," I interrupted. "I'm sorry, but I really need to ask you to calm down. We'll forget Takwa and Ghofrane. Just keep your eyes ahead. Please."

"It's okay, Dr. Jack. Those are just my thoughts, you know. They even—"

"Mansour. Please, I insist. Let's just forget the girls. I'm sorry I brought them up."

He became quiet, his chin tight and conspicuous. The whole thing felt so strange. It made my skull tight, as if too many rubber bands were snapped around it. It wasn't so much what Mansour said that shocked me, but the fuss. And it all just came out of nowhere. It rattled me airless. I yanked a stick of gum from its tiny wrapper and shoved it in my mouth in one nervous move before twisting my wedding ring repeatedly, ruminating emptily.

A spacious covering of a grin sported Mansour's face, and his tone shot to normal, leading me to suspect he sensed my inquietude. "Don't worry, Dr. Jack. Americans say we Moroccans sound like we're mad, but I assure you we're not."

I didn't know how to reply. It's true, I said to myself, Moroccan Arabic, Darija, can convey a mordent edge to those not used to it. And maybe his English had been hammered out over its unadorned center. But that didn't explain everything. His agility between scary and calm swung too easily, and I wondered if he knew the difference. This wasn't the Mansour I had remembered in America.

The counsel my wife once gave me came to mind. After the tangle at the university, she had recommended I give people the benefit of the doubt. The marketization of education's effect on teaching was driving me near mad. To such a point that my "inner self," as she put it, had become "spring-loaded." It all came to a head one day when my eyes shot like blood at Karl during a departmental meeting. He had made a comment to which I had injected malice, and everything escalated from there. The whole thing went to HR, and after all was said and done, he stopped being my friend. Turns out, I had misunderstood him. And ever since, I've whipped myself for my draconian reply to the guy. So, I decided to give Mansour the benefit of the doubt.

The egrets and herons in a manmade aquafer ignored our droning car and the minutes passed. "Dr. Jack, are you still with us?" Mansour said, his voice cracking through my escape.

I wetted my lips on account of the dry air. "Yes sir, I'm still here."

"Dr. Jack," Indela said.

She was mid-breath into her next sentence when I stopped her. "Please feel free to call me Jack. I like to avoid titles unless absolutely necessary."

Indela didn't reply, and the suddenness caused me to fall forward mentally into concern that I may have said something contrary to my intended sentiment—although I couldn't imagine what. My eye pivoted haltingly just enough to notice her algid glower out the front window into what appeared to be pure nothingness. And the emotional space within me compressed, creating a vague fragility.

Finally, she spoke. "Really, are you sure?"

"Yes. I insist." I was happy just to hear her say anything.

"Okay. I'll try to remember to call you Jack." Indela laughed a hearty chuckle and it refreshed me. "Anyways, is there some special place you want to go in Marrakech?"

"Not really." In fact, I really didn't spend a lot of time looking at possible places to visit before I arrived. I was kind of distracted by my preparations, so I'm depending on Mansour to know. Isn't that right, Mansour?"

"More than happy to help, Dr. Jack. I know the city well."

"I want to visit at least a couple touristy dives," I told Indela. "After all, I did promise the Mrs. a doodad."

"A what?" Indela asked.

"Souvenir," Mansour clarified.

"Oh. Okay," she said. "Ah, Dr.—umm—I mean—Jack." She giggled. "See, I made a mistake already."

"No problem," I said. "Go ahead."

"Anyway." Then she brought the volume and pace of her voice way down. "If you need help finding something for your wife, I'm here for you, okay?"

"Thanks, I may take you up on that." Even though that's what I said, I had already decided to accept her offer, being what my wife once called, "The worst shopper on earth."

I grabbed my phone to check for messages, but it looked back at me with a frozen stare. And my solid strategy to beat the phone in the palm of my hand did nothing to thaw it out. Looking at messages was just a distraction anyway—to give me a quiet moment to allow the vagarious reactions ping-ponging in my head to settle down. Just then, Indela sat forward, her face near mine. And the arm, which had been a forceful charm at an hour earlier at La Croissanterie, appeared again and, slipping over my shoulder, gently lifted the phone from my hand. And my tension became like old pavement markings in the rain.

"What's wrong with it?" she asked.

"Oh, um, none of the buttons work."

"Just restart it."

"Restart it?"

"Yeah, you didn't know to do that?" She spoke in a tone of disbelief.

"I'm a rolodex living in an iPhone world."

"You're what?" she said with a featherlike laugh.

"Oh, nothing at all."

"Here, it's working now." And she handed it back.

A kind of breathless tranquility came over me then; of eternal motions in thought, gently awake to what I was feeling about my new friend.

Chapter 2

We continued southward. Heavy rays of sun splashed the arid places and the juniper, fir, and pine. The sound of marching was in the tops of them, and a lonesome cloud came and went, and no one knew where. Wind formed around us, great gales of it, without beginning or end.

To Marrakech we came in the shadow of father Atlas, and the palm and citrus trees ushered us in, saying welcome, be our guest, in the hand of Komisa's protection. We dropped the car near the Mamounia Hotel at a little parking slot and walked through the Koutoubia Gardens and around the great Koutoubia Mosque, stopping to catch our breath at the heavily trafficked Avenue Mohammed V.

The vibrancy caught me unprepared. The city was palpating in clusters of machinations: dark-skinned traders, chalk-faced poorlings, business types brokering through their Bluetooth headsets, and young, stylish denizens skating around the slow walkers laureled with 35mm cameras.

The Slat Al Azama Synagogue and its courtyard caused me to reflect how the ambience of history dwarfed us—that the Jewish corner was built the year the Spanish Inquisition drove out the Jews from Spain to Morocco and Columbus came to the Americas. A sidewalk became the temporary home to a young boy warming something in a tiny, charcoal fire.

Time to cross the rue had come and I looked back just in time to see Mansour bolting dangerously across without looking. The mad rush of pedestrians, taxis, bikes, and donkey carts, was so intimidating, I froze in my tracks. "Come on," Indela encouraged. She cradled my arm and ferried me across.

We entered the ancient medina and into the Jemaa el-Fna Square. "Jemaa," I would learn, probably refers to an ancient mosque that once occupied the site, but was destroyed many years ago. The utterly massive square was filled with row upon row of juice stalls, water sellers dressed in traditional Berber costumes pouring fresh water from traditional leather waterskins into brass cups for thirsty tourists, and snake charmers sounding their hypnotic spells in every direction.

We took a quick espresso at the Café de France. The fragrance of sweet spices filled the air from the local herb stores at Place des Ferblantiers. But my allergies kicked up and Indela, mistaking the cobra-like arms of a sneezing fit for a gag on a morsel of food, beat me on the mid-back several times. I would have told her to stop if I could have stopped sneezing. Mansour walked speedily ahead of us as if he had been put off by her attention to me. Indela caught up to him and gave him her full consideration.

They walked the predictable, touristy routes, chatting and pointing, turning tight alleyways locked at the hip, showing interest in the same repetitive items on display. The picture struck me as odd because I thought it all so typical to them. Then the reason for their intimacy came to mind. They just liked being together. I could see it.

A pearl-shaped bead hit my earlobe, but I barely noticed. Maybe a passing shower is coming, I thought, looking up and around.

"Do you mind getting a little wet, Dr. Jack?" asked Mansour.

"No, not at all. Bring it on."

To my left, standing tightly erect under a little, tongued jut of a blue and white awning protruding from a merchant's shop, was Indela, hiding from the rain.

"Afraid you're gonna get wet?" I yelled over to her.

"I don't want my hair wet." She spoke fearfully.

"It's just going over," Mansour said. "Come on out." She ran to me and pressed her shoulder hard on mine, ducking her head as if I were her shelter from the rain.

"What are you doing?" I laughed. "I'm not an umbrella." That got a few peals of laughter from her.

"Just walk," she guffawed. She kept one eye up and the other ahead, seemingly determined to keep her hair dry. The skies stripling in patched puffs would never even develop into a hard rain as she feared.

She strolled closer to me again. And with Mansour leading the way, we canaled the narrow streets past the mudbrick buildings, deep in the medina all the way to the spice market. Moving tenderly over the slants and tilts of the winding alleyways, I found myself looking down more than up, unsure of myself; vulnerable. We picked up the pace just a bit, and a woman carrying a sack on her head along a narrow street attracted my attention. Not watching where I was going, I did the very thing I was trying so hard not to do. I stubbed my foot and stumbled, causing Indela to stretch for me.

"Are you okay, Jack? Did you hurt yourself?" Her hand met my chest, trying to straighten me up.

"Sorry. It's this back of mine. Hitting—that thing—right there—really got it going." I rolled up in a spasm.

"You hurt your back? You need to sit?"

"No—I mean—I hurt it many years ago and I've had some surgeries so it's not the best." I grunted.

"What happened to you?"

"Well, I don't wish to make a big deal."

"No, please, I want to know."

"You're such a dear."

"Please, I want to know everything," she pressed, her tone sweet.

Giving a slight nod toward a step, I said, "Let's sit here."

"The step is okay?"

"It's fine."

She helped me sit through a tender vanity of uncontrived "oohs and ahhs," and once I was comfortable decided to take her back in time. "In my 20s, I was a competitive weight-lifter, but I didn't know I was born with a defect in my low back. One day, I lifted too much weight and a vertebra became unstable."

Her face ricked with sympathy, she cradled the small of my back with the palm of her hand, and said, "I'm so sorry. I didn't know." The second her hand rested on my back, my tension broke, starting with my forehead and, pouring down to the bottom of my back, it rilled through her warm fingers. Leaning back just a little on my arms, I stretched out my legs to tell her more of my arduous story. As I spoke, something both unsettling and freeing happened. As long as her hand remained on my back, it was as if I had raced back in time through a wormhole, standing illusorily as an observer to my own history. When I had finished, she removed her hand and I found myself firmly in the present.

Accompanying it all, a clear and irrevocable interpretation of why I had suffered so many years welled up within my heart. Pain is a teacher making us who we are. For what else is a diamond except a piece of coal that withstood the pressure?

Mansour walked back to us and asked, "Is Dr. Jack, okay?"

"I'm okay," I said, getting up.

"He told me how he hurt his back," said Indela. "Lifting weights."

"Yes, I knew about that. You look in really good form, sir. Much more muscular than what I remember when I saw you in the States."

"Yeah, I've been lifting again."

"That's okay for you?" asked Mansour.

"It actually helps me a lot."

"I need to return to the gym myself," Mansour said.

3:31 p.m. I was starving. "Say, when are we going to eat?"

"We can go back to the big square. It isn't far," Indela said, half asking.

Mansour looked to see where we were. "No, I know a better place." We passed a blue sign in a metalworkers' souk to a little haven of a café and, walking the narrow, winding staircase inside, we passed through a dining room and up to a shady roof terrace with tables. Both Indela and I ate the rate au viande hachée. She gobbled past the glistening, oil-filmed shimmer and I had sense enough to take a pill for my stomach beforehand.

"I have an idea," Mansour said, just as I was really getting into the goopy density I had plastered with some lemony sunshine.

"What's that?" Indela cudded, hand over mouth once more.

"It's less than three hours to Essaouira. Instead of staying the night, let's see if we can make it. That way, we'll have plenty of time tomorrow."

"Oh, we're going to Essaouira?" muffled Indela in total surprise. "You know, I never asked where we're going."

"Dr. Jack asked me to take us along the coast," said Mansour. "He loves the beach."

"When'd you guys decide that?"

"Before he came," Mansour said. "We discussed it."

"I haven't been there in so long," Indela said. "I'm for it, Jack. If you want."

"Oh, you know what?" I said, alarmed and thinking through how to make up for my forgetfulness.

"What is it, Jack," Indela said.

"I forgot to get something for my wife."

"There's plenty of time for that," Mansour promised.

"I should have reminded you," said Indela.

"Oh, it's my fault," I said angrily. "I do this so much." My right heel pressed the floor firmly.

"It's okay," Indela comforted.

than friends. That partly explained why Indela was along. Settling at least that much, I felt good about their relationship.

A barren pause immersed me. "Where are my sunglasses?" Snapping my head around several times, Indela's hand gently tapped my shoulder.

"You looking for these?"

"How'd you get them?" I asked.

"You left them on a wall at the Citadel and I put them in my purse and forgot them. Sorry."

"No. That's okay. At least I have them."

"Um, Mansour," I said. "I should have stopped at the Citadel. But is there a men's room somewhere?"

"I think there's one right here. But you may have to pay."

"Oh, I don't care. I'll be right back; just hold on."

Mansour pulled over and parked in the street close to cars parked along the curb. Just as I was getting out of the car, Indela snapped, "It's so f—ng hot," which made me think she wanted me to move it.

I walked through a winding corridor of disarranged shops and found what passed as a public bathroom. An abstemious woman sat outside its doorway and raised a shabby bowl full of paper money and change and shook it at me. I knew what that meant. Really, I wanted to pay anyway because she was nearer the ideal work ethic than were many of the sunless merchants. But I needed more dirhams.

I looked around for a bureau de change and found one. But there was a problem. When I asked my wife to pick up some money for me to exchange in Morocco, I forgot to specify new bills. A big problem because, frustratingly, most Moroccan banks and bureau de change do not exchange pre-2000 U.S. notes. What to do?

Not a second later, a short, rather well-dressed fellow, wearing a pair of wire-rimmed glasses draggling near the tip of his nose, approached me.

"You look lost," he said. "Can I be of service?"

"Actually," I replied, "I'm looking for a place to exchange money. But I only have older U.S. notes."

"How much you need?"

"Not much. Maybe twenty dollars."

"I might be able to spot you."

"Really?"

"Yes. Give me your old twenty and I can give you a new one."

"How about two, ten-dollar bills?"

"I can do that too."

"You're sure?"

"Of course. And I can save you the exchange rate."

"Well, that would certainly be helpful. But I want to see the money first; not that I don't trust you."

"Perfectly understandable. Let's walk back under the canopy for some privacy. He handed me two, crisp ten-dollar bills. In return, he got two old ones. Both of us were satisfied.

"Thanks so much," I said, and off to the bureau de change I went. The line of people waiting was thick and loud. But I waited, concerned that Mansour and Indela were surely wondering about me. I got my money and darted off. I gave the woman in front of the bathroom a single dollar bill, and her face rounded bright like a perfect planet on a cold winter's night.

I was back at the car now and jumped in and turned my head but Indela didn't look at me. Her look was stern now. A sheath of concern covered me and the air felt suffocating. Then it occurred to me that Mansour had said something to her about the cursing and that it had offended me. I wasn't happy if that's what had happened, because her dirty word wasn't that big of a deal, and I didn't want our time at the Citadel to be overshadowed by pendulous branches of misunderstanding.

≈ ≈ ≈

We entered the riad, and the majestic ambience so astounded me, I stopped breathing momentarily. When I could breathe, I breathed double my amazement, but half the beauty.

My eyes moved slowly to Mansour. "This is a riad?" I said to the heavens.

"Yes, Dr. Jack. This is a big one with many things."

"Mansour, "Indela said. "Who are these people?" Even Indela seemed stunned.

"The riad is for sale. It's owned by people my father knows. But we can stay one night. It's fine."

We walked farther inside. The inward-focused, Andalusian-style, garden courtyard was pure majesty. Zellige tile spread from foot to the top of the walls. A gallery of lush, green trees columned evenly through the courtyard, each tree surrounded by a tiled island, and a green and white, octagon-shaped fountain burbled a little bird to sleep. Intricate stucco cornices and trim, called gebs, joined walls and ceilings. Light of dusk flooded through the roof open to the peerless blue. Two mature queen palms stood opposite us on each side of the massive, Islamic-patterned entrance to a dining area; itself adjoined by delightful arabesque patterns of Thuja wood. Tadelakt plaster shined in all the inner rooms. Thornily carved, moucharabieh screens, influenced by Art Nouveau and Art Deco, apportioned various spaces. And though I tried to count all the details from room to room, they were as many as the sparkles on an emerald sea.

During the evening, we sat together in a small room with T.V. It had been an incredibly full day for Indela and Mansour. That, together with and the lateness of the night, made Indela's heart-shaped mouth sling open, her head bobbing continually, struggling to stay awake on a wide, fluffy chair.

Mansour nudged her to decide it was time for bed. "Need a little help?" he asked gently. "No," she groused. She got up and noticed the clutter in the room—the safety caps next to my vitamin containers, Mansour's rumpled fatigues shoved halfway in his Army-Navy colored backpack, my shaver with some residue I hadn't cleaned in a while, and the overlapping mess. She gathered her blue checkered blanket, threw it around herself, and headed off to bed like an overstuffed pigeon, sleepwalking.

That was the first chance Mansour and I had to be alone. He was picking up a few things, straightening this and that, and since we were departing in the morning, I had thought it okay to leave my junk where it was. Except I stuffed my pills away in my sack in two big handfuls. Moments before bed, my familiar crankiness began to surface, this time regarding the blowzy way Indela came along without advance notice. It wasn't her presence I minded, but Mansour's blithe failure to tell me she was coming.

"Dr. Jack, can I get you anything; something to drink?"

"No sir. I'm fine. Thanks." Mansour remained quiet, puttering around for a few more minutes.

"Say, why don't you just leave your things for now and have a seat?"

He continued to rustle among the jumble, appearing to think through my invitation in delayed movements. The shared space between us felt intense to me, like I had just asked a shy girl on a first date.

In the waiting, I relapsed to the time my young son joked, "Dad, you wear your underwear too tight." I disagreed, choosing instead to believe that I possess a valuable, mechanized nature. But after he left home for college, I had to admit my capacity to be viscerally reactive to even isolated stressors. Mansour fidgeted and fiddled, and I wondered if he knew what I wanted to talk about and if my gift for brittleness had been so obvious as to keep him at bay.

"Sure. It's been a good day," he said after some time. He sat opposite me on an old, armless, black leather chair.

"Mansour," I said. "You know, I don't mean to get too personal. But do you mind if I ask how you and Indela met?"

"I met her at school and just decided to show her kindness. Things developed from there."

"That's wonderful. I'm happy for you guys. Now, what exactly is the plan with Indela? I mean, it's not a problem. But I'd thought we had agreed that only you were accompanying me."

"I'm sorry, Dr. Jack. I should have said something before now."

I was sure to keep my tone friendly. "No problem. I'd just like to know the plan."

"Well, you know we're both still in school. I'm completing my master's and Indela is expected to graduate university next year."

"What's her major?"

"Sociology."

"Sociology? Wonderful."

"Yes. And when I told her you're coming, she immediately wanted to meet you and to come along."

"Why is that?"

"She said people in her field have a lot of interest in how the forests are challenging local economies. I don't know, she'd have to explain it to you."

"And not just the people near the forests," I said. "All of Morocco."

"And she'll take care of herself. You don't need to worry about her."

"Well—you see—if she's along on our trip, I feel I have some responsibility and, if I may say, not worrying about her isn't so much the issue."

Instantly, he left his black leather chair and our chat in misted spectacles. He splattered his belongings in his backpack on the floor and spread out all of it in little island patches in a florid search for I knew not what.

"What are you looking for?" I asked.

"Just something." His back to me, my spirit deflated in the recognition that Mansour must have sensed a faint silhouette of my son's portraiture of his father. Nothing more was said between us about his lack of communication.

I went to bed, my mind skipping from thought to thought like a flat rock across a crystal-clear lake. There were his feelings. My feelings. Having already decided to give him the benefit of the doubt. But now not so sure.

Or was it all me?

Chapter 3

Seagulls mounting the new day cawing their nostalgic song of the seaside sounded from early trawlers coming in first to sell their fish. The miasma of morning cacophonies—urchin street hawkers, dogs chasing public transportation, and a jam honking worthlessly just outside our riad because a fool had decided to sell from his fruit wagon at Bab Doukkala. The brightness of the morning sun cloaked the chaos. Effortful wrestling with my recurrent back pain had seesawed me back and forth periodically throughout the night. At 4:30 a.m. I had consigned my mind to the message once given to Job that the world has order and beauty, but is also fiercely dangerous.

But I did dream. A dream of dreams. I was a very old man. Dying. Then she came. Indela slowly approached the side railing of my bed. She looked down with a smile and combed my hair ever so gently with her fingers to make me look a little more presentable. I gazed up into her face. A subdued hush befell the room as a ray of light entered through the blinds covering the side window. Hers was the last face I saw before I saw the face of God.

I bravely rousted myself and looked from the balcony down to the courtyard below. It beckoned me. Standing near the fountain, I looked straight up at the sparkling show of stars arrayed lazily in dawn yellow. Mansour said that because the place was for sale, we couldn't disturb the kitchen. But there was a café immediately next door that opened at 6:30 a.m. Now, just a few minutes before opening, the glare from the picture windows of the café caught the reflection of the rising sun ricocheting. The waiter appeared and brought me coffee without me even asking. It was strong, just as I like it. Tunneling my eyes through the corridor to the outer world, the colorless prosaic of traffic and pedestrians unveiled the day's expectations. The sun. The coffee. My nervous system enlivened. I took a deep breath. I was right as rain.

"Good morning, Jack. Sleep okay?"

I recognized the voice immediately. "Indela, I didn't expect you. I thought you were asleep in the riad. You come for coffee?"

"I thought I heard you walk past my room, so I just wanted to come down and greet you."

"Oh, that's so nice."

"Have a good night?"

"No, I didn't sleep very well dear." I spoke raggedly.

"Oh, your back?"

"No. Something else. Can you sit a minute?"

"Of course." She sat and I hemmed and hawed some words. "Something wrong?"

"No, it's just that I had a dream last night."

"A nightmare?"

"No, nothing like that. It was—a vision of sorts."

"A vision?" she said excitedly.

"I really don't know what it was."

Her voice hushed decidedly, her body inclining toward me now. "I want to know, Jack. Please tell me." I would have answered her right away, but the vibrations of her voice transmitted through the air so low and strong, they penetrated my chest, and I couldn't understand how I had missed the resonance of her beautiful contralto before that moment. The crisp air stilled peacefully.

"Well, Indela, I dreamed I was dying. And yours was the last face I saw before I saw the face of God."

I waited.

"Wow. What a dream, Jack," she said, her head orientating afresh. And my shoulders, which had been pinned to my ears, relaxed.

"Oh, Jack, you won't believe it. That's so bizarre. I had a dream, too." Her voice was excited now.

"Really? About what?"

"I dreamed I came to New York City and you met me there." Mute several seconds followed on account of my usual insecurities. I cleared my throat.

"Well—you don't know, but I was born in New York City."

"Oh, wow."

"Yes. So, what happened next in your dream?"

"I don't remember exactly. I think that was all there was to it." Indela spoke the whole time with her hands wrapped tightly together.

Concerned for her I asked, "Aren't you a little cold? You okay?"

"I forgot my scarf. But I'm fine. Let me go and get ready. I just wanted to come down and say good morning. And I'll make sure Mansour is up."

Indela dashed, and as I watched her disappear, I reflected the salient fact. We just got along.

A morning shower guy, a shock hit me that I'd better get cracking and take my chance-upon, hot water shower—the bane of every world traveler—or else I might miss it. But Indela had left me swimming slow and methodical in my thoughts. Something consequential had transpired between us about the dreams. But what was it? The harder I thought, the more I found myself stuck in sort of an intellectual, Chinese finger trap. The idea that something behind the scenes to bring us closer together, call it a priori and mystical, had broached my rational mind. But I wasn't ready to accept that such a world even existed. Not yet.

Moments fleeting, I broke my laser-like trance and ran back into the riad and upstairs to prep myself. That woke Mansour who was operating on what I sometimes detractingly; sometimes jokingly, called Africa time. The equilibrium between slowing for Mansour, who I could hear moving as fast as a tortoise on its back, and the clock hammer in my German head prodding us to get going, tilted slightly toward patience with the satisfaction of hot water from the shower cascading.

Half-dressed, I staggered my fidgety wanderlust to match the sound of what I had perceived through the sonic air to be Indela cocooning through shower, hair, splash of Huda Kattan, rigmarole. Packed and piddling in the hallway, I yelled, "Guys, are we ready to leave yet?" My head was occupied by a small child bouncing and writhing in intoxicated impulse in the backseat of a car.

In the waiting, I walked up the hallway and noticed a framed cover of the *Old Man and the Sea*, by Ernest Hemingway. Hemingway? What was he doing in a Moroccan riad? My mind began to drift. I recalled the few facts I knew about him. When he lived in Key West, he rose at 6:00 a.m., wrote 600 words until 12:00 p.m., then went fishing until 6:00 p.m. Then he joined the old salts down at Sloppy Joes until the dead of night. It all repeated the next day.

Porous memories of drinking at Sloppy Joe's, back when my buddies and I were underage, began to gel. We drank ourselves sick, I remembered that for sure. Then I recalled us walking around the corner to our VW Van parked in a lot which, back in those days, was okay to do. We slept until one of us woke up, all of us hungover for several hours. I couldn't imagine why I drank so much. But young and stupid, I loved it.

Something about the Hemingway cover gave me perspective. Halls of time compressed, and I could see across the decades to my life when spontaneity ebbing and flowing could decide on the wisp of a whim to grab my buddies, a keg of beer, and take off for Truman Avenue. The mirrored face was that of an older, impatient, pressing, emasculated shadow of that young man. Had I become the old man of the story, struggling with my own marlins? I put my head down. It was too much for me.

We got our boards at a local surf station, not far at all from where we were standing. I purchased a set of floppy swim trunks and rented a short wetsuit. Mansour, God bless him, went in his underwear. I never laughed so hard. But I was impressed he was willing to withstand the cold.

"You ready for a lesson in surfing, sir?" I asked.

"Sure, Dr. Jack. Whatever you say."

We paddled out and I was surprised how fast Mansour made it past the break. I tried hard to hide my huffing and puffing.

"So, when's that lesson starting, Dr. Jack?"

I would like to have wiped that Cheshire grin but figured it best to dispel his misconceptions about my prowess on the playing field. The first swell was on its way and, looking over at Mansour, I thought he had positioned himself a little too far to the nose. He started, then stopped.

"Don't worry," I yelled. "They come in threes."

I had learned the ropes years ago when as kids we surfed for hours and then rested under a palm tree sipping coconut milk from a can for strength. The stuff possessed tons of minerals and the most important were the calcium, magnesium, and zinc oxide. I had learned that testosterone can be increased by fifty percent just by ingesting these three consistently. This day, decades later, a fifty-gallon drum of that stuff would have been just about right.

The second swell was right on schedule. I decided to go for it. The longboard moved heavy but made a fine entrance. My tail raised sooner than expected. I just knew Mansour was looking. I started freaking out. The wave was at risk when something inside me screamed, just get up! My fused lower back added a half second to the pop, but I did it. "Woah!" I yelled. Perfect timing. Atop a watery hillside, I crouched and pressed my right foot on the tail and, angling left, my thighs clamped steely to hold me from falling off. I was in full flight. Seconds passed. Every nerve from head to toe electrified in unison burst and even a hint of a barrel canopied over my left shoulder.

Slowing oblique to the coastline, a glimpse of Indela jumping joyously on the beach at my minor success refracted through the haze of my saltwater eyes.

I was immortal.

I remounted my board and looked back at Mansour. He had caught the third wave in the set. Cutting, slicing hard, back up the face and down again with studied composure, my perpendicular sheer of a ride contrasted amateurishly. Mansour got back up on his board and looked at me with a self-assured smile. In jest, I bowed my head and fanned my arms up and down in the universal sign of veneration. He paddled over to me chattering guy stuff and we exchanged a high five.

Indela came running. "You really can do it, Jack," she yelled. "I'm impressed."

"Not bad," Mansour said.

Self-effacement was just a little difficult to muster, but I found it. "I have to admit. Mansour has me by a little."

"You both did so good," Indela congratulated.

We recovered the road and the sun was lopping west of its zenith. The changing landscape through my dust-crusted sunglasses passed quickly from seaside resort to P2201, a shortcut hugging the coastline back to N1 to Agadir, a treat-in-itself. Men on donkeys were selling bread and fish. A middle-aged woman, her face and arms roast-graveled and peeling, a red bandana hanging from her convertible pants, and lugging an internal framed walking backpack, approached us at a stop. She asked Mansour for the nearest pharmacy. Her back, she said, was covered with bites from mosquitoes or sandflies. It just so happened that I had some extra repellent and was more than happy to help her out.

Our boyish frolic made the thinning threads of the old rag arrive late at Agadir, and I was fine with the hour without even a trace of juvenile impatience. But I was desperate for coffee. Indela went to add minutes to her phone and Mansour and I spared old surfing conquests at a roadside café, our hands animated and recollections larger-than-life.

I sipped a slurry espresso and enjoyed watching cats sitting stoically at the edge of the gravely road and pretentious men sitting cross-legged, smoking hookah. Fascinated by the process of smoke cooling and filtering through a water reservoir, and flexible tubes extending from the body of the hookahs, I asked Mansour. "You think that maybe those pipes have a little something in them?"

"Oh, you mean hashish? No, I don't think so."

His voice seemed strangely loud in public. "Shh," I waved my hand.

"Oh, it's no problem."

A truck filled with day workers and riding excessively low in the back bounced and jiggled past us close to the roadside, kicking up some dust in our faces. The secondhand smoke and dust stimulated my asthma and a sense of foreboding gripped my stomach.

"Think it's about time we get going, Mansour?"

"Whatever you want, Dr. Jack."

"But where's Indela? She's been long."

At the edge of my question, Indela appeared through the old, painted Berber doors of the café just as two men dressed in traditional djellabas cut in front of her. She relented with a forced smile, eyes down—the way children do when they know they're to keep their servile place. And she didn't make eye contact with either man. The image made me feel elusively invaded.

Then she approached Mansour with her typical affiliative smile—lips pressed together and making those little dimples at the side of her mouth show. Nearing our table, she burst open into her sweet, crescent smile, and with each step toward him, it seemed to expand as far as possible. I guessed she was showing him affection. But Mansour didn't appear to notice her, punching a phone call instead. No one was answering. And as I sat listening to the muffled dial of his phone, something in the unchivalrous confluence at the doorway between the men and Indela, and Mansour's disregard for her warmth, was reaching for me. But I couldn't put it together.

He put the phone away and, half-asking; half instructing, he looked at Indela and me. "Maybe we should go to the apartment now?" I heard him, but didn't reply right away. "We can go right now," he repeated as he stood, his body torquing rotationally like a Botticelli sculpture.

"Ah, sure," I responded as colorless as the fumes in the air. "If you know people, we can just go."

The place was close to the beachfront promenade, away from the sterile, concrete-covered inland quarters of the inner city. Pleasantly satisfied, as I strolled the main room, I said, "You know, Mansour. I need to travel with you more often."

He popped me on the arm with a double-quick slap. "Welcome. Any time, Dr. Jack."

The glazed transom window at the back of the room pulled me through a looking glass. Moroccan culture, I reflected, contains the worst and best of everything—the worst and best conversations, the worst and best friendships, and the worst and best kinds of unspeakable pain and joy.

Dusk was settling into its restful hammock. I walked outdoors to the Picasso blue streaking the twilight spectrum upward and the floating moon was larger than life. The remitting of the day to the stars and the promise of newness was hours away. I stood beneath the mutable canopy and the busy fireflies of concern slowing prefigured her appearance.

"Night is almost here, isn't it, Jack?" Indela said.

"Hey—yeah, how are you? Yeah, it's coming. And what a beautiful night too."

"You have a minute?"

"Certainly." Just as I spoke, the high-pitched squeak of a night Gecko could be heard close by.

"I don't know. I just felt like I wanted to share something."

"Sure, what is it?"

"Well, remember I told you I'm adopted?"

"Yes."

"Well, a few years ago, I found my mother. I went to her to ask where my father was. I said I just wanted to see him, that's all. She told me to get away and that she'd call the police if I didn't leave."

"What did you do?"

"I left. But I was so upset. It's hard to say this. But I really wanted to give up." Indela's dyspeptic face undraped the pain of her personal struggles.

Her candor so overwhelmed me, it was all I could do to say, "Really?" Gravity pulled my legs down hard and I took a deep breath through my nose and exhaled out my mouth and added, "I think everyone feels like giving up at least once."

"A friend told me I just need to humble myself; think less of myself. And I've learned to move on."

Initially, I felt it best to check my avuncular nature from saying more and just hear her out. But she stood looking at me with big eyes, the type in desperate need of a life-preserver. As well, I was reminded that my words to her at the Citadel had helped.

"Dear, may I offer a thought?"

"Please."

"Humility doesn't mean thinking less of yourself than other people. It's the freedom from thinking about yourself at all."

She looked as though a revelation had dawned on her and nothing more needed to be said "Thank-you so much for your understanding." Her eyes misted tender as a Lorient morning.

"Indela, I'm always here for you." My hand touched her shoulder sympathetically in a gesture of assurance.

"Jack, I don't know what it is. It's just that I feel such good vibes when I'm around you." She took a long pause and then in a slow and systematic manner repeated, "You know me better than anyone."

"That's so nice of you to say."

"Can I say something else?"

"Of course."

"You're the father I should have had." Feeling the need to respond, my reason in full flow up to that second adjourned, and the harsh squawk of an evening bird signaled in the distance.

Indela's face then grew puzzled in my prolongment. "Jack, I hope I didn't say something wrong."

"No, not at all. I can't tell you how much that means to me." I didn't know if she wanted more from me. I needed time to think, my guard timorous to the hem of her admission. But what my mind had yet to work out, my heart had already decided. Her unrepressed brokenness had imputed to me. And there I stood. Melting in the perfect silence.

Morning came. And all I could think was that my head must have been eavesdropping on my heart throughout the night. Because the immersed veil of sleep lifted to a warm realization. She had become important to me. As I sat up in the fuzzy white light of the old, Moroccan tray lamp, the fulsomeness burned down to the glowing embers of mixed emotions rapidly. I was married after all. What kind of love did I feel for Indela?

Just then, she knocked on my door. "Jack, are you awake?"

"I'm here."

"Don't you want some breakfast?"

"You guys go ahead. I'll be out shortly."

She left and I returned to my antechamber of concentration, and an investment of an old teacher of mine fell from my brain like a soft drink after you put in the money and push the button. Mr. Rollins, a man in his early fifties at the time that I knew him, and a sprinter in his college days—so good, he could beat any of us kids in the 100-yard dash—had been both my sixth-grade teacher and my Sunday school teacher at the Presbyterian church. He used to joke that God had blessed me with Saturdays. He had taught us in Sunday school about three kinds of love—agape, phileo, and eros.

Which one did I feel for Indela?

A light knock came at the door again. "Dr. Jack, are you okay in there?" Mansour said with concern in his voice.

I opened the door. "I'm fine. Just working."

"If we're going to keep your schedule, we need to go soon."

"Just let me grab some coffee and we'll go."

Always unconvinced of the new day, my back required a bit more medication as a rasp to edge the pain before our caravan pulled out. The old rag was ready to go, and I patted her on the hood before getting in. Truthfully, I think we winked at each other to keep our respective chassis going. With only my left foot on the floorboard of the passenger side, a small girl, followed by an elderly woman and a small tribe of goats to their side, passed us by. I froze, my body neither standing nor sitting. She looked back, turned, and walked toward me.

She wore a long kaftan and tan sandals. Around her shoulder was a small satchel and she reached inside and removed a book. She opened the book and between its pages was a crushed flower. She removed it slowly. Cupping the flower in both palms of her hands, she looked at me with wide set eyes and offered it to me. Gently, almost surgically, I took it. She spoke sparingly and Indela translated. The flower was an Iris, the national symbol of France. She simply wanted me to have it. I thanked her and she rejoined the others.

The three petals of the flower were violet blue and lightly spattered yellow with an inner tongue of glazed yellow only God could paint. The flower's beauty brought the gestating question to fertile clarity. Instead of three kinds of love, I saw in the Iris but one love with three expressions, each expression sharing the same substance, but manifesting uniquely. Because the three love manifestations share the same substance, it's possible, I admitted to myself, that love is a mystery that defies Mr. Rollin's compartmentalization.

The question plaguing me had been answered. My love for Indela was like the Iris. It was beautiful. It was good. It just was. And similar to the unfathomable design of the flower resting in the palm of my hand, I would never comprehend it fully. If she needed a father, I would be that man.

Chapter 4

I felt in my bones that I knew the meaning of Indela's breathy sigh in the car on the way to Agadir. All the talk of goats had pinned her in the cuddle of her youth. The animals were tangential to my study. But making her happy had become important to me. To treat her, I agreed furtively with Mansour to take us to the best spot to see goats.

Approaching Taroudant, the city deigned in the specter of the High Atlas, its violet soil hazed atmospherically in outline. We came to a roundabout by the Metro warehouse on Marrakech Road. Turning off a drive of about twenty minutes Mansour said, "You'll see goats on the left, Dr. Jack."

"What? Where?" Indela replied with excitement. "Oh, we're going to stop to see the goats?"

"Yeah, I just knew you wanted to see them again, so I worked it out with Mansour."

"Oh, it's been so long since I saw them. Thank-you, Jack."

We pulled over and a man walking along the edge of the road crossed over and approached my side. His eyes were piercingly hazel. The sagging waves of facial skin enmeshed his eyelids forming a monolith. His cheek bones were high and narrow, and strong, deep lines cut to the rim of his jaw. His hands were soft and his digits round at the joints and sheeted in callouses to the fingernails.

"Don't worry about him," Mansour said. "He wants something."

I knew what he wanted. The old man was prayerful for a few dirhams to see the goats and I gave him a few and his smile protruded barracuda teeth.

"Jack," Indela said. "A professor at school told us that the goats are why the forests are in trouble. Is that true?"

"Good question. Mansour told me you're interested in the problems with the forests and how that's affecting people, economies, and all that."

"Yeah, that's right. Rural communities especially. I want to talk with you and see what you're doing. I hope it's okay. Mansour said it'd be okay."

"No, that's fine. Anyway, your question. A lot of the forests have been cleared for crops, cut down for firewood. Large-scale irrigation and irregular changes in climate are also considerations. Years ago, it was to the point where only remaining patches of forests were left. So, huge areas of land in Morocco are now under protection."

"What can be done?" Indela asked.

"I hope to do some follow-up work in the Souss on an argan fruit biology database that some of my colleagues have been working on. We're checking for progress because further decline of the forests could have devastating consequences."

Indela appeared flummoxed. "I don't understand everything you said. Sorry, my English."

"Oh, I'm sorry. We'll get to it and then you'll see."

"So—why exactly are the goats a problem for the trees?" Indela asked.

"They're famous for scurrying up the branches to eat the argan nuts. The shepherds let them because the almond nuts are big and hard and the goats digest them and poop them out and that softens the hard-shells. But in more recent years, the fruit is hand-picked and the oil is pressed. And you probably know that argan is then sold to produce argan oil, cosmetics, a bunch of stuff."

"Sure. And it's mostly women who do that part."

"You mean it's women buying the cosmetics?" I asked.

"No, I mean it's mostly women who make the oil and that supports a lot of homes."

"Oh, you're absolutely right. And—I forgot the other big problem for the trees.

"What's that?"

"The problem is that so many tourists come just to see the goats that some herders actually position the animals up in the trees on planks of wood virtually year-round in order to make more money. It's like a sideshow for profit. But because the fruit is ripe only during certain times of the year; and the goats nibble the leaves before they've had a chance to mature, that stuns the growth of the trees. The trees never have a chance to recover. So, a lot of them are dying off."

"Is that happening here?" A look of concern radiated from her eyes.

"Well, I asked Mansour not to take us to those places, so I doubt it."

"Can you get my picture with the goats?"

"Sure, I don't think anyone will mind."

Mansour shuffled his feet sideways in my direction and I inched around for just the right shot. He said, "Dr. Jack, I'm happy you wanted to come off the beaten path, away from the tourists."

"Me too, Mansour." I kneeled to get my best photo of Indela before the eight, tightrope-walking marvels atop a seventeen-foot tree, one more raw-boned than the others. As I clicked, the tree branches sprang up and down under the weight of the goats, a flicker if the goat was close to the trunk, more if the goat was far out, the way a diving board does when one is testing its springiness.

Indela broke her pose and walked to Mansour. "Jack was just telling me how some farmers put the goats on sticks of wood. What'd you call them, Jack?"

"Planks."

"Yeah, planks," she said. "And too much climbing damages the trees."

"Yes," Mansour assured us. "I overhead you guys and I'm aware of these things."

A swath of concern showed on her face. "Do you think the forests can be saved?" She spoke with a delay like a pencil scraped out at first contours.

"Say, don't you want to take some more pictures?" I asked in an ersatz attempt to recoup her mood.

"Nah, that's okay."

"Dear, look, I don't think we can restore the forests to their pristine condition. But many experts are at work to conserve them, and possibly regrow large patches." I reassured her with the type of familiarity that typically blooms over time between a father and daughter.

She appeared to take momentary comfort in the fact that a phalanx of cool-grey, reserved specialists was piloting the problem. But I could see the auricular truth cutting her deep. The goats, important symbols of Moroccan culture and life, were being stage-managed by their possessors and were menacing the trees. Feeling deflated because I wanted so for Indela to enjoy the spot, amusement vacated my interests and the subjugation of the goats weighed heavily upon me also.

The rammed earth ramparts, weather-beaten from the squall of years, stood their mediate position between the snow-capped High Atlas and Anti-Atlas ranges as we approached the ancient medina of Taroudant. A passing shower spangling a jogger in Deraa and Nikes mixed a cultural tagine.

We took the day to peruse the medina and I was more relaxed than in Marrakech, so much so, I didn't think of goats or trees or science at all. An old man sat alone outside the Bab el-Kasbah and sorrow bled though his blue eyes. I wanted to ask him about life because I thought he knew much. But I felt I could learn more, looking deep into his blue eyes and not asking a thing.

The souqs and squares healthily sprinkling the Maghrebi mystique wetted my sense of wonder the way a spring rain kisses the sun-exposed petals of a M'Goun rose before the perfume is lost. I tasted life and when I did, I heard the sounds of little children in the dancing of the air, and deeper still, the soft and sibilant voices of women passing in the alleys. At a certain point it all cut through and I breathed in the scent, heady and sweet, with notes of honey and treacle. When Mansour asked for some minutes to visit an old school-teacher of his who had a small shop, Indela and I strolled the grand sidewalk and discussed life, and other things. I saw the medina for the last time in my cracked side mirror, the wall lightened to a lover's dream.

The day of surfing was still fresh on my mind as we landed the old rag at an apartment residence in the M'Haita area on the outskirts of Taroudant. Mansour had said his sister was out of town and that we could have the place.

Hours passing, my mind directed inward to the varied landscape of reactions, feelings, and sensations, set in motion since the moment the three of us started out together. I was trying hard to resolve something; everything. But my every attempt only created my own competition. The ancient Greeks told the myth of Sisyphus, whom the gods punished by forcing him to drag a giant stone up a hillside, only to have it roll back to its origin so that he had to repeat the task for eternity. Was I my own punisher?

"Dr. Jack," Mansour said.

"Yes."

"I think you need a hammam."

"A what?"

"A hammam. It's a like a—how do you say—a spa. And they work on you. You look like you need it."

"Oh, that would be good," Indela chimed. "Jack, you need to go. Is there one in Taroudant?" she asked Mansour.

"I'm certain."

"Wait," I said apprehensively, "what are we talking about—exactly?"

"Let's not talk about it," Mansour said. "Let's just do it."

In the far reaches of my gray matter, a kernely recollection of Erol's Spa was trying hard to surface through layers of forgotten years. My dad took me there when I turned eighteen and I swore never to return to such a place. The spa was owned conjointly by two pornographic store owners—Erol even flacking for the dual combo of store and spa on T.V. Forebodingness filled me. Surely, I thought, that couldn't be the case in conservative Morocco. To my shock, the wabbly window knob then came off the door in my hand. In my tension, I must have broken it right off. I raised it to Mansour.

"Indela, look," Mansour said.

"What?" She moved forward for a look.

"Don't worry, Dr. Jack. It can be fixed," Mansour promised.

Holding the knob so Indela could see it, I said, "I broke it."

"Oh, Jack, you do need a hammam."

"Okay, let's do it," I agreed while spinning the knob in little circles. But then, little flakes of plastic, unable to withstand the g-forces, started flying off. So, I slid the broken handle in the side compartment of the door.

The hammam was old rustic clean and not fussy. A non-English-speaking, older man, handed me a bucket, a mat to lie on, black soap, and exfoliating gloves. I could have paid extra to have someone exfoliate me. But since I didn't know what exfoliate meant, I took the gloves. I never used them. It turns out, I was to go totally naked. Great. But I did get a paper thong and some flip flops. Mansour had told me just to be myself. That would be—uncomfortable. Sitting in what seemed like a steam room with two totally nude men with facial hair, I closed my eyes and imagined Indela's voice patting me gently into a state of relaxation, which produced the darndest thing: a vision of myself at breakfast on Lake Como eating a morning baguette.

The old man then returned and splashed a big bucket of water on the floor and flapped his pointed hand for me to lay on the floor. Oh gosh. Lathered everywhere—and I do mean everywhere—I was sloshed with water, twisted, and slapped several times, re-soaped, and re-sloshed. It was as if he had been following the directions on the back of a shampoo bottle. Now, I was wondering if Indela and Mansour hated me. After a fairly soothing massage and sitting on some heated tiles, I was led to a cooldown area and served some mint tea. Since I only swim laps, I passed on the little pool.

As I was getting back in the old rag, Indela asked, "So, did you love it?"

"Wonderful," I punctuated the air with a fist pump. But my fist hit the out-of-date air freshener and broke it, so I stuck it in the side compartment with the door knob.

"Are you just saying that?" Indela asked with an ariose lilt.

"No, it was fine, dear. Thank-you guys for the idea. Think I'm ready for a nap now." At least it wasn't Erol's.

Now at the apartment, I looked out the back window. The backyard of the building, fitted with a clay wall, separated the clothesline condominium behind, but not from site. The modernistic balcony, far too focused on materials base theory to bow to such human-comfort sensitivities as refuge and outlook, much less vital air movement, served a temporary distraction. From my vantagepoint, I spotted something.

A solitary Brugmansia of oscillating orange, its coarse-rimmed floral bells and peeling inner clappers, swaying elegantly from its limpid branches, perfumed the moonlit evening into a magical fairytale. Wanting a better look, I rushed down the stairwell, detangling myself spasmodically from several strands of a spider's webbed netting, and lurched quickly through the toxic smell of half-opened paint cans and out the bleached white back door. There, I was startled by the added sight, lurking reticently around a wall corner, of a secluded Datura arrayed in purplish red, its flushes of blooms in Fall ascendance like the military signal flare of Roman majesty, but soon to be molten in the face of winter.

An Angel Trumpet tree and a Devil's Snare tree. How fitting, I thought. The respective positions of the trees: good more prominent and desirous; evil more concealed and shocking in its advent. Nothing else occupied my garden bare, save sapped years streaming the island grasses. Ant mounds and bounteous creepy-crawlies also joined the common evolutionary struggle.

Midnight approached. I laid on my bed and the inconstant lightbulb dangling from the center of the ceiling pressed a somber mood. Eyeing the lightlessness through my window, I hoped a pleasant idea to call me so I could go out to meet it. I stood and walked to the glass and put both hands squarely on the sill, my nose touching the dust-filled screen.

The outside world was not what I had expected. My room was higher up than I had anticipated, and it looked out to the horseshoe ends of the building, jutting outward to my left and to my right. I was standing at the flat, squared, dead-end of the building, a place where, if I were a kid, I'd hang out with my buddies planning cool stuff. The windows on both sides of me were agitating in design: some linear; others squatty, that is, beneath the others and weirdly roundish.

A sound was outside my window. I looked out. The romping and wrestling of two cats among the garbage and storage bins below had resulted in quite a racket. Thinking nothing more of it, I turned away when an ear-splitting *rrrreeeeer* stopped me cold and my shoulders raised near my ears. The guttural meowing sounds of screeching, hissing, yowling, and growling, followed. Oh boy, I said to myself. Something's brewing. No doubt. The penultimate predatory stare and dance exploded, and the fight was on.

Rupturing the unsettling duet below, a stentorian lament, further back in the field of sound, and acoustically dissimilar from the sound of the cats, tousled me. I looked through one of the rectangular-style windows at my 2:00 o'clock and saw a hand silhouetted flat against a windowpane, an interior light from behind the hand annotating the fingers upon the glass.

Just then, a lunette appeared from behind the clouds and the light of it revealed a woman at the window. She screamed. She screamed again. Louder. Louder still. Her other hand then hit the glass, hard, but the pane didn't break. Her upper body lunged forward. A hand then appeared from behind her and covered her mouth and her screams stopped. A sudden jolt forward of her body again. I was determined to comprehend, when unbalanced forces tugging and pulling from behind the window transformed the ambient night into horror. The woman was being raped. Shock overtook me. Near total exhaustion, I collapsed on the bed and passed out.

Morning clamor through my window woke me. Indela was already up. She called, "You up, Jack?" I looked. My alarm clock failed to go off. Then I realized, I hadn't turned on the alarm the night before. Wait, I thought. Oh no. Had Indela heard the cats? No, I corrected myself. Had she perceived anything of the woman? That's right. The woman. Fragmented deliberations refused to form a simple thought. Coffee, I said to myself. I need coffee. And I need to say something. I can't be supine. That's not me.

I walked out to the shared area. Mansour was also just up.

"Sleep well, Dr. Jack?" he asked.

"Well, not really," I said in a fuddled way. "Say, did you hear anything last night?"

"Just some late traffic. Why?"

Moving closer to Mansour so Indela couldn't hear, I mouthed, "I almost certain, no, I'm sure—why—a woman was being attacked last night. I saw what I could see through my window."

"Truthfully, Dr. Jack?" Mansour reacted in raw bewilderment.

"I think she was being sexually assaulted," I continued, keeping my voice low. "Yeah, yeah. I think so. Is there something we can do?"

"Where'd you see her?"

"I'm pretty sure on this floor, but around the corner to the right. Yes. I think I can spot the exact windowpane from last night and perhaps we can find the room."

"Let's eat breakfast and we'll go look."

Mansour returned to the stove cluttered with small, inharmonious accoutrements. He turned on some music. I had hoped it wasn't for me. The easy vibe in the room, over and against the invariant vision of the night, doxed my tetchiness, and I could only wonder when those blasted eggs would stop their infernal sizzling.

"How you like your eggs?" Mansour asked me. "Scrambled? I hope so. Sorry, I forgot to ask."

"Don't worry. Say, you think we can hurry please?"

Hearing me, Indela asked, "We going soon?"

"Sorry, dear. No, I was talking to Mansour. We're just going to go out a second. We'll be right back."

I wolfed my eggs. Indela ate some crunchy bar from her giant travel bag. And the smell of mint tea filled the air. I started to feel sick, my heart beating irregularly sometimes hard, sometimes pounding. My eyes flashed a side squint at Indela, checking if she could hear it.

"Mansour. Think we can go please?"

"Jack, are you okay?" Indela's question transmitted in my hearing dully as if through a pillow.

Mansour and I entered the hallway. He moved coolly and I walked, ebbing behind him. The farther we walked, the longer the hallway seemed to stretch. The terror of the Bled es-Siba, the old domain of violent passions, the sphere men create to suppress reproach—was pulling me through. I reached in my pocket for my hand sanitizer for no reason.

A door opened and a young man emerged. His beard was black and trim, and he wore dark colored business attire, and a starchy white shirt hugged his slim frame. His collar was open just a little, and his narrow tie matched his black shoes that glistened off the hall lights. He had thrown his coat over his shoulder before he locked his door, and the sound the lock made was like a big barricade falling into place.

"Puis-je vous aider ?" he asked.

"Salam alaikum," Mansour replied. He followed in English, "Hello, I am Mansour, and this is my friend from America, Dr. Jack."

"Hello. I am Yousef," he said, moving his eyes back and forth between Mansour and me.

Oh good, I said to myself. He speaks some English. In mild panic, I moved toward Yousef. "Sir, did you hear anything last night. I think that room. Right there." I pointed at the room.

"Oh, that room," Yousef said, his voice calm. "Yes, they did marriage not long ago."

That the couple was married rocked me back mentally. But I stayed on track. "I heard something bad last night. A woman screaming and in trouble. In fact, I saw it. Any ideas?"

"I don't think going to them can do much," Yousef said. "I know the woman. I talked with her myself. When she was nineteen, her parents forced her to marry a man she feared. She didn't accept this relationship. She said, 'Every night, I told him, I don't want you as my husband.' But he hit her and raped her. Sometimes he would order her to undress in front of him, and if she delayed, he beat her. She told me, 'I can go to the police. But because he is my husband, they will not do anything to him. He has the right to do sex.' She doesn't know that even though he is her husband, this is still rape."

"How is this possible?" I asked.

"I'm a lawyer. And I work with women and I saw a lot of terrible things, especially in the countryside. Many men don't work. Mostly women work. And every night they give the money to their husbands. The problem here is that marital rape continues to be a question in our laws. The women should stand up to their husbands. But most don't. They don't resist."

Mansour looked around at me and I shook my head minutely in incredulity. "I'm sorry, Dr. Jack," he said sadly. "It's really bad the way some men treat women in Morocco. I'm ashamed for them."

"Sir," I said to Yousef. "I want to thank-you for your time. Appreciate it very much."

"You are most welcome." Then he walked down the hall and disappeared down the stairs.

Mansour and I walked back to our place. But before we walked through the door, I stopped. "Mansour, can you add anything more to what has happened? If this had happened in America, the man would very likely be arrested and charged with rape."

"Dr. Jack, I understand. We need to hope for change. I'm so sorry you saw this thing. Some men in Morocco feel like they can treat the women very bad."

"And nothing happens?"

"I think the laws will catch up."

"But it's not only the laws; just common sense not to rape your wife."

"Sir, I know. Let's go back in and plan our day. That's the best we can do right now—and I don't think we need to say anything to Indela. Women here don't need to hear these things."

"Fine."

Inside the apartment, skies of anger descended on me, and when I couldn't hold it any longer, my being collapsed into hollowness, of being desolated by the Zagora.

Although restlessly avid to gain ground on my studies, the incident had created such a plosive encumbrance in my inner voice that I felt the need to delay my morphological work in Taroudant. I asked Mansour if he'd be willing to drive us to the rural commune of Amskroud, in the region of Agadir Ida Ou Tanane. It was there that a woman's cooperative prepared argan seeds, and it just so happened that the leader of the group was a friend on social media. I contacted her and she was more than willing for us to come and join her group for the day, and for Indela to take a hand in helping the women. There was also a place nearby for me to take some plant samplings if I wanted.

"Indela, dear," I said.

"Yes."

"I have an idea. I think we can have you do a little on the job training today."

"Do what? Sorry, it's my English again."

"Your English is good. I just forgot you don't know all of our American slang. What I meant is that I have an idea for you do some work today and learn at the same time."

Her appearance perked. "Work? What kind of work?"

"I've decided I want to go to Amskroud, and you can help prepare the seeds. I'll explain everything."

"Oh, I've never done that before. You mean like the women do?"

"Pretty much. But you'll be fine, and anyway, I have an acquaintance, sort of, who leads one of the women's cooperatives. The women know everything about taking the almonds from the argan so you don't need to worry. I asked if you can join in and she agreed."

"Really? Oh, I can't wait." Indela's excitement volcanized and my heart permeated with joy at the sight.

Lenticular clouds reached in the vague distance as we headed across P1708. A sudden, light rain scattered on the car roof and snake-like sheets of rain kissed the arid desert landscapes of burnt-orange slabs and slags of rock.

"Mansour, see those clouds way out?" Mansour put his head out of his window in an effort to see the flying saucer-like objects patrolling the abstracted elevations in the distance, and his face disfigured, straining in the recusant wind. He drove about one hundred meters, his eyes off the road, the tires sheering the stony edge of the road, and some small rocks spit up. I kept waiting for him to notice.

"Don't worry," I insisted. "You don't need to find them; they're over there. Just keep your eyes on the road, please."

~ ~ ~

We arrived and to my surprise my acquaintance had left for Agadir. But she had asked a woman, advanced in years, to supervise Indela. When the old woman walked toward us, she walked with a slight limp, smiling a Madonna smile—its width revealing deeply scored nasolabial folds. Approaching Indela, she reached her cauliflower hands, and the women embraced.

"Smyti Zohar," said the old woman.

"Her name is Zohar," Indela said, her face a beam of inspiration.

"How are you?" I asked Zohar, but she didn't know a lick of English.

Indela spoke with her, and I was fascinated by Zohar's traditional purple djellaba and matching scarf tied around her head in the old-fashioned style. It matched her bloodshot eyes, and in the sun, her furrowed skin looked to complete the set. The women continued to speak as if they had known each other for years. The outline of a tattoo nestled beneath Zohar's left eye, and another tracked tattoo extended from her lower lip to the bottom of her jaw. It charmed me, and I don't think I'd ever seen a more beautiful woman.

"Mansour," I said. "Why don't we go and you can join me in the collection and sampling of plants. We'll leave the ladies to get to know one another."

We walked, and Mansour said to me, "Why again are we in Amskroud?"

"More of a diversion. Last night and this morning really got to me. And I want to do my real studies with a clear mind." A significant fact suddenly hit me about the region. "Oh, I just recalled something."

"What?" Mansour appeared overly concerned as if I had left something at the apartment.

I placed my arm on his shoulder to reassure him. "No, no. It's only that it might be good we're here. The Amskroud area is one of the more important for argan."

"Oh, how so?" He seemed relieved.

"Amskroud is one of the highest yield areas in all Southwest Morocco for large argan nuts."

"Studies bear that out?"

"Absolutely. You know, as a former student of mine, I'm a little surprised you didn't know that."

"Life took a turn for me after I returned to Morocco. The family."

"Oh, I didn't know that. Sorry. Hope nothing serious. We'll have to talk."

"That's fine."

"Second, the people of this area were the subject of a study on the usage of many plants, including argan, for human health benefits. Most of those interviewed were older because they've known about the medicinal benefits of the plants for many years. In fact, now that I think about it, I'll bet Zophar was interviewed.

"There's a little town very far from here called Errachidia," Mansour said. "And I think some studies like that were done there too."

Noon had caught up to us, the sun hot and unyielding even in its lazed autumn position. I opted for a break. "Mansour, can you put away the tools for now? I don't want to leave them out, and I'm going to find Indela for lunch. Come find us."

When I found Indela, she was wearing a blue headscarf and sitting next to Zohar in a room full of hard-working women, and the look on her face was one of priceless joy. I snuck up shiftily and whispered, "Want something to eat?"

Indela side-glanced at Zophar as if for approval, but the master was deep in her work. "I think I'll just stay here for now if that's okay," she whispered. "Oh, but wait, I want to tell you something." Indela stood and, pulling me by the arm like she loved to do, walked me away from the line. "Jack, this is just amazing. I'll tell you more later, but I want to thank-you so much for this." Her eyes showed her meaning in ebullient shades, the way people do when their heart is attached to something.

"Dear," I said. "I'm so glad you're happy."

Hours flipped by and the scaffolds of the day lowered to the daubs and lines of soft-hued sky. Mansour put away some things in the building used by the women, and Indela and I walked back to the old rag.

"So, what all you do today?" I asked.

"The day was so full of interesting things," she said, "and I learned so much from the women, not just about the argan process, but about life and culture."

"What did you learn about the argan?"

"I learned all the fine details: how the women collect the seeds and bring them to the villages where they sit and do everything in an assembly line."

"Yeah, you were in one of those lines today."

"Yes, but one of the women said that now there are other ways to get the oil. I didn't quite understand that part." Her brown eyes alighted on me, teasing me for an answer.

"We talked a little about that. Maybe you forgot. It can be done mechanically now. In fact, maybe you know that a Moroccan woman pioneered the modern process to get the oil."

"Oh really," she said excitingly. "The women didn't tell me that part."

"Yeah. And she worked out ways for companies that profit from the mechanical production of argan oil to pay women like Zophar who still do it manually so their families can have some income."

"I wasn't aware of that either. See, we Moroccan women are not to be held down." She followed her declaration with a confident bob of her head.

"You bet," I said, firmly placing separate weight on each word.

"What else did you do today, Jack?"

"I spent some good time with Mansour. And I explained why Amskroud is important for our research, and other things."

"Guy time, right? Like when you were surfing?"

"No, not quite that fun; more important things. But yeah, it was good."

We reached the old rag, and Indela put her light jacket away. "Jack, you look a little worried." Her eyes were pearly with concern.

"A lot of things went through my mind today. For some reason. I don't know. One rather troubled me."

"What is it?" she asked. My usual anxieties were clamping the idea shut behind my teeth.

"Just try," she prevailed on.

I replied, "It's just that, you meet people, and they mean a lot for a while. But then they just disappear. They move on to other things. You never see them again. I just don't want that to happen with you and me. And Mansour too. I always want to know you as a friend and a daughter. Please don't slowly fade away."

"I won't let it happen." She spoke with immediate assurance.

"Promise?"

"I promise."

Chapter 5

We returned to the apartment, and it felt later than it was. Papers in hand, I sat on the couch to work. After some time, Mansour went back out and Indela sat next to me to talk. I marveled. How could two people, separated by so many years, by such different cultures and experiences, care so deeply for one other? It was a simple thing really. We felt safe together.

Afterwards she went to her room. Sometime later, Mansour reentered the apartment quickly, his eyes evident and determined. He moved forward. Tigerishly.

"Where's Indela?" he bit.

"She's in the bedroom," I replied with a trace of concern.

Mansour walked into the bedroom where Indela was sitting on the bed looking at her phone. Unaware to Mansour, I could see both of them from my primed angle at the end of the couch. Mansour approached Indela, said some words, and it happened.

He grabbed her by her shirt and threw her halfway across the room in the most violent fashion, and I heard her body hit the floor. Numbness enfolded me. Ringing split my ears. Straining. Wanting to move. Lactic acid teemed my legs in concrete.

For goodness sake, Jack, I said to myself, louder and louder. Get up. Get. Up. Get back there.

Then Mansour started for the bedroom door, but stopped just short of it when he saw Indela walk around the other side of the bed. My eyes began to blacken in pinpricked vision. What the hell. Get up, Jack, I said to myself again. But I was unable. Like a fragile, Maidenhair Fern in a dry, bright sun, I shriveled there in my own self-contempt.

He chased her down and pinned her against a tall chest of drawers with his torso and, stabbing the air by her left eye with his fat, index finger, chewed her out and Indela stood frozen, appearing petrified. He walked out of the bedroom into the kitchen, and Indela ran and closed the door behind him with a loud thud.

Is it over? I thought. I can't believe it. What just happened? I had just witnessed Mansour attack Indela. Why, why? I cudgeled myself, was I inert?

Mansour moved placidly into the room where I was and asked, "So, Dr. Jack, what would you like for dinner?"

Did I hear him right? I thought. "Um, I'm really not sure," I replied mechanically.

"Okay, well, there's a fast-food place near; that sound good to you?"

Still trying to find my bearings, and without an appetite, I muttered, "Whatever you want is fine by me."

A sudden flash and Indela bolted from her bedroom, unlatched the apartment door, and flew down the stairs. I watched Mansour go right after her, and had hoped she had found the night. Alone now, it was all a haze. And I can't remember if I had been sitting or standing.

Lonely minutes passed. The couple returned, and Indela looked totally deflated, playing the good soldier. To the kitchen, Mansour and Indela walked with the food and set it out on plates. Indela pulled out a liter of water from a bag and tried to sit it on the kitchen counter. The container must have been awkward because she struggled with it. Then I watched it fall from the counter. It hit hard against the floor and bounced before water poured from its broken side.

"Indela, what is wrong with you?" Mansour yelled. The blunting of his voice against my skin snatched my shoulder blades up to the bottom of my neck. She leaned her back deliberately against the refrigerator door. The heels of her feet rose, and her back stretched up the side of the refrigerator.

"I'm sorry," she said, her face white as terror.

Mansour thundered at Indela. "What's wrong with you? Mop. It. Up." Instead, she sat at the little wooden table where the food was to be served, hands folded in her lap like a scolded schoolgirl. "I'm sorry," she repeated. I felt myself being pulled into her fright.

Mansour continued to yell.

"I apologize," she reiterated. "I'm sorry."

It didn't matter if she had obeyed him. Mansour had gone blank, in a pure, white-hot rage.

"I'm offended," Mansour boomed in thunderous slugs.

Finally, part of my voice returned. "I'm offended too," and I looked directly at Mansour.

But Indela, taking my remarks as a criticism of her, said, "Then I will leave, and you two can travel without of me." She spoke graciously and measured.

"Sorry," I said. "I didn't mean you." But my words seemed to brush off Mansour's skin.

He then stood and moved to my left, looking Indela directly in the eye, and in a cold and calculating tone, said, "If you ever fail to obey me again, that will be the end of you." The energy charge of his words overloaded my capacity to absorb.

Mansour calmed as fast as he had enraged. And the three of us gravitated toward the couches.

"You attacked me," Indela lamented, standing up for herself now.

"And what were you doing before I came back?" Mansour answered angrily.

"Can't I talk to other people?"

What were they talking about? I thought. Was it that she had communicated with another young man when I saw her on her phone earlier? Mansour looked green with jealousy, morbid jealousy, the kind that turns the will rancid dark. If so, then he had been suggesting the incredible: a moral equivalence between his death threat, and her having other male friends.

Mansour seethed. Indela tried to interrupt, but his jaw jutted forward, and he extended his left hand, snapping his fingers and convulsing the air like the sound a board makes when busted in half. A shudder ran through my entire body at the sound if it, and Indela stopped speaking instantly. She sat back in her chair; eyes large as saucers.

Indela spoke only when Mansour permitted, and I was lost in the pain of it all.

Suddenly, Mansour asked, "So, Dr. Jack, what's the plan for tomorrow?"

Nonplussed, words fell from my mouth. "I'm not entirely certain at the moment."

Mansour grabbed his plate of food and sat. "Now I can eat," he said, looking at Indela and me sitting side by side on an adjacent couch, his grin, unmissably inappropriate, portending that a great tempest not of his making had passed.

My breakers off.

In a reflexive, sideward scan, I caught Indela sitting affectless—her face painted the most god-awful, mannequin smile at Mansour. Then Mansour took a long bite and I was surprised to see her purloin a little wink my way, which I took to mean, "I'm okay."

"Dr. Jack, you'll let us know our plans in the morning?" Mansour asked, masticating broadly, his eyes pinned wide open as though he were checking me to make sure he hadn't unlocked some hidden force in me.

"Yes, in the morning. We'll have plenty to do. Tell you what. Let me go to my room a little early. I have some stats to compile, and I'll figure out the day tomorrow." All of it came out of my mouth too hurried to have sounded sincere. But I needed space.

Entering my room, I looked back at Indela, her face dimly lit. "Good night dear," I said. "See you in the morning."

"Good night, Jack." Her aspects sheeted sympathetically as if I had been the one in need of emotional support.

I rolled over the handle to my bedroom door and pushed it gently until it stopped. Dexterously, I released the handle mechanism, and it engaged without a clunk. The brake on my heart released, and I laid on the bed, feeling like I was trying to measure the radius of a black hole.

Hours later, I woke, fully clothed, my right leg dangling off the edge of the bed. Slowly, I sat up rubbing my face. Did I imagine it all? Oh no, it happened. Tears began to form. Anger mounted at Mansour, but mainly at myself for not having stood up to him when Indela needed me. Little fits of pain crossed my chest and forced me to calm down.

Now what? My wife, Beth. She always knew best. I emailed her. Spelled it all out.

My favorite smell popped my eyes, and I walked out and grabbed a cup. I radared the place. Neither Indela nor Mansour were around. They must have gone out, I thought. Right then, the sound of my phone's ding distracted me.

> To: Jack Lockhart
> From: Beth Lockhart
> Date: Wednesday, October, 17, 2018 08:15:01 EST
> Subject: It's me.
> Hey. I'm so sorry for what happened. Poor Indela. But I don't think it's wise for you to speak with Mansour right now. You're in a foreign country, maybe not the best place if a big confrontation happens. Be careful. Luv u.

Not more than a second after reading her email, the front door opened. "Well, good morning, Jack," said Indela. "How are you?" She started to put some stuff away that she and Mansour had grabbed while they were out.

"Dr. Jack. Good to see you, sir," Mansour followed. "We didn't know if we should leave you or what."

"Did you sleep all night in your clothes?" Indela asked.

"Well, I guess I did." I watched them now. Moving through the kitchen in tandem, they actually looked like before. Why is Indela acting so nonchalant after the events of last night? I wondered. She had tried to leave. Looked terrified. Now they were moving smoothly around the place as if nothing had happened, and a feeling akin to rays of hammers pulsated my head. Had she found a way to justify what had happened? Fear for Indela's future with Mansour consumed me. I determined to field her opinion about the attack. But how? Especially without Mansour suspecting my involvement.

"Indela dear," I said calmly.

"Oh, what are we doing today?" she asked.

Keeping my back to Mansour in an effort to keep him from hearing me, I half-whispered, "I'm not totally sure yet. Think it's possible we can go to a little café?"

"But we just picked up—" Lifting my brows glaringly, I intercepted her mid-sentence.

"Okay," she said. "Just a minute."

Her burst of energy for her purse told me she knew what I was thinking and she wasn't afraid to talk. So as not to splash up our mutual thoughts, I turned unhurriedly to check Mansour's guise. Little moves, a busy nothing, was all I saw, and I feared his foxy awareness would tease my doubts.

"Mansour, we'll be right back," Indela said, light bag in hand. "Just follow me, Jack." Mansour remained silent.

Scarcely did we enter the stairwell, then she said, "He can hurt me. But he wouldn't hurt me. He wouldn't do that." The lineaments around her eyes belied reality. I didn't say a word at that point. Indela walked the narrow sidewalk dogged, her pace quickening and difficult for me to match. Punctuating the morning air, she blurted several times, "I don't feel right." Her fast stride said it was starting to hit her hard now, and because she was saying what I was thinking, I stayed my opinion temporarily.

We sat in the sun, my mind boiling in thought. I feared that were I to speak, every thought would gush out. I kept waiting for her. Sadness filled her face and she looked at me as if to say, if you're going to be the person I need in my life, now's the time.

My fatherly instinct cycling, and with no headroom left, I placed my elbows on the table and stated, "Dear, I think you have a problem."

"Yeah, you think?" She spoke worriedly, not sarcastically.

"Yes. Without question. I'm in absolute shock over what happened last night. Has he ever done that before?"

"No, never. But I can handle him." Handle him? I thought. Hours earlier, her body was strewn on the bedroom floor. How will she handle him should his combative state worsen? Perplexed in suspension, I couldn't tell if she was simply confused, or if this cheetah turn was indicative of a true change of attitude.

"You heard him," I said, pushing my voice forward. "He said he'll hurt you."

"He did say that, didn't he? What should I do?"

"Dear, I don't want to tell you how to live your life, because I would be involving myself too much." Truth is, I felt she needed to run from him, and I wanted to say that so badly.

"Jack, I think you need to talk to him."

"I will. But it may not be a good idea for me to do that so far from home."

"Why does that matter?"

"Sometimes when we try to talk to people about really touchy subjects, you know, people get emotional and an argument happens. I think I need to wait." Indela didn't respond and her mouth set in a great arc as people often do when they're thinking something through.

"I understand," she said reflectively. But her appearance said she wasn't convinced. Neither was I. It was then that I felt the little finger on my left hand begin to twitch. I held it as it flicked in my hand several minutes.

"Dear, can you call the police?" I asked. "In America, women do that."

"I can go to the police, but they will do nothing." Her words merely touched my comprehension. I struggled to understand her. The idea that the authorities would have done nothing was foreign to my way of thinking.

Indela cried.

Passerby movements vignetting around us, I reached my hand and, gently squeezing hers, she looked up at me, her eyes bulbous and moist, sharpening my care and concern for her.

≈ ≈ ≈

We returned to the apartment in silence. She walked quickly toward her room to get some things for the day, Mansour staying right behind her. The door closed and voices fulminated. Not loudly, probably for my sake.

The bedroom door opened. "Dr. Jack, are you ready?" Mansour spoke calmly now, and the feeling I had of his dissembled words cut me deep.

"Ready when you are," I yelled out from within my room.

Moments later, Indela exited her room, her face a sheet of turquoise ice. "So, what's the plan today, Jack?"

"I had planned to meet an old research contact at Argana today. But the morning is already half-gone, and Argana's a ninety-minute drive. So, how about we just try more of what we did yesterday? Same location."

"Oh, will Zophar be there again?" Indela asked eagerly.

"I'm not sure. But let's just go and find out."

The atmosphere in the car was leaden. I needed a distraction. Shimmers of gossamer light through a raggedy cloud transported me to a better place.

Anyplace, Morocco. I woke to find Mansour and Indela asleep, still in their respective places. I tried to make sense of the kitchen. In the refrigerator was some mortadella and some sort of bread in the freezer. There wasn't a toaster, and I wasn't sure how to operate the oven. I started pressing buttons. Big mistake. The more buttons I pressed, the more buttons I needed to press to undo the buttons I had already pressed.

"Jack, what are you doing out here?" Indela asked, emerging from her room and shutting off the oven before I burned down the place.

"I was trying to make a little breakfast," I replied bashfully.

"But what were you trying to do?"

"Well—I found this bready-looking stuff in the refrigerator."

"That's Harcha. I'll take care of it." She placed it back on the counter, grabbed my arm, and directed me out of the kitchen. "Just do something for a minute, and I'll get us something. Maybe wake Mansour."

I felt like a little boy. But for some reason, I liked it.

Mansour was snoring melodically on the living room couch, the cadence almost enchanting. I made a little song out it, and Indela laughed. I began motioning my arms in 3/4 time as if I was conducting Strauss. "Jack, stop," she said, grinning ear to ear. Sauntering toward her, I gently grabbed her arms and began to Waltz, all the while singing my extemporaneous tune to Mansour's rhythmical kip.

"Jack, really! What's gotten into you?" She had a grand smile while pushing herself away.

A silhouetting figure grew slowly on the kitchen wall. "Good morning, Dr. Jack." Taking for granted it was Mansour, I swung around, gabbed his arms, and began to dance.

Mansour, barely half-awake, marveled, "What are you doing, Dr. Jack? You okay?"

Indela stood, shaking her head. "He's just silly this morning."

Indela walked to the couch and, sticking some harsha in my hand, insisted, "Eat this." But then tricking me, she suddenly stuck the stuff into my mouth too far and I choked. I stood and returned the favor in kindness, and we played like children in the sedgy grass of autumn days.

"Come on over here and try some of this bread," I spoke to Mansour with a side wink to Indela.

"Alright," he agreed. He walked toward me, but rather than put the bread in his hand, I tried for his mouth but his head flinched right, and the bread smacked him right in his nose. "Oh," blurted Indela, her reaction more pushed out by her diaphragm than intentional. Mansour's bare laugh fractured just above his breath at the realization. That freed Indela to laugh, then me, and the synergy intensified to such a degree that not a single one of us of us could breathe, holding our stomachs and crying a heave. The carnage of bodies strewn one on the floor, another on a chair, and Mansour shot with arrows of mirth over an arm of the couch.

The weight inside the car then shifted like a house sliding unexpectantly into a sinkhole, and I returned to reality. "Mansour!" Indela requested urgently. "Can you pull over please?"

"What's wrong?" he asked.

"I just need you to pull over."

"But what's wrong?"

"Mansour, over there. Please," she repeated, pointing to a roughly strewn, off-road location.

"Can you wait? There's a gas station not far."

"No, please, Mansour."

Concern mounting in me, I asked, "Is she okay?"

Mansour shook his head. "I don't know." He pulled over. Indela exited the car and started vomiting on the side of the road.

"Oh my," I said. "Looks like she's sick."

"Maybe something she ate," he speculated.

Indela got back in the car and said something in Arabic to Mansour. We proceeded but didn't get very far.

Indela walked back to the car and asked Mansour, "Is there a gas station somewhere?"

"Yes," he said insistently, "it's just ahead. Just get in."

We rolled into the parking lot of the gas station, and Indela started to exit the car even before we came to a complete stop. "Wait. I haven't stopped." Mansour sounded put off. He continued to drive farther than I would have expected for Indela to exit the vehicle.

"Can you please stop?" she cried.

Mansour and I followed Indela inside the station. "What do you think is wrong with her?" I asked.

"I don't know," Mansour said. "I hate all this drama." Right then, my head blazed with the sound screeching tires make on hot asphalt.

What? I thought in stunned credulity. Indela vomiting on the side of the road is a girlish drama? A feeling of pressure built rapidly inside me. I stood hastily and moved away from him to the opposite side of the store, keeping my back to him. That was it, I determined. Mansour and I were going to have a chat.

Indela exited the bathroom and walked in my direction, her face flaccid. "I'm so sorry. I'm not sure what happened. I think I'm okay now."

"Indela, I think we need to go back," I said in firm resolve.

"What? We're going back? Why? I'm okay."

"Look. Something happened, and I think I'm going to go ahead and have that talk with Mansour. I can't go on until I do."

"What happened?"

"I just ask you to trust me, okay?" A swathe of care spread across her face. She reached her hand and gently touched my arm. "Jack, is everything okay?"

"I'm okay."

"Well, whatever you think is best."

Mansour was up and walking toward the exit.

I turned to him and said, "Mansour."

"Yes sir."

"I think we need to go back." Mansour was deadpan quiet the entire way back, and I warried of his resilience. The depths of winter sheathed my exterior, and there was no music.

Halfway up the stairs to the apartment complex, a man walked down passed us wearing a gandora. The image of the man reminded me that I was indeed in a foreign country and to speak to Mansour gentlemanly. Perhaps this will be a first pass, I instructed myself.

Inside the apartment, and before I could say a word, Mansour said, "Dr. Jack, I know you were offended about last night. I'm sorry about what happened, but really it was necessary. Her behavior has been bad."

Fire shot to my head. My heart pumped faster with each step toward him. My plan to be thoughtful went out the window. I stood directly before him, and his eyes reeled inevitability. I spoke on Indela's behalf.

"Necessary? So, she needed a good beating—is that it?"

"But all I did was go into the bedroom and grab her to get her attention."

"Absolutely not. You don't know, but I was sitting on the end of the couch and had perfect line of sight to everything that happened. You attacked Indela in the bedroom in the most horrific way." Mansour stood openmouthed; exposed.

"Dr. Jack. Please listen. We went out this morning for food and we both apologized. She said she was sorry for talking with another guy and I apologized for I did."

"I can't believe my ears. Mansour, let me be really clear about something. There is no moral equivalence between her talking with another young man and you physically attacking her and threatening her. Those two things have nothing—and I mean nothing—in common."

"But you don't know what her friends have been saying about her. Just before you arrived—"

"You are doing it again—trying to find a way to justify your actions. Sir, I don't want to hear from her friends. It is the height of cowardice to try to hide your actions behind what she did rather than stand up like a man and take full responsibility. Then you stood right here screaming at the top of your voice, terrorizing her. Didn't you see the look on her face? She was petrified. Or was that necessary too?"

Mansour was utterly flummoxed. "But I—"

"Do you understand the sheer terror a woman feels when she's attacked physically and verbally? Complete panic grips her heart and mind. She has no idea what more might happen to her. Her whole sense of safety and self-esteem is injured. It can take years for her to recover, if ever.

"Sure, I was jealous. But you don't know that in our culture many women want a husband or boyfriend who's jealous."

"But love is not jealous."

"Wait—"

"No, you wait. There's a good jealousy and a bad jealousy. You can be jealous for someone—that she does great things. Or you can be just plain insecure—that everything she does and everyone she talks with is somehow a betrayal of you. So, if you're going to apologize, you go it alone. This isn't about her friends, her calls, or the man in the moon. It's about you."

No projecting, fantasy world had ever been so exposed or so fatally torn down by reason's sword. The blood in my neck was its Avatar—pulsing measured rhymes of reason. Indela stood speechless. Mansour stormed out on the edge of my final word to him.

"Jack!" Indela said loudly, her appearance grave.

"What? Where's he going?" I asked. "I thought he was going to say something, to talk things out."

"I think he's hurt," she said.

"Hurt! What do you mean?" She started for the door. "Wait, where are you going now?" I asked in perplexity.

"I want to see if I can find him," she said halfway to the open door.

"Indela. Wait." She stopped at the top of the stairs. "I think right now I need to go to a hotel and try to pull my head together. You do what you need with Mansour, and I'll wait to hear from you, okay?"

"Let me see where he is and we'll talk later."

She went right after him and black ribbons of uncertainty over what I had just done hung in my heart. I was thirsty also, so I walked into the kitchen and poured a glass of water. My hand shook so hard, I had to lay the glass back on the kitchen counter. My body weakened.

Chapter 6

I found a cheap hotel. Pacing. Laying. I knew all too well how to think myself into a good sickness, and I was well on my way.

In the small hours, my phone rang, waking me from a light sleep.

"Hello."

"Hi Jack. It's Indela. I'm sorry to call you so late."

"Indela. Where are you?"

"How's your back?"

"My back is okay. But where are you?"

"Jack. I need you to listen to me. I'm so upset." Her voice was rising gradually and the more it did, the more my fears stuck to my tongue like glue.

"Upset? What do you mean?" Blood pushed hard through my entire body.

"I've known Mansour a long time. But we haven't known each other that long. Why did you talk to him like that?"

"You asked me to."

"I asked you to talk to him. Not to—well—confront him like that." Her voice continued to rise upwards toward the top of her anger.

"Indela. I'm sorry. But I think I need to ask you to lower your voice." It was just a little reaction I had to her anger, but the crystalline echo in my head was that of my own voice saying to me, Jack, what have you done?

"I'm not yelling," she reacted.

"You realize what he did to you. Don't you? I saw it."

"He's won't do that again. He was just jealous."

"Jealous? They're all jealous."

"Do you know everything Mansour's done for me? Do you?"

"No, I don't. But what does that have to do with him throwing you across the room?"

"My family knows Mansour. They love him. My adoptive father gave him a job once."

"Men who abuse women have jobs. They go to school. They even help people."

"But it's more than that. I—" She cried diffidently now, and it was a sad form of crying.

"Indela, I'm sorry—" She kept on crying, and I braked my mouth. The pause, in a sense, allowed my reason to gain ground on the emotions flooding everywhere. I pushed my glasses up onto the bridge of my nose and focused my attention on how to recover the conversation in a way that would help her.

"Indela, I'm so sorry. But you know I think he's dangerous. Why are you doing this?"

"Jack, look, I have to go. I'll call you again later."

"Are you sure?"

"Yeah, I'll call you back."

"Okay, well, if you have to go. We'll talk later. Call me tomorrow. Okay?"

"Okay. Bye."

I sat in such utter confusion as to imagine the Jinn of smokeless fire gripping me. It had all been too much for her, I explained to myself, opting to think she was working it through. Exhausted too much to sleep, I began to count the number of half-circular designs in the shell white ceiling paint, images of everything that had happened from the time I disembarked the plane in Casablanca, interspersing the count. Wait, I thought. Beth. It's hours earlier back home. I shot her an email to update her. But no speedy ding this time.

Raucous children outside my hotel door alarmed me early the next morning. Rousting, I grew more cognizant of the past twenty-four hours. The battle to distinguish sweet sketches of the past days from surrealism nestled barbs in my skull like a crown. Either I had spoken to Indela's doppelgänger or she had spoken to me overwrought. The other option rimming my mind. Mansour's fingerprinting on her had spun reality in her mind.

Perhaps Beth had replied by now, I deliberated. I looked only to see a text message from Indela.

> Jack. Mansour's mother got really sick, and we must to leave late last night. Mansour got another driver for you, so everything is good now. He calls you this morning. I am sory jack. I will reach you later when Mansour mother ok. We hope for rest of time here in Morocco will be good for you.

My whole being hobbled. An immediate perspiration, fetid and clammy cold, surfaced on my face. I cupped my phone in the palms of my hands for fear that I could drop it. But it fell anyway. My heart began to cry. My mind on fire, I recalled a man arguing with a woman on a train from Rome to Florence, and how he raised the back of his hand to her. When the train arrived, two men got out and beat the man silly.

My hands on my face, a steady flow of tears cataracted the crannies of my face and seeped through my fingers to the floor, each drop aqueous with questions. What had happened? Was I too harsh with Mansour? Stabbing guilt overwhelmed me as in a bad dream for having killed someone by accident only to wake to find it had really happened.

I cried until I was cried out in the center.

My strength emaciated, I opened my shuttered windows, and UV rays pranced off a cragged wall onto my face. Dust particles pirouetted in the ribbed beams of light, angling across the courtyard. How I envied the dust. Studying the dancing powder, I realized that the shadows were thick and foreboding in the inner corners of the building, far from the sun's ribboned rays, but gauzy closer to the light because the light made them so. Knowing the reasons Indela had suddenly made our new relationship raven black evoked me. But not for so superficial a reason as closure. The vision outside my window had enlivened me to consider a higher calling. Could it be, I asked myself, that some hand of immanence was at work in my circumstances to make me more like the light in order to fray the darkness?

Eyes trained on the light, I decided right then and there to abandon my forestry studies and travel the country in the hope that time and events would school me in the problem of gendered violence, so I could now be a change agent for Arab women.

Rather than go with the driver Mansour had arranged, I walked into a car rental agency to get an old, dust-mangled buggy like the old rag, so I could replicate the feeling of patting the roof with a brotherly wink. But I came to realize my real motivation. Chasing something lost. Suddenly, memories of Mansour and Indela raced across my mind like billboards. That was the first of the flashbacks.

"Are you okay, sir?" Mustafa asked. I raised my head and standing across the rental counter was a youngish man, the front of his long, non-layered hair falling forward over the top of his wire-rimmed glasses.

"I'm okay. Is there a place I can sit please?"

"Yes, absolutely. Please, take my chair. Is good for you. Just come over here. You're sweating. You want water, sir? We have water for you."

"I don't want to be any trouble," I replied, gasping for air.

"Let me get you something to drink. Sir, you want some tea?"

"No, no. I'll be fine. Just give me a minute. Oh—water would be good."

Mustafa vanished behind a wall and returned a few minutes later with bottled water and a young woman wearing a niqāb. Seeing the shamrock green of her eyes effervescent against the black cowled backdrop so startled me that my composure returned. She never spoke a word. I came to see the old rag as a trigger, and Mustafa's recommendation of a late model SUV drove out with me behind the wheel.

I traveled East.

Flowering purple crocus sativus, source of the world's most exorbitant spice, marked late October in the village of Taliouine and its trailing hills. Passing to the East of the stirring Glaoui kasbah, I saw locals picking flowers in preparation for the saffron festival, and they waved at me. I waved and smiled back, currents of liberty oxygenating my being. But the uncharged experience didn't last. I opened my window all the way and turned up the radio loud. It didn't help much. Intermittent tears could just hit me without warning. None overwhelmed except once, and I had to pull over.

I always love the feeling of driving into a new town. And Ouarzazate proved every bit as lifting. Nitta, a Moroccan woman whom I had met when she taught for a brief period at my university, now worked for a contracting consortium at the world's largest, solar-power generating plant in Ouarzazate. There fields of curved, firmament-reflecting mirrors, matrixing linearly, rise above the golden sands of the desert. She said she'd be delighted to see me after so long.

"Jack, it's been too long," Nitta said, meeting me right outside her place. She greeted me with an affectionate, three-cheek-kiss. Even though I met her "comment vas-tu?" with my compunctious "ça va," the intuitive engines of her mind saw through me. "Jack, is something wrong?"

"I tried to seize the day, but somebody greased the handle."

"Oh, what happened? Look. Just come in." Then in a motherly way she added, "You hungry; something to drink?"

"No, I'm fine for now. Thanks."

She went to the kitchen to get something for us, and I strolled her family artifacts hanging on the wall the way people meander art galleries, stopping at old photos of her. She hadn't changed much since we had worked together, and I pointed that out to her: hair still stunning black with just a few white streaks now, and not too long. She had kept herself up also, her athletically toned arms obvious in her white, short sleeve blouse.

"Nitta, do you still have that cute little anchor tattoo on your inner wrist?" I had remembered it and couldn't believe that I had.

"Of course, I do," I heard from the kitchen.

"Say, you still workout like a maniac?"

"I do. When I have time."

She entered the dining area with a platter of refreshments. "Jack. Come. Please sit. I made some tea. I know you want some; come."

I sat and watched in psychic reserve as Nitta poured mint tea in the traditional Moroccan fashion—the pot's spout primed close to the tea glasses, increasing the distance and arc of the stream upward and outward in a continuous motion, then returning the pot to the edge of the glass in a single, grand gesture.

Ready to burst I said, "Nitta, something happened, and I want to tell you."

"I'm listening."

I told her everything I had experienced since arriving in Morocco and watched it all go straight into her attention out of sight into her heart. And I was happy to see her listening because I thought it meant a possible theodicy.

She scrutinized me with an uncomfortable frown. "Jack. That was a very hard experience for you, and I'm so sorry. As for the young women, well, we haven't seen each other in a long time. But if I may say. Do you think that maybe you became too emotionally involved with her?"

"Maybe you're right. I don't know. Really, Nitta, I don't understand what happened. I thought I was doing the right thing, trying to stand up for her."

"Almost everyone does who says that. But relationships between men and women in this part of the world are very complicated."

"That's what I want to learn."

"But why do you want to know?"

"I don't know exactly. All I can say is that the breakage I feel is driving me to understand. Can you help me?" I wasn't prepared to relegate the things I had seen and heard to a self-interpreting ink blot. I desired truth, if such a thing could be found.

"Of course, Jack," she said. "But if I can make one more observation."

"Sure."

"You look shaken; white like a ghost."

"Nitta, something happened to me the night of the attack, and I'm not sure what is was. I tried and tried to get up to help her, but wasn't able to move. And it's killing me. Maybe that's part of it too."

"Maybe you're in shock? PTSD? Maybe you need to see a doctor."

"No, no doctors. But thanks."

"Are you sure? I know a good one."

"No, no, please. Let's just talk." I started to cry.

She warmed my tea and said, "Drink some. It will help. And I'll talk freely."

I wiped my eyes.

"One problem area is that many men here consider romance a drawback and say romance is for the West. In Morocco, when the wife asks for love and feeling the reaction can be a stabbing look or worse. Here women become angry and begin to get mad. Here many women are exposed to violence. Most men here don't know romance and love. They think, I'm a man and I don't have to do this. It's enough to say the words, I love you. And many don't even say that. That's a real big reason you find violence. It's cruelty of grief."

"Mansour and Indela," I said, "were affectionate and it seemed very spontaneous. But who knows?"

"The men can appear very loving when they want a woman. Then after marriage it goes away."

"That's true in America also."

"It's worse here, Jack. I think that the reality of women in North Africa and the Middle East today is determined by one of the most complex issues, namely society which didn't fully understand the new reality of women.

"Society?"

"Yes, our lands still see equality as the appropriation of men and women's freedom as being drawn from their own desires.

"You mean there's been no forward movement in women's rights in the broader society, just among the women themselves?"

"There have been some changes in law. But very few.

"Wow."

"Nitta's phone rang unnervingly just then and she picked it up, pronating her forearm and her thick tendons flexed and were prominent. My body rotated gradually at the sound of unexpected rain and it settled me into an impromptu imagination of the trodden women reaching for rainbows with their feet stuck in tar-caked pits.

Nitta was talking fast and smiling widely, her low back rounded and legs crossed the way comfortable ladies of old, southern American tradition sat in highbacked wicker chairs. Assuming she would be on her call for a while, I walked to the window to see the rain. The final drops were big and hit the roof loudly and left no trace of daubing in the air. The passing sunshowers in Florida were different, I recalled. The humidity caused steamy vapors to rise above the sidewalks like smoke after the rain. As a child, I imagined the humidity as a magician preforming a trick just for me.

My thoughts were like hummingbirds fighting for territorial rights now and I wanted to organize my thoughts. A side room invited me and I entered among old paintings and a white couch covered with plastic. There I realized the continuity among my reflections: the idea of society, Nitta mentioned. I had come to her place looking for truth. But what is truth? Does it change from society to society? Or is there an absolute standard for traditions and societies? Without one, how could I know I wasn't imposing western standards of justice for women on a foreign culture?

"Jack?"

"Oh, sorry," I said, reentering the dining area.

"Sorry, that was my sister. Now what was I saying?"

"You were talking about society." I took my seat again and Nitta warmed my tea.

"What I was saying is that society in general and men in particular knew that women's freedom was a fact imposed by economic realities. The transformation that has taken place in the country drives women to work because society needs their help."

"You mean because of economic forces women have to work to support the families, but the men somehow struggle with that?"

"Exactly. Our lands continue to view women's work, especially in textile and sewing factories, as an escape from their original duties at home. The men need the women to make money but think the women's natural, God-given place is at home."

"How do the men deal with the internal tension within their own beliefs?"

"They say, you can work, but don't think you are more than that. So, the employment of women is usually poor pay, poor work, and long periods of social guarantees less than men."

"That means the changes aren't systemic. Just practical. It's like the few changes to this point are still within the bubble of male authority."

"And the irony is that when women are treated as inferiors it affects the entire workplace. Not just the women."

"How's that?"

"When men treat women as gross inferiors the men are destroying themselves. We have skillsets, vision, we're career builders, we're gifted in multiple area just like men. We're on the line with the men and we want to see the workplace flourish and productivity go up like anyone else. We've got skin in the game. One of the things businesses in the West have learned is that women's productivity is near impossible in a stressful atmosphere. How are you going to be relaxed when you're constantly worrying about sexual harassment, lower pay, being treated like a hireling, and are regarded with contempt? But what if a whole society is like that? When you hurt women, you lose the value they can add to a culture. Music, the visual arts, industry, education, medicine, everything, is squelched. There is one truth I have come to embrace. A country that oppresses women will inevitably oppose the progress and greatness of a nation."

"Well said. But I'm not sure if this applies to Indela. She's graduating university and plans to do her masters."

"She can experience the same problem at that level. You know my educational background. But in my country, I've known great discrimination."

"I understand. Now, you think we can focus more on the issue of violence?"

"Because the salary of a woman is not allowed to buy a house and a decent life, she is silent on violence and doesn't speak or she can be in the street. Or when a woman tries to enter into a dialogue about her rights, or even ask for attention from the husband, then she can be attacked.

"Indela was attacked for doing something small."

"Jack, women here are exposed to violence for the most trivial reasons. I work with a forty-year-old woman who is subjected to violence from her husband for reasons she doesn't understand."

"Trivial reasons. Yeah. That's what I saw."

"Now you understand."

"But not all men are like this here, right?"

"Men who are open to the world treat women with respect and love. But the majority of men in our lands reject equality and women's freedom. The land refuses to change."

"I see."

"And then there's the problem of treason."

"Treason?"

"Yes. Adultery. A large percentage of women seek divorce because of treason by their husband. But when she confronts the husband because of betrayal she can be subjected to violence from him. And, she remains satisfied with little, and violence also, because she doesn't want to hear the absolute word in the society about the status of divorced women."

"The absolute word in the society? What exactly do you mean by that?"

"It's the concept of shame. Moroccan men are very concerned about their honor and self-respect and how their actions hit the family, including extended family. I think this is true everywhere in our lands. People work very hard to uphold their personal dignity."

"Oh boy," I said disconsolately. "I think I may have blown away Mansour's dignity."

"You probably did if you were too harsh."

"But again. This idea of the absolute word. You mean divorced women can be looked down on by the broader society?"

"Yes. Divorce can shame the woman and, by extension, bring shame on the extended family; really even people in the community if they find things you've done to bring insult."

"But Indela isn't divorced or facing divorce."

"But it's possible she took off for a similar reason. Maybe she reacted out of fear of somehow drawing attention to herself should she make a big deal out of what happened. Like I say, people here are very concerned with how others perceive them. If she thought she could be shamed, or draw unwanted attention, then it's possible."

"Nitta, I've heard some of these things before. But it's hitting me fresh like something you've read a thousand times, but then the next time it all comes together."

"It's your recent experience. Don't you think we learn best in real life?"

"Yeah, life is the best school."

Wanting to play the contrarian, but not from some principled high ground, I asked, "So, what would you say to the person who says we have the same problems in America?"

"I'd say you don't have so much of it, and it's not embedded in your culture like ours." My head dropped in dampened heaviness.

We chatted a little longer and I said, "Nitta. You can't believe how much you've helped me. And I can't thank-you enough. I don't want to intrude longer."

"Jack, you're welcome to stay as long as you wish. We can talk more. Besides, what's your plan?" She asked looking fretful.

"I'm not sure. But I know there's more out there for me. I'm going to keep moving until I find what I'm after."

"I hope you find it, Jack. And let's not wait another ten years."

"Deal."

Nitta walked me back to the car sprinkling convivial questions about my family. Helping me close the car door, she said, "It's all good, Jack." That made me smile so big because that's exactly what Beth always says when she sees me glum.

Fall marched on crisp and cool laden with the hints of winter. I looked up at the sky searchingly and imagined in the cycles of the seasons the promise of blossoming, spring apple trees and valleys lush and green. As in all things there is hope and new life. I decided to carry on in search of spring.

The lack of human contact unmoored my focus and within the hour my thoughts returned to Indela and Mansour, and my whole body went taut, my hands gripping the steering wheel with the force of steel clamps. And the picture of a metallic ball juddering off flippers, zig-zagging in helpless accelerations at the say-so of a pinball player—his machine a compressed torrent of Vegas strip marquees—appeared in my mind's eye. I pulled over and rolled down my window just to breathe. Some tears returned but not so many this time. Then my phone rang and buzzed and I was shocked by the abrupt distraction. It was Beth.

"Hey," I said.

"Hey, what are you doing?"

I explained my change of plans, my words hitching vainly in an effort to throttle back my feelings.

"What do you mean you left your studies?" she asked with her tone raised. "Why didn't you call and tell me?"

"Dear, try to understand. Look, after what happened, I feel like some kind of destiny is calling me—"

"Destiny? Jack, what are you talking about?"

"Well, let me finish. I have to know what's going on with the women here; the mistreatment of them is so big here."

A silence, the kind that makes your stomach knot up, followed. Then she said, "It's Indela, isn't it?"

"That's part of it. But there's more. Please try to understand. Look, I promise to keep in touch."

"Where are you going?"

"I'm not sure exactly. I've just decided to travel."

"And what do you expect to happen?"

"Well, already I've met an old friend who really helped me understand some things. And I think I'm going to learn a lot more. And I'm just going to go where things take me." My internal sensor was flashing red, that not a word I was saying was convincing her of my change in direction.

"Honey," she pined. "I've never known you like this. I'm concerned."

"Don't be. Listen, I love you so very much. And I'll keep in touch."

As a college student, Beth had visited Morocco and reminded me that parts of one of my favorite movies had been filmed in a city not far from where I was parked, thinking that a visit there might be a welcome distraction. "Then," she said, "you come home." "Let me think about it," I replied. "You're so bad," she retorted, and I just knew she was smirking. We said our goodbyes, and my northward trac made heading over the mountains a fait accompli. A freeing breeze gave rise to my wings and the road was brave.

Chapter 7

Sketch people and scrabble terrains, the famed ighrem of Aït Benhaddou, and its Ksar pyramiding in disarranged buildings above a broad stream, unapologetically commands the infinite blue in bas-relief. Pell-mell streets meandered, and the sun cast a russet pink on the village similar to the color of an antique Moroccan, covered soup tureen. The aerial, ziggurat designs above me aggravated my arthritic neck, a whipped-hose bequeath of my lumbar fusion. So, I focused my eyes downward and spotted a young woman.

She was painting a Moorish, closet door in work clothes, and her brown hair was in a messy bun. Her nose was broad and flat, her lips full and prominent. Her dark-skinned face was narrow across her high cheekbones, and her symmetrical jawline spoke of strength. Crumpled near her by the entrance of a keyhole archway was a piece of paper. Drawn to it, and for what purpose I had no idea, I walked slowly in its direction to pick it up. The young woman pronated her back and flexed her shoulders backward in a good, long stretch, then spoke to me in fine English—my pale, European features, Florida Seminoles tee-shirt, and khaki pants—an obvious giveaway for the patch-dressed tourist. I didn't have time.

"How are you, sir?" she asked.

"Oh, I'm sorry. I didn't mean to disturb you. Is this where you live?"

"It's okay. No, I don't live here but I know the people. Can I help you?" she asked, rubbing her hands with a towel.

"Silly, but I was just reaching for this piece of paper." She looked at the paper, then looked back at me, hesitant, checking me. I wondered why she was taking so much interest in me. I started to walk away, feeling cretinous, but the piece of debris allured me. I turned back and scooped it up.

"What does it say?" she asked.

"Ahh. Looks like it's written in Arabic."

"Can I see?" She stretched her scrutiny over my left arm, her hands folded in the wipe of her towel.

"Know what it says?" I asked.

She continued to read the paper. "Yes, it's Arabic." Then I thought I noticed her curiosity peaking, and she asked politely, "May I see it please?"

"Most certainly." She took a long time to read it. "So, what does it say?"

"It looks like a poem."

"Ah, okay."

Feeling I had taken enough of her time over nothing, I was about to thank her and move along. But she said, "It's about what men should know about women."

"Women?" The possibility of a dark horse sequence leading me to this piece of paper was, I reasoned, insurmountable.

"Yes. And I think I know who wrote this," she said as her eyes were auditing the doorway where the paper had lain. She then stood very close to me and, handing me the paper, her right hand touched just below my elbow and I felt her closeness. "I think the woman who lives here wrote it," she added.

"Maybe she wants it back; maybe she left it here," I replied, taking a step backward.

"Are you just here for the day? I can translate it for you if you like."

"I'm not sure what I'm doing. But I'll be here for a while at least."

"How can I reach you?" I sensed her interest.

"Look. Just let me give you my contact. I'm Jack, by the way."

"Nour," she said, her tone poised.

"Pleasure, Nour." I acknowledged her with a handshake, and her handshake was weak. "Guess I need to find a place for the evening."

"I know where you can stay. My uncle has a riad. You'll like it." She started to write his number on the back of the paper and then realized she still needed it to translate.

Nothing to write on, I said, "Just write it on my hand."

My mental exhaustion bundling in a catacomb niche, I found a little place and enjoyed a café cassis. My phone rang and it was a man representing Nour's uncle. At Nour's request, he cut the putative price way down. I was staying for sure.

The riad broke with tradition. Instead of an inner courtyard, its outer hallways and bared windows looked out to an aquamarine pool contained by red-berried mistletoe, yew, and date palms. A young man vectored me into the office, and Nour's Uncle Ahmed met me in a full beard, sans moustache, and his head was covered with a rotative shaal turban wound unevenly over a taqiyah. The typical roulette of possible languages by which we might communicate flipped between us rapidly, and I was shocked to learn Ahmed spoke some Italian, so I enjoyed exchanging duvet moments with ease.

Dinner was upon me and I thought how much work eating can be when Nour called.

"Hello, Jack. This is Nour. We met earlier."

"Yes. Hello."

"I hope the room is good."

"Fine, thanks."

"I have the translation, and I can just give it to you if I can stop by."

"That would be great. See you in the lobby in—say—twenty minutes?"

"That's fine. I'll meet you downstairs."

Nour arrived and handed me the translation right off the bat and went to talk with her uncle, and I read.

In my homeland there are five things men should memorize—
Man's stronger than woman. To times, three times, and four times
But women are very cunning to stay alive
For the male, God give twice the chances what the female gets
For the female, God give for the mind and religion
Men lack for love and apathy

In my homeland, five things men forget—
The good ones in you, will be good one in their families
Take good care of women
Only generous people can be generous to women
And whoever mistreat women will be very unkind
Women will not be equal even when they care

In my homeland—
love is haram, forbidden
Insulting is halal, permitted

In my homeland
Habits = necessity
Worship = a reward
Women = sin
Men = authority
Kind people = stupid
Confident = proud
Gifted people = are buried

In my homeland—
the flower woman can be assaulted
The vegetable woman can be raped
The grocery shop woman can be injured
All the good men in my homeland are few, except many are the ones who
sold our homeland; whom are the ones who live the good life

In my homeland, the one who don't deserve to die, die,
By the hands of the ones who don't deserve the life

In my homeland—
the chest of our hairs is filled with bullets,
And the stomachs of the betrayers are filled with money

Arctic desolation ran through my veins as I tried to internalize the poem. Nour reemerged in the lobby.

"Nour," I said. "This is incredible."

"I know."

"You said you think you know who wrote this?"

"Yes. The woman who asked me to redo her door; you saw me working on it today. I know she had much trouble in marriage. I spoke to her and she said it's hers. Hayat is her name.

"I want to talk with this woman. Do you think it's possible?" I asked full of primal doubts that a stranger like me could be trusted.

Nour looked at me with an examining eye, the seconds exsanguinating. "Why exactly are you interested?"

"I'm chasing something, I guess." My words were absorbed in sadness.

"I can see. You're wearing it on your shoulder."

"It would really help me if I could see her," I said pleadingly, and feeling a headache coming on.

"She doesn't speak English. But I'll ask her, and I'll translate if she agrees."

"That'd be wonderful. But I don't want to do anything to upset her. In that case, I'll just go in the morning."

"She's always up early. I'll call you."

"Thanks, Nour."

"You are very welcome, Jack."

Doubtful Hayat would meet, I moved through the morning light in little hobbling circles, repacking my things. Then my phone buzzed, and it was Nour.

"Good morning, Nour. How are you?"

"Good morning, Jack. I'm Fine. Jack, she agreed to see you, and I'm really very surprised."

"Wow, that's great!" I think I was even more surprised.

"But she wanted to know more about you. I told her you're a writer."

"That's fine."

"Can we meet you at the same café you went to yesterday, maybe in one hour?"

"That should work. And thank-you for arranging this."

Just inside the entrance to the café, I was waiting on the women, my mind manacled in indecision over what to ask Hayat. My head lifted then to see a man setting a glass bottle on the bar top. The bottle rocked in little circular motions as he walked from my sight. I watched the bottle. As it began to spin on its invisible, vertical axis, the limits of its motion grew greater. The bottle began to wobble and tilt, gravity exerting torque at the top to help the bottle stand. The bottle slowed and spun faster to maintain its angular momentum. The wobbling worsened just before it fell from the counter. Plummeting to the floor, everything inside the bottle was in free fall motion, air and water attempting to fall at the same rate. Pressure inside the bottle dropped and the air and the water inside it began to mix. It crashed. The sound of it rather than shock me drew me to its valiant effort to survive.

A sound behind me. The two women walked in. Nour said, "Good morning, Jack. May I present Hayat."

"Good day," I said to both women, purposely paying more attention to Hayat. Her head remained down; still, and I could see her face glowering a daunted shadow of pain that goes on and on until it can no longer remain. She wore an abaya in black tones and a glittery exterior below the shawl. Her shirt jutted down her arms just above her wrists. She looked vulnerable beyond her years, one coarse front tooth projecting sidelong over another.

No one tutting anywhere in the café we sat alone, and the café was dark. Before I could preface my reason for wanting to speak to Hayat, she began to recount her days of terror and even Nour appeared unprepared for the sudden monologue. I had asked Nour not to render Hayat's words into a more understandable form of English, but to translate word for word as close as possible. I wanted to hear Hayat's heart. Nour began,

> It all start on my wedding night. All I wanted is what other woman want, respect for each other and love. But he started beating me, yes, on our first night together. I went to the bathroom to prepare. And he yelled where I am. When I exit, he treat me with extreme violence and cruelly. He seize my head and hair and hurl me on the wall. I was hoping that my marriage to someone I loved make me happy and I never saw that the man I decided as my husband abuse me while we were on honeymoon.

> We came to our home but for me it was a jail. Painting. I like painting. It was for me a place to escape; to close my eyes and imagine I am in the painting, trembling in fear that my husband is still coming and tormenting me. He come sometimes to my painting and I didn't move. But he push me down and destroy my works. All was a nightmare of nightmares. It not stop ever.

> I marry him although my family not approve. Finally, my father say yes. But he always drinking alcohol. He drag me on floor and hold me and I cry so much to let go. Torture and oppression. I ran to rooms and throw things but nothing stop him because he drunk. He hurt me so bad. Then I was struck by complete nervous breakdown and my sister take me to hospital. And I was shamed in my heart and family. Everyone know and I was shamed. I ask for divorce and I pray and pray. God give me divorce and I found it, my freedom. But I live in memories, bad, bad memories.

Insentience impaled my heart. Even the concept of certainty abandoned me transitorily. That a man could beat his wife on her precious wedding night was so far beyond my comprehension, I communicated my stupefaction to Nour through mute codes of gawking.

I asked Nour, "How can such a thing be?"

Nour stalled for a second as if she didn't want to say, then spoke. "To let her know he's in charge. To show his strength, to always be scared of him."

"How ridiculous." I felt like I was vomiting my words.

Compassion filled me and I said, "I'm so sorry." Hayat seemed to understand me because she smiled small as if to say thank-you. Then she looked over at the entrance of the café and seemed lost in her gaze. I thought she wanted to leave, but she turned her head back and said one last thing, which Nour was averse to translate.

"Nour, can you please tell me what she said? I want to hear everything."

"She said, 'I'll give you everything I have if you can take me with you.'"

My heart broke for Hayat.

"I think maybe I'll walk back with her now, Jack." Nour expressed her own sorrow with communicative eyes.

"I simply can't thank you enough. And please thank Hayat for me."

"Where's your next stop, Jack?"

"Toward the light, to be like the light."

"And I know you will find it. Because there is a light. We are not the light. We can only reflect it to the world. Let your light shine, Jack." Covering my mouth with the palm of my hand my eyes swelled.

"I don't know what happened with you. But I pray for you," Nour said. She smiled and the two women departed arm in arm.

Out into the unlimited sunlight I walked. Hope fenestrate beyond my doubts and fears culled my tears into a bucket of forgets. Now what? The bridge back to my reality was short. I was in Morocco to work. But purpose was finding me. It found me in pain, and it was taking me through the darkened halls of others' pain. I was willing to walk the palling galleries of darkness if by its ugliness, or beauty, it mattered not, purpose brought me into the light. Life is a series of decisions, I thought. The common ruble of banality could wait.

∼ ∼ ∼

The ghostly desolation, disturbed only by enclaved dots of mountain villages, captured a continuum of colors, from bright yellow, to light violet, to deep red. Rock walls, sharp switchback turns, five-hundred-foot drops, and possible consequences. No lack of souvenir stalls and tourists. I was going over the mountains. Something in my heart had said to go north. Fez. Maybe Tangiers. The map made it pretty clear. Getting there was really only practicable by returning to Marrakech over the mountains and then to—wherever.

The sense of adventure I feel entering a new town for the first time is nothing compared to the exhilaration I get navigating a tortuous mountain pass. The Tizi N'Tichka Pass made my adrenaline charge on high and no sooner did I begin to make the bend, which can knock the metrosexual out of anyone, then a tour bus met me and peril fluttered inside my brain like playing cards clothespinned to the spokes of a bike wheel. I pulled over in a utilitarian parking space cut out in the hill designed for sightseers.

The panorama rapt my attention. Exiting the car, I stood motionless. But it was then that the unmovable parts of me permitted my ever-active fears to question whether I should just go home. The vista remaining in my visual field, my memory faded back to my conversation with Indela at the apartment in Taroudant the second night.

"Jack, can I talk?"

"Of course, you can. Let me sit over here with you on the couch."

Abruptly, I released my body onto the couch and waited expectantly for the springs to do their job. But the handful of material passing itself off as a cushion drowned me next to Indela.

"What are you doing down there, Jack?" She laughed. We both laughed.

"I tell you what. Just let me sit here and we'll talk."

"I've been thinking about the dreams," she said. "Isn't it bizarre I had one about you, and you had one about me, the same night?" She looked perplexed like some revelation was lapping at her consciousness. Slowly, I reached for my barrel coffee cup and gently stroked its rim like a kitty with big paws and, taking a big breath, tried to conjure my loosely configured memories about the dreams.

A busy quiet passed between us. And I almost said something that probably would have been stupid but thunder in the distance spared the certain gaff.

"A big storm's out there," Indela said. "There's so much power in a storm. I feel so small next to it."

I also knew myself differently in the mirror of the storm and a calm draped the moment. Everything was in its proper place.

"Jack, I think I understand the dreams."

Some apprehension eclipsed me. "What are you thinking?"

Indela gazed at me in silence. Her upturned eyes had always looked like windows into her soul, and I believed I could look right through them to some hidden meaning inside her. This night was different. Her eyes seemed to radiate from within her, articulating some transcendent value and which had made me their object.

"Jack," she said in an urgent tone. I was about to reply, but she straightened her spine and, with the most resolute conviction, said, "Father, will you embrace me?" My thoughts swam in search of her meaning. Her upper body, not waiting for my reply, rested fully against my torso, and I instinctively wrapped my left arm around her deltoid and squeezed her body close to mine. She relaxed, and I thought it was for the first time.

My attention then returned fully to the splendid view, and I realized that it was on that couch that I had heard, though indirectly, her interpretation of the dreams. And somehow, the realization touched me like an unseen voice to persevere. It was the catalyst to keep me on the narrow path. I got back in the car.

The afternoon sun arched its predetermined vault above the parallel folds of limestone ledges and marls and had cast a reddish hue. An increasing number of trees came into sight, and past the alee side of the mountains the winds were strong. The site of a rocky-height restaurant overlooking the Oued Tichka River surprised me, and I pulled over to see a lithe waterfall inspiriting from the riverbed into an abyss in the distance. A couple of selfies were in order to send Beth. But seeing my image before the river had the unanticipated effect of sparking a hallucination. And the perseverance that had been restored not moments earlier was tested there.

I saw Charon paddling his boat down the River Styx, his eyes like fiery darts, delivering the damned to Minos. Can it be? I exclaimed. The condemned spilling out of the ferry were all the women without hope of liberation—the Boatman thwacking the women with his long oar should they refuse their hellish end. In my daymare, Minos took the form of all the men directly responsible for the women's Sisyphean hopelessness.

I dropped the phone. Fear inexplicable radiating my nervous system externalized and a feeling of demoralization weakened me to the point that I felt I had to sit in the car. Bracing myself, I walked around the trunk hoping to make it. My head laid back on the headrest and, looking up at the lining, I held my breath and let out a scream in anger. Grabbing the steering wheel, I banged my forehead metrically in three even whacks on the top of the wheel. I must have passed out because later I found myself rousing from a self-induced nap. I scratched the near surface for signs of people versus figments and then checked my watch, wondering how long I had been out.

The titled rearview mirror revealed a small mouse under my right eye. Ratcheting concerns for my safety made me consider that the two-hour drive to Marrakech was achievable for the car but less than achievable for me. Aware of my skin, a valuation of a possible poser who wasn't as strong as he pretended, was confronting me. Maybe I should go home like my wife wants, I thought, and avoid some Faustian bargain for understanding if it means impaling myself on my own pigheadedness.

A bygone objet d'art entrance wall to old Col du Tichka had caught my attention a few kilometers back and looked welcoming. But the café restaurant with a view was right there. I thought, wouldn't it be better to sit there to recoup than to binge watch myself self-destruct in extraordinary shivers? I parked and went in.

A gentleman came to take my order. There was a little menu. But not having the energy to look at it, I assumed my default position of whatever's easy. So, I asked the waiter's recommendation and minutes later kebabs and chips arrived.

In the throes of purposelessness, I recalled how I like to ask my more progressively minded students who think they're going to overturn the system why they too assume their own default positions by sitting in the same seats all semester without anyone ever assigning seats. In the end, we're all conformists, I tell them. Wiping my mouth quickly after seeing a woman sitting nearby pointing to her face in effigy of my sauce-bathed chops, I smiled at her without feeling the least embarrassed.

I watched her group leaving, and to my surprise, the same woman turned back and stopped at my table. "Excuse me," she asked, "but are you American?"

"Yes, I am," I replied, now self-aware of my bad eating habit. As I wiped my mouth, my eyes scanned how very tall she was, and I thought her light brunette with subtle peekaboo highlights was something my wife should try.

"I'm from Florida," she said with a disarming smile.

"You're from Florida?" My face must have looked like a kid at his own surprise birthday party. "Small world. I'm from Florida too."

"Oh, I met another man from Florida last week. How unusual."

"Pardon my excitement. It's just that it's so good to meet someone from home. Oh, excuse me. My name's Jack. Nice to meet you."

"I'm Robin." She reached over and shook my hand, and her handshake was much stronger than Nitta's. Then she readjusted her gray-black sweater and stood motionless like she wanted to say something.

"If you have a minute," I invited, "please, have a seat."

"Well, as you can see my friends are preparing to leave." She motioned a man in her group that she'd be right along, and then sat on the edge of a chair sideways like she didn't want to glue down. "I have only a minute." She spoke regretfully.

"Well, I don't want to hold you."

"Say, I saw you outside. You okay?"

My face now ribboned flush, I realized why she came over and how much I needed to get off this mountain. "Well—yeah—I'm okay. Just a few things have been on my mind lately." She didn't reply but sat congealed as if she knew I was a good actor.

"So, Robin, you vacationing?"

"No, not really. I'm in Morocco for my work." She glanced over her shoulder at the entrance to the restaurant, and said, "Well, I probably need to get going. My group's waiting. So nice to meet you and have a good time here."

Something in me said I needed to know more about her. "Say, before you go, can I just ask what work you do?"

"I'm a cultural anthropologist and I'm living here for a time to do fieldwork for my doctorate."

"Really. Can I ask your specialty?"

"I'm focusing on the everyday lives of Moroccan women."

"No."

"Yes, you look surprised."

"Please, if I can just ask. Where are you and your friends heading now?"

"Marrakech."

"Marrakech?" My emotional palate was riveted. "Why, that's where I'm going. Um—is there a way I can contact you in Marrakech, possibly for a brief conversation? You may just be a person I need to talk with."

"Sure. But we're very busy you know. We travel. Say, I've got to skedaddle."

Robin gave me her card and I stood watching as she walked away, and the scabby days of sadness seemed a shade sunnier. Still, I wished for an even easier time of music sweet and summer kind, at home with my familiar things. But I had seen too much, the impress of the designs of time and fortunes amalgamating their timeless rhymes and I wanted to be their horn. What to do? In a scent of confidence, to Marrakech, I averred, to turn the next page and play on.

Chapter 8

The gentle road lay ahead. Light traffic and a montage of valleys wide and narrow, villages, children near the road, and sounded ruins communicating epochs and values, charmed me. I passed a car broken down alongside the road. The Forêt Toufliht, its trees tall and strong; elsewhere opening its checkered lawns and glades among chocolate plains, and hilltops ascending— some rounding, some pyramiding. The road straight through misty green hills before me and a portentous wall of gray behind me. I was engaged again. My soul was blessed with a rake.

Marrakech was just as it was before and memories of my time here with Indela and Mansour percolated through the myriad of sights. Suddenly, a little boy jumped in front of my car and I slammed on the brakes just in time. Getting out, I went to his aid, but his mother, I had presumed, slitted and lathed me in Arabic, making short work of me. When I offered an apology in my broken French, she retorted, and with a crowd looking on, I felt like the poor fool blamed for the fall of Constantinople because he had left open the small Kerkoporta gate in the Land Walls. Every effort to calm her down went nowhere. She was a wrecking ball of motherly tenderness.

Immediately, a short, youngish man, wearing business casual and a pale-grey blazer, his smile a thin, down-turned arc, walked into the street and chased away the woman and the boy, and urged me to get out of the road. Seeing my discreetly complicated expression, the guy clued me in to the presence, though illegal, of a cottage industry in his city that exploits children for money in a variety of ways.

Having seen similar tricks in Europe, I asked him, "So, do these women do this on their own or are they put up to it?"

"Sir," he cautioned, "Many, I think, are working for some kind of men. But maybe they do it alone."

"Great" I said somewhat sarcastically.

"Oh, well, they are very poor, sir. But it is wrong what they do."

"Look, you've been helpful. You think, maybe, you can suggest a good place to stay for the night?" I asked, my brainwaves slouching.

"Oh, you are in Marrakech."

"Yes, but any ideas? Oh wait. I didn't get your name. I'm Jack."

"I am Yassine, sir. I am at your disposal. Welcome to Marrakech."

"Well, thank-you—Yassine."

"How long you are in Marrakech, sir?"

"I'm not sure. I don't know the city. But. Maybe. Well," I said, in sporadic blips. "Perhaps a moderate hotel or inexpensive riad."

"Oh, there is a riad not far. And reasonably priced for you."

"Nothing too expensive. Please."

"No sir. Not much money and very nice. You like it and do private room for you." Yassine wrote down the address on the back of a business card for an Italian restaurant.

Taking the card, I said, "Is this good Italian? Boy, if its anything like the one in Cairo, this is one place I don't want to go to."

"Why's that, sir?"

"Everything is fish. No real Italian dishes there. And no wine. Frankly, I need a good red right about now."

"Oh, no. I know this place. This is good place. With everything. You like." Yassine spoke in swelling pales of confidence.

Not able to distinguish truth from rhetorical flash in my new friend, I said, "Maybe I'll try it."

The heavens began to shine perfunctory little droplets, and I thought that the ominous clouds over the mountains on my way into the city had followed me.

"Looks like rain," I said. "Thank-you so much, Yassine."

"My pleasure, sir. Welcome."

I punched the address Yassine gave me for the riad into Siri and, pulling back onto the road, swerved so as not to hit a donkey dressed in a burlap sack which almost made me hit another donkey not dressed in a burlap sack.

The door into the riad was lined with young people coming and going, a fateful indication that Yassine's characterization of the place was more ambition than reality. Once inside, everything changed. The place was absolutely gorgeous, and I feared beyond the size of my wallet.

A young woman met me, and the boutique chambers dampened the Schoenberg discord of minion sounds outside the door. Her blouse was cut just low enough to reveal her long, strutted collarbones, and her neck flowed as if from the hand of Leonardo.

"Welcome, sir. I am Sanaa. Would you like a quick tour please?"

"I think I need to see prices."

"Please, let me show you around first."

Sanaa walked just ahead of me and floated through the hallways, posing her body left, then right, her eyes so big, I could see them from the sides. Extending her gracefully cool arms, she showed me the lounges and the arcaded interior courtyard. Each time we passed a wall or arch, she purposely touched the sheathing of her left hand on the paint and then slid it along, making the sound one might expect from the finest possible sandpaper, until the tippy tips of her fingers tripped off one by one. Then to the roof terrace and the chambre berbère styled as a Moroccan tent with outstanding views and a distinct hot tub. The scope and beauty were way beyond my meager means, and I told her so. But I got the impression she wanted to show it off anyway because doing so fit her personality.

We followed a different flight of stairs back to the front entrance, and Sanaa kept an eye on my footing over each step. Her sweetness helped to wash the dust of days. The entrance was full now. The youthful crowing of silly banters had come in from outside and filled the space. Recent events and the dissonance in the room met in the way that two busy oceans meet but never mix. I tried hard to wrap my brain around it all. Sanaa looked back at me with a sweet smile like she knew I needed peace. My upper back and neck muscles began to tighten, and I could hear Beth say, it's all good. I became pliant.

Sanaa disappeared into a room off the entrance and I waited on the sumptuous price. A man's hand showed from the same area and clasped the doorjamb, and the man's voice sounded familiar. He walked out and I said, "Yassine," and my tone was half stunned; half amused.

"Hello, sir," he said. "Very good to see you again."

Laughing through my words, I said, "Yassine, you're the—?"

"Yes sir, I am the manager here. I trust the accommodations are fine, sir."

"Yassine, I've never seen anything like it. But I'm concerned about the price."

"We take good care of you." He wrote a price on a piece of paper and showed it to me. My proverbial jaw hit the floor. I was staying.

My first order of business was the hot tub. But I didn't bring a bathing suit. It was then that I recalled Mansour surfing in his underwear. Oh, what the heck, I thought. A young woman had just finished adjusting the calcium levels as I walked up with a towel wrapped tight around my waist. She showed me three fingers and I took her to mean to wait three minutes before getting in. I waited less.

The jets of warm, circulating water made me swell in extraordinary comfort, and the feeling tunneled me back in time to surfing with Mansour at Sidi Kaouki. Indela out of our audible field, I encouraged him to marry the girl—that regardless her fight for love and independence, to work out their individual problems together, and to climb the stairs of life as one. "You think I should marry the girl?" he said with a sparkle in his eye that outmatched the sun-reflecting waves. The jets pumping around my solid calves recentered my attention on the tiling, and how I hoped they had found the stairs to the clear blue heaven.

Before I parboiled myself, I got out of the hot tub, slipping a little on the slick. I had wanted to contact Robin. But I had just seen her, and a turnaround call felt inappropriate. On the other hand, I had returned to Marrakech only because some ephemeral voice had prompted me to do so, and I certainly had no reason to dawdle there. In a moment's impulse, I decided to dial. She answered.

"Hello."

"Hello Robin, this is Jack. I met you earlier."

"Oh yes, how are you? You made it to the medina, okay?" Her voice was lissome.

"Well, yes, I'm in the city. How are you doing?"

"Oh, you won't believe it. We had a flat tire as soon as we left you."

"Is that right?" I said, sheepishly, recalling the broken-down vehicle I saw on my way from the mountains to Marrakech.

"So, what about you, Jack?"

"But you made it to Marrakech?" I interjected.

"Yes, we're here. We're staying at our place near the medina. You know where that is?"

"Not really, no."

"We're planning to go to dinner. If you're available, and you think you can find the place, why don't you join us? And like I said, we travel lots, so I don't know how long I'm available in the city to talk."

"Well, I better check my calendar," I said, fist-pumping.

"Oh, are you busy?"

"No, no. I'm joking. In fact, I really want to talk if you think we can squeeze that in."

"Oh, no problem. Happy to chat. But there's going to be a group of us, and I have to give attention to others, so please factor that in."

"That's okay. Where do I meet you?"

"If you don't mind, let me call you back, because I need to find the directions. And we have some things to do here at the moment, if that's okay."

"Perfect. Thanks so much." I spoke in accentual pitches. "I'll be waiting."

I sat on the edge of my bed, thinking how well my spur-of-the-moment call had turned out. My hips let up, and a release of tension flowed to my neck and out my eyes like carbonated water fizzing over the lip of a bottle after popping the lid. Ideas of what I would ask her then refused to assemble in my mind, and I had a reverse reaction: my muscles tensed from my neck to low back. Then with a sudden yell, I erupted out loud, "Stop, Jack." Too loud, apparently, because not a moment later I heard a knock at my room door.

"Yes," I said.

Standing at the door was a tall, young man dressed in sheer black. He looked as far as he could into the room without actually entering the room, and asked, "Okay?"

"Yes. Everything is okay."

He walked away with a stare. My teeth clenched as I closed the door, I realized my emotions were still on high alert and that I just needed to come down. Feeling languid by so many sights and emotions, I decided to grab my phone and scribbled some general questions for Robin.

My phone rang. Robin asked if I'd meet her group at an Italian restaurant in the medina and I was almost certain it wasn't the one on the back of the card Yassine gave me.

Needing a few dirhams, I asked my taxi driver to stop at a money exchange on the way to the restaurant. The woman took a long time to make the exchange, and I had hoped her dillydallying wouldn't cause me to be late.

I arrived on time. The carved wooden door entrance of the restaurant portaged me into an alternative reality and I felt lifted. Lemons, the main catalyst for other Italian ingredients, hung from trees shading an open patio and, stimulating my taste buds, made my mouth water with expectation. This was no knock off Italian place like the one in Egypt but an extant invitation to explore.

Before the maître d' could assist me, Robin walked up. "Hi Jack. Glad you made it. I saw you coming through the window."

"Wow, what a nice place. Love it. And great to see you."

"Happy to see you also. We're over this way." I followed her and couldn't get my nose off the array of Italian smells flirting with my taste buds.

It was a large, round table. Laying her left hand on the back of my shoulder, she made introductions to her group, and the introductions were cordial. But all I could hear was the nervy disquiet within me. How could I talk with Robin on a touchy subject at a dinner table full of her friends? Robin inspected my outward appearance, and I knew, she knew, I was jumpy. Our eyes spoke to each other for at least three seconds.

Then she shifted herself on her chair, I guessed to accommodate me, and said, "Jack. I think you're wondering about cultural anthropology?"

"Not exactly. I'm an academic. I've some sense of what it is."

"Oh really. What do you teach?"

"Forestry."

"Oh, how interesting. And you're in Morocco for—?"

"I came to do follow-up studies on the argan forests. Some personal work." Everyone at the table was listening to me, and I didn't want others to know why I was there. So, I said, "I have some technical questions about cultural anthropology," at which point, everyone turned away.

Feeling my alone time with Robin was limited, I jumped the loop and gave her an abridged version of my time in Morocco. After I had finished, Robin looked at me like she had just slid backwards off her chair.

"Jack," Robin said. "I'm really sorry you lost the relationship with this couple, especially the young lady. The way you describe her sounds like she is a very caring person."

"I cared a lot about both of them, really. The young woman especially. She has a really big heart."

"Do you think anything else played into your feelings for her?"

"The attack. It's hard to explain. But it's like it caused my care for her to explode inside me. And I can't get over the feeling of guilt that I failed her."

"You just got too emotionally involved."

"I've heard that before."

"You didn't want to talk to me as a psychiatrist. I'm sorry. You had questions about women in Morocco. How do you see me helping you?"

"My experiences enlightened me to the plight of women in this part of the world, especially the issue of domestic violence. If I can just use Indela as an example, why do you think she seemed to have sided with her abuser?"

"Jack. I would honestly say that women in all cultures often side with their abusers and that this is not unique to Morocco. But there are some added pressures here. It sounds like if she was already an adopted woman, she was probably doubly marginalized in society from the beginning and might have felt like she would fit in better in her society if she maintained the relationship with the boyfriend."

"And you think that could be said of any young woman in Morocco?"

"Definitely."

"I heard something similar from Nitta, a Moroccan woman I've known many years. She spoke of the ways women continue to find themselves stuck between the older expectations society places on them and the newer reality of the need of women to work."

"Well, that's a different pressure but similar. It sounds like your friend feared being ostracized through too much of the wrong kind of attention. And remember this, before I forget. It's also frowned upon for women to openly have boyfriends."

"I did not know that," I responded in staccato pulses.

"Yes. Because for more traditional people, a female is not considered a woman until she's married. So, sex is reserved strictly for marriage. In fact, sex before marriage is illegal here."

"By law?"

"Yes."

"I didn't know that either. But I don't think they were having sex."

"It doesn't matter. If a couple's dating, traditional people assume they're doing something sexual even though they may not be. So, any kind of romantic touching or kissing, even holding hands in public, can be taboo in certain quarters."

"So, it's not universal in Morocco?"

"No. It's like the observation your friend—Nitta, I think? made about how working women are trapped between the old ways and the new. More traditional people, mostly in the rural regions, can frown on dating. But in the big cities that attitude is loosening up. So, in the villages you see young, unmarried women in traditional dress, and they don't date. But in Casablanca or Rabat, it's become more common to see friends out clubbing and so forth. It's a very fine line women must walk in order to fit in."

The waiter was taking orders and I hadn't even looked at a menu. "Do you know what you want, Jack?" Robin asked.

My favorite dish was on the menu. An easy choice. "Spaghetti alla puttanesca, per favore."

To Robin, I said, "And I'm licking my chops."

"I think we met because I noticed you licking your chops." She chuckled.

"Really, I remember." I couldn't hold back a big guffaw.

Then the man sitting on the other side of Robin, his long gray hair tied neatly in a ponytail, leaned in, and said, "Pardon me. But I couldn't help overhearing some of your talk with Robin."

"Jack, this is Jeffrey," Robin said, "in case you forgot." I had forgotten but pretended like I hadn't.

"Robin's being very helpful," I said to Jeffery.

"I'm sure she is. Just let me add that women in Arab nations generally react to violent men differently. There are women who actually favor violent men because they think they can protect them. Others fight it and don't put up with it at all. And then there are those who try to handle their violent lovers diplomatically."

"I bet they do that for the reason Robin mentioned," I said. "They feel stuck."

Jefferey took a second to think and said, "Yes. But remember. There are various reasons for that also. Women can feel stuck because they don't feel they have options to be independent. Or they feel caught between the parts of the culture trying to be progressive, and those parts with its more traditional expectations.

"Exactly," Robin said.

Jefferey politely waited to see if Robin was going to say more. She sat as though she was gardening thoughts. So, he included the idea that, "This is an honor/shame culture. In a law-based society like America, a person might ask themselves, "Is what I'm doing right or wrong?" That view weighs the conscious in light of law and punishment. In an honor/shame society, the question is more, "How will people look at me if I do x?"

"I got it," I said. "And from what I've heard and seen, the honor goes more to the man and the shame to the woman." Jefferey and Robin looked at each other as if I had just threaded the needle from thirty meters.

"You have a point," Jeffery said.

Robin then reentered the discussion. "Jack, I don't know if you're familiar with ethnography. That's part of the work of the anthropologist. The researcher observes society from the point of view of the subject of the study. In women's studies, the status of women is frequently invoked as a barometer of the country's progress. So, listening to women; seeing things through their worldview, is critical for what we do."

"But why are women used as the gauge of a nation's progress?" I asked.

Her cheeks tightened. "Because a chain is only as strong as its weakest link. I don't mean the women are weak. I mean that what a society fails to empower jeopardizes the whole. And women are no small link. Women birthed us, some died in the process, they nursed us, they hope and pray for us, they teach us, especially at odd moments, and they love us."

For a moment, I sat quietly, remembering my mother, my wife, and my own daughter, at home. "I get it," I said. Eager to explore one more area, I took a breath as Robin looked at the others seated around the table, then asked her, "Another minute, maybe? Sorry."

"Oh, no problem," she said. "But I probably need to get to the others soon."

"I'll try to be brief. I'm curious about the recent changes in law to protect women here."

"The laws in Morocco have changed in the favor of women. There are associations abused women can go to and that help to protect these women and follow their cases in court."

"Do all the women take advantage of these associations?"

"No. The problem is that many women don't have the money to resort to the police or the courts. Others just accept their destiny for fear of attracting attention, so they simply endure."

"Well, wait, going to police costs money?"

"The associations are very helpful and don't cost anything; they mainly facilitate the women. Lawyers can cost money though."

"I see. Now my friend, Nitta, also said there's been little change in the society to help women. But you seem to think change has happened."

"I don't know what Nitta was referring to. She may have meant that the public laws haven't seen much change. Where change has in fact occurred is in the political or secular laws."

"Oh, I see. So, there's a difference here between the public and political, kind of like the difference between church law and secular law in America. Is that close?"

"That's sounds about right. I don't know how close it is, though. I'm not an expert in the laws here or in America." The open atmosphere of discussion on the topic was dissipating. Robin said, "Jack, I think if you want to know more about the legal aspects, there's a lawyer here in Marrakech who knows both the secular and cultural laws. I can contact him to see if he's available if you want, but I don't know how long you're here."

"I'm here as long as it takes. Can you please give him my contact?"

"I will. Tonight."

The dinner and the setting had been a Neapolitan dream. But releasing the conversation with Robin allowed my memory to scuffle through layers of time to that dreadful night. My nervous system ratcheted me and a man, whom had not said a word to me all night, stared at me. Just then, I noticed my right eyelash fluttering in butterfly rhythm as against a strong wind, and I was sure the mini-spectacle had colored the man's perception of me. The affect metastasized from my eye to my right cheek, pillaging my confidence. The restaurant insignia on the white cloth napkin laying crumpled across my lap served as a good focal point, so I looked down at it and said to myself, it's all good, Jack. A man-tear formed inauspiciously, and I started to feel exhausted. I left my unfinished plate.

Wiping my mouth, a final time, I said. "Robin, I'm going to go. I want to thank you so much. You've been an absolutely tremendous help."

"Going already?"

"Not feeling so great. Sorry. Please say goodnight to everyone for me."

"Okay, Jack. Good luck. And I do hope we meet again someday. And good luck with all your research."

Chapter 9

The taxi dropped me a block from the riad. The remaining walk was littered by kindles of kittens snooping though the days' garbage scattered helter-skelter along the art felled sidewalks and curbsides. What struck me was the absence of molly cats and clowders. Where were the bigger cats? I wondered. The riad came into sight and an old man was shingled over the steps leading to the front door, his head snugged tight in a San Francisco 49er cuffed hat. His things were wedged tightly between his bent legs as if he were a professional wrestler finishing off his opponent. A single light from the adjacent building spotlighted him, and I thought he was laying there for safety. I had to step over him in order to ring the bell, and I was surprised to find Sanaa answering because the hour was late.

Sanaa had changed her dress to a long, gray housecoat and light headscarf. She didn't respond to my greeting, her head buried deep in the bone of her chest. She relocked the door without looking, and it must have been from pure instinct—I just knew something was wrong. As she turned to walk away, I reached my hand to her arm. "Sanaa, are you okay?" She brushed off my hand angrily, and a cold vacancy stilled me.

"I'm so sorry," I exclaimed as she ran into the voided halls. I followed the sound of her cries until I reached the hollow of the grand room and the air stood still. Then a sudden heave of tears shattered the stillness and I ran in its direction. She was sitting on a cushion by the pool drinking a cup of tears.

With worry and thoughtfulness, I sat beside her, bending my knees slowly and keeping my distance.

Sanaa took three, distinct deep gulps of air and spoke three short sentences. "I'm. Sorry. Sir." Then, she said, "I did not mean to push your hand. I'm not accustomed to the warmth."

I restrained myself from touching her again, and the mystery of her heart unraveled.

"Is there something I can do?" I asked.

"No sir. I feel huzun."

"Huzun?"

"Sadness, sir. So much sadness. I should return to my room. I stay up because you're the only one right now."

I listened through the heavy air for a solitary sound. Nothing.

"Yassine's not here?" I asked.

"He lives close." Sanaa spoke through the spams in her diaphragm.

A sudden feeling of self-consciousness hit me of being alone in a riad with a single woman. "But he's not in the building?"

"No."

"Dear, I'm going to my room. If you want to talk, I'm here. Okay"

My hand reached up and laid gently against a blue and white tiled pillar as I prepared to leave. But I was discomfited at her tears. Being careful to check on her one last time, as if doing so made the situation less intolerable, I looked back, then made a final turn toward my room.

It was then that Sanaa screamed, "They have torn me." As if my feet were not touching the ground, I raced to her side. She reached her hand and clutched her throat.

"What is it?" I pled.

"They've torn me. They've torn me. They've torn me." She yelled, her voice rising with each repetition and reverberating strongly off the riad's tiled interior.

I implored her. "Who's torn you, dear? Who?"

She opened like an old, unread book full of promise and pain. "I'm trying to find my second life. I didn't even know I was given in marriage until it happened. I was fourteen, sir. I was just a child. No one told me that I had to agree to be married. My family just did it. My parents signed the papers without me knowing and told me I had a husband. I was miserable. I knew the old man from our ville. He was forty-seven years older than me. I told my parents; I screamed at my mother not to do this. I didn't know my parents had agreed to the marriage. He was old enough to be my grandfather."

"Wait," I said, my face feeling blushed as a sunburn. "You were forced to marry a man forty-seven years older than you?"

Just then, a light in the grand hall went out. Sanaa started to get up. "Oh, I should change the light." Her eyes were purulent testaments of her grief.

"Let's not worry about the light right now." I searched my jacket for some tissues. "We'll get it later." All at once, I noticed my lower lip in pain from biting down hard. I rubbed it and said, "Please continue."

Sanaa gathered herself. "The man gave my father the dowry. We call it sdaq." She looked up at me, her eyes streaked in dolorous red strips like the atmosphere at sunset. "Life was a horror. Sometimes he would hit me, beat me, sometimes rape me. I never told nobody. Who could I tell? People would say what they always say. You deserved it. What did you do?"

My jaw was hanging. "Did you tell your family what he was doing?"

"No. My family knew what he did to his first wife. One time I came to them and they saw the bruises, and my mother said, 'Your husband has money and many good friends. Do not worry about these things,' and she was stroking my hair."

"What kind of work does he do?"

"He owns buildings. But I never saw them. All day he sat with men in cafés, smoking and talking about nothing. He came home at lunch, and if the food was not right, he hit me. One time he pushed me over the divan and hit me so hard with his belt. I tried to run away, but each time he found me. Where I can flee? Then I became pregnant. We had a little son. I was very happy. But I lived in fear; fear for me and my son."

"You have a son?" I said to my surprise.

"Yes. But then a friend at the market saw my bruises on my arms. She spoke to me and asked how old I was when I married. She told me I can't be forced to marry unless I agree. No one told me these things were illegal. I didn't even know about sdaq, that it was for me."

"What happened to the bride price?"

"My father took it. I've never seen it."

Becoming angrier by the moment, I focused, and asked, "Have you gone to the police about the beatings?"

"The lady at the market said I need proof. She helped me go to a store and the man there took good pictures. Then I get help from friends, and I divorce the man. I refuse to call him my husband." Sanaa needed to wipe her eyes and so did I. Some tissues were in a hidden pocket in my jacket, and I reached to the bottom of the pocket and pulled them out. Sanaa took the entire packet and handed me one. "Mister, I don't want to trouble you."

"No, please, please, go on." I wanted her to get it all out as much for her as for me.

"I got a job as a maid in the city. The man; he owned house. He was married man; always picked me up and brought me to his apartment. One day, he started to take me a different way, and I said, 'Where are we going?' I started to cry because I knew. He took me to a place, and he raped me. I could hear the voices of other men in another room, and I prayed and prayed they not come in too. When he was finished with me, I ran. I ran as far as I could run. I wanted to die so much."

Sanaa grabbed my hand again and held tight. I wiggled a few more tissues from our shared packet in her hand and waited for what was next.

"Now I had no job," she went on to say. "I went in the medina and did prostitution."

"Prostitution?" I was stunned.

"Yes. I would take off my long, headscarf and put on a red sweatshirt and jeans, and touch myself up with heavy red lipstick." Assuming, perhaps, I was ready to judge her, Sanaa was quick to add, "But I always used condoms, not like some of the other girls."

"Sanaa, why did you do this?" I asked in an understanding tone.

"Because in our country, if a divorced woman remarry, the husband can take all the children, and I was willing to do anything to keep my son."

"What?" I was incredulous. "If a divorced woman gets another husband, the husband can take the children? Is that what you said?"

"Yes. Is Morocco. Many divorced women with children in big trouble. They need money. So, they marry again. But then can lose children."

Things were coming together in my head. To keep the children, they must work. But people in the community know they're divorced and won't give them work. So, they go into the medina to prostitute. Wow.

She blew her nose. Then, as if I hadn't heard enough, she said, "That's when I met Mr. Yassine."

"You mean—" I said ending with a deliberate tenuto.

"Yes. Mr. Yassine was a customer. Regular. But he good man. He not like the others. He was nice." With just a flicker of self-respect she added, "Then one night he come to me and offer me this job and I do it." Sanaa grasped the sides of the cushion tightly. "Today," she continued, "I saw my father. I went to him to get the sdaq. I need it for my son. He laughed at me and said I'm nothing but a prostitute. He threw me down on the floor and said that he sold the sdaq long ago and there was nothing left for me. I told him I have friends now and I can go to court. He said I am wasting my time. I know he's right."

"Why would you be you wasting your time?"

"My father can pay the judge and he make decision for my father." It was all a revulsion.

Never had I heard anything like this before. Sanaa's fervid pleas and loathsome past flagged what little remained in me of the day's strength.

"Mister. I will go now. I hope for you pleasant evening. I hope I not bother you."

"Oh, my goodness. No."

Sanaa stood to her feet, and her eyes exuded a flaming torch of self-assurance. But I felt it wasn't real; only that she was releasing me. "Bonne nuit," she yielded the night and moved from me.

"Sanaa," I said as I stood also. "I really do not know what to say. I'm beyond words."

"I hope we meet again, mister." She replied in a demurring tone. And with that she vanished into the douriya, or servant's quarters.

Back in my room, two hours of rigid wakefulness dissolved into the tender burbling of late-night streams, and I was whisked kindly to where fairies never tire.

≈ ≈ ≈

"Ring," sounded my phone near dawn. I reached to shut off the hellish torment, but my zigzagged reach knocked over a glass of water. "Hello," I gargled through the evening's reservoir of mucus.

"Dr. Jack?" the voice intoned.

"Yes," I acknowledged, clearing my throat.

"I am Jamal, friend of Ms. Robin. She says you want to do some questions." I fought so hard to realize what this guy was talking about that a picture of Trümmerfrau, the German women who helped to clear the wreckage in the aftermath of World War II, blazed across my hippocampus.

"Sir!" Jamal said in an insistent tone. The laws affecting many women in Morocco."

"Oh, oh, of course." I replied while straining to raise myself into a semi-sitting position in bed. "Yes, how are you?"

"Fine, sir. I apologize to call you so early." I looked at my watch. It was 5:45 a.m.

"No, no, that's quite alright," I muttered, my eyes narrowing to enhance my visual discrimination.

"I have busy times now. But I know Ms. Robin and am willing to make time for you this morning if you desire. You're welcome."

"That's fine. When and where?"

"I will send you text with information. You can get taxi?"

"I dropped my rental. But of course. I'll walk if I have to."

"Oh, no need, sir. I hope to see you later."

"Yes. Thank-you."

I struggled not to fall back to sleep, recalling the dream I had had. The night's recounting with Sanaa had twilled a denim of my own, of better times, but all was lost. Before old man sorrow had his way with me, I decided to rise and meet what the day had planned. I was halfway to the bathroom when I heard the phone ding and knew that Jamal was eager, which was fine by me. I was getting closer to the kernel than to the husk. A deep breath and alveoli allowed inhaled oxygen to surge, and my face danced with life.

The riad seemed completely empty and I couldn't find Sanaa. For some reason, I imagined I'd never see her again and deep sadness worked from the inside of me out to the feeling of doleful eyes.

From a side door, a Rubenesque woman appeared wearing an apron and pushing a cart of coffee and croissants. She fixed her hennaed hair falling out the side of her barrette, and resituated a croissant tobogganing from the top of the pile to the bottom.

My first sip of coffee is always my favorite. Light glinted covertly across the rim of the glassed dome top of the wustadar and caused the pastel blue of the tiles on one side of the room to show off. Brushing even strokes of crumbs from my shirt onto the cart, I was interrupted when the same woman who brought out the breakfast pointed to the corner of my mouth paddled with mess from gobbling too fast. Wow, I have a problem, I thought. I waved a thank-you, headed outside, and flagged a taxi. The driver was so big he had to dip his head down to see through the windshield. He took my phone and read the directions Jamal had texted me.

A single flight of stairs led into the entrance of Jamal's apartment where he kept his office. A boy sat halfway up the stairs and appeared to be playing a videogame. He had on kind of a cool grey tee. His hair was matted and face a little dirty and he looked like he knew his way around. He had a sandal on one foot and a shoe on the other, and he noticed me looking.

"I lost a shoe," he said. I could tell from the way his eyes moved that maybe he knew I was surprised by his English. "Yeah, I speak English." He spoke with an agile smirk, and I sensed this kid was cagy. He donned a gritty appeal beyond his years.

"So, kid, how'd you learn English?"

"I learned reading comic books."

"Wow you're pretty good from reading comic books."

"And TV pumped in from America on a free streaming URL."

"Impressive," I responded with a big grin.

"My dad's waiting for you. He said to let you in, but the door's open. Go to the third floor."

"Thanks kid."

The entrance to the building led to yet another set of stairs, an L-shaped climb, zhooshed up a little with inlaid, Moroccan flutes. Only then did I realize that the initial entryway was some kind of an exterior shell. The mysterious climb led to a big, green door which opened up to more stairs. "Keep going man," I heard from way below. "You got it," I yelled down to the kid, my slight fear of heights catching my attention as I looked over the banister. The big, green door was heavy, and I had to place my right hand on the wall for leverage to open it.

The door opened to an interior stairwell of the actual building and no sooner had my right foot touched the first step, then I heard, "Dr. Jack. I'm sorry I don't know your last name. I hope the walk up isn't too much."

Stretching my neck backwards, I said, "No, not at all. And Jack is fine. Please." Just three steps before the landing, Jamal reached down and pulled me up the rest of the way. He gave my right shoulder a brotherly smack and then shook my hand so hard I thought for sure it could register a 150-pound dynameter squeeze.

"I see you met my son, Nabil." We continued up to the next set of stairs to the third floor.

"Yes, I did. He seems like a nice kid."

"I'm afraid he's lost a shoe. We were all young once."

"Yes, I guess we were." One more floor to go, I was huffing a bit, but tried hard not to let on.

The apartment was surprisingly large, and Jamal escorted me to a bedroom he had converted into an office. A man of some years, the determined, eagle-like, supraorbital ridge of his brow made him appear confronting even when his glossy bass voice stoked gently. His white feathery bangs looped coolly over his right eye and softened his florid complexion, giving him a youthful appearance.

A touch of exoticism filled the office and vied for my attention. The many furnishings boasted the Moroccan heritage in distinctive geometric shapes and handmade lattice work, and they mixed evenly among collectibles from China to Paris. Jamal sat stiffly behind a gray desk of old, Moorish design with inlaid motifs and, pinning down both of his elbows strategically at opposite ends of the spotless inkblot, gave me the jitters as I thought he may have mistaken me for a paying client. Then he said, "Let's sit on the couches. Robin said you want to chat," and my imagined bulrush of problems vanished.

"If my English is not perfect, please do not mind," he said. "And I did a call early because I go to Germany later today for my work."

"The hour is fine. Thank-you for making the time on such short notice." I was sure he saw me speaking and noticing his many plaques appended to the walls, some in English.

"Robin said you do research on our argan trees."

One of his plaques was his law degree. "You're a graduate of Cornell Law?" I was astonished.

"Oh yes. Many years ago. I first met Robin at Cornell. But let's not get sidetracked."

"As for me, yes, I'm a professor of Forestry in America."

"But you want to talk about legalities around women?"

"Yes. Robin said that I could ask you some legal questions about how things are going for woman in Morocco, especially their rights in a marriage, divorce, and so forth."

"I've handled some divorce settlements, although that isn't my main area of practice. What exact things do you want to know?" He sat perplexed, his chin in the palm of his hand and first two fingers across his upper lip.

"I'm mainly interested in laws related to domestic violence."

"Okay," he granted with a nod. "Can I ask, please, why you want to know these things?"

"I experienced something that opened my eyes to women's rights in North Africa, Morocco especially. It's a long story."

"I can say things about domestic violence. But one can only understand that if one understands the larger issue of women's rights in Morocco. Maybe you like to hear some of these things?"

"I don't even know enough to know the right questions. Anything you say can be of help."

"Then let me talk a little about marriage in our country. When a woman comes to the time of marriage, she has been under the control of her father's guardianship. When she reaches eighteen—and you may know that the legal age of marriage is now changed from fifteen to eighteen—legally her status is now under her husband."

"If I may interrupt, I met a woman who says she was forced into marriage at fourteen. She lost everything, including the dowry. Quite a story."

"That's illegal," Jamal insisted, his voice tightening. "Both her age and forcing her to marry. But," he continued, adjusting himself on the fat cushion, "the old ways do continue in our country."

"How so?"

"Everything in our culture falls under the moudawana."

"The what? I'm sorry."

"The moudawana," he reiterated, stating each syllable in distinct breaks. "The personal status code of legislation of women in marriage and divorce. It dates back many years and stayed unchanged until reforms came in 1993 and 1994 and then again in 2003 to 2004 to make us, you know," Jamal grinned, "more modern."

"I take it you don't think that being more modern is good?"

"I'm in favor of some changes, but not all. But no doubt the modifications are controversial in Morocco, you know."

"How has this code made marriage more modern for women?"

"Well, as I said, the minimum age for a woman to marry was changed to eighteen. And unlike your friend, a woman is not to marry against her will. And the woman no longer needs a wali."

"What's that? I'm sorry again."

"That's fine. I don't expect you to know our ways. A wali. He's a guardian, usually her father, who speaks on her behalf in the marriage contract. The contract is then signed by all parties before an adul, something like your American notary. But if the woman hasn't a father, a guardian is usually sought in her nearest male relative. The 1994 changes to moudawana state that the woman now has the right to choose the wali, and also that the wali cannot give her away in marriage without her consent. A little different from your American context."

"I'd never heard any of this before. Is the wali used in every marital context?"

"This is one point where some controversy enters. In the Maliki, Shafi'I, and Hanbali schools of religion, approval of the guardian is necessary for marriage to be legal, but to a much lesser extent in the Hanafi school. In fact, many religious scholars argue that the wali is not mandated at all by the religious texts but comes from jurisprudence, the Fiqh, and so the guardian's permission is not needed at all for the marriage. But the guardian is so much a part of our customs, he continues, you know."

"I understand. But how do you explain what happened to the woman I met at the riad, who lost everything?"

"I have practiced law for many years, and I see that because the guardian is not absolute in our sacred texts; I mean, the moral context is missing, many bad practices of patriarchal authority, coercion, and abuse of power, happen. A family, or especially a father, can decide many things for a girl of fourteen, you know. What are you writing there?"

"I'm taking notes on my phone if you don't mind."

"That's fine."

"Please continue," I said politely.

"Also, there is the mother-in law. In our country, a woman is not considered a full woman until she reaches the age of marriage and in many families she doesn't have full status until she's beyond her child-bearing years, at which point she herself is able to dominate her own daughters-in-law."

"Dominate? Sounds like the system is ripe for problems and abuse."

"Yes, and that's where I usually come in. You see, originally, the guardian's role was intended to protect the woman, to make sure she isn't marrying someone who can create harm to her, or to the families, or in the case she's— umm—how do you say—?"

"Incapacitated?"

"Yes. That. Or she suffers some mental problems, you know, to make sure she's making the right decision for herself."

"I see."

"Now the marriage contract includes the sdaq, or the dowry, as I think you say. That too is there for the woman."

"What do you mean, it's there for the woman? Most Americans assume that the dowry system in foreign countries is for the father of the bride; for his retirement—something like that."

"Yes, yes, but that's not how the dowry was intended, at least according to our customs. When the suitor gives sdaq, the woman's father, or the wali, keeps the money or the possessions in trust in order to keep the man's feet in the marriage. Because if he leaves, he can lose the sdaq. Also, if he does leave, the sdaq is to go to the woman who may not have good education or resources as a means of support. So, always we want the woman's security. But, between of all of the pressures surrounding the marriage, and because the marriage is essentially a contract, and money is involved, problems and abuses can and do happen."

"Like in the case of the female employee at the riad whose father stole her dowry."

"That sort of abuse is more common than many people say."

"But why would a father, and a mother for that matter, want to marry off their daughter who's too young or who doesn't want to be married?"

"Even though by law a woman must now be at least eighteen, some fathers go to a judge and pay some monies because a family wants their daughter to wed a rich man. Or because they have many children and think a man with money can help relieve their burden with so many children. Also, rich men count in this country. In business and in dealings with local government, family connections can make for favorable considerations."

"I see," I said in long strides. "And domestic violence? The worker at the riad said that that happened to her too."

"There's too much of that, and it happens for many reasons. That is a reason for the strong marriage contact. Without it, a woman taken advantage of in the beginning is usually treated quite bad from then on."

"Are the new laws working well?"

"Overall, yes. But understand this." Jamal leaned forward with his hands folded as if to pray. "Despite our updated laws they continue to rest on a man's kindness. I mean, women are really allowed freedoms just as long as her choices don't go against male interests. Women from middle-and upper-middle classes and those with more education or higher employment can say I am free from what is expected of me. But underneath we are still very much patriarchal on all levels of our society."

"I don't mean to be insulting. But it sounds like all of the changes are really just the façade of modernity. Women are free. But on a long tether."

"I'm trying to be honest with you. A woman can go to university, can work for a big company, can wear modern clothes. She is given these freedoms. But these freedoms are just on the surface, you know. She's still expected to take care of all of the things at home; not to test the male foundations of our culture. You know, people are always talking about how 'We are more European.' That's true only on the surface."

My scientific mind drifted momentarily. What happens if the Cosmos is locked into determining influences? Is human freedom this way? If the women are free only insofar as the men determine, then in what sense are they truly free? Then, I recalled how Nour said we're not the light. It's objective like the light that came to me through my window in Taroudant when I was so sad. That must be true or else freedom is an extension of myself, a mere circular farce. Or is freedom the grant of government? But how can that be considered freedom if the same can take it away? Neither can an impersonal force be the source of liberty, for how can an impersonal force serve as the standard for personal freedom? Freedom must find its radical origin in something outside me that is infinitely free, personal, and all-loving. And I am in its likeness.

"Then there's the problem of polygamy," Jamal said.

"Polygamy?" I said in shock.

"Yes. But not polyandry. As long as the first wife approves of the second woman, and the second woman knows about the first wife, the man can go to the judge and seek approval. In fact, a Moroccan man can have up to four wives, a number which has been reduced by law. But again, all we are doing, in my opinion, is adding layers of problems."

"Wait. Did you just say that a man can have up to four wives in Morocco?"

Jamal didn't seem the least embarrassed and said, "This is a lot, I know," as if there was an intricate underside to four wives I hadn't understood.

"How did I miss this?" I verbalized aggressively, as a criticism of myself.

"Not a problem, sir." Most westerners don't know. It might make you feel better to know that Tunisia is different. According to the Code of Personal Status of that nation, polygamy is illegal, and many Tunisians think that is a gain in Tunisian and Arab civil law. The law to prevent polygamy in Tunisia is fixed despite renewed calls for its abolition."

"Okay, a question about the marriage contract."

"Yes."

"You said it's been revised several times."

"Yes."

"At the beginning you indicated that some of the changes are not fully accepted by many Moroccans; in fact, I think you said that you don't accept all of them. Why not?"

"Sir, you need to remember a single phrase. The Moroccan way of life. The moudawana is so much wrapped up in our society that for many, change to the moudawana is to challenge the very foundations of Moroccan culture. Many say it can bring fitna, or social chaos."

"I'll bet that most of the people saying that are men."

"Ha! Yes, but some women too."

"It sounds like women must strike an incredible balance. There's family, tradition, society, religion, law, and modernization."

"The path is difficult," Jamal conceded readily.

"One last thing, please. Marital rape. I've heard about this both from the lady at the riad and elsewhere."

At that point, his eyes were knives of exasperation, and I felt like I had crossed a boundary. I wanted to crawl into a bottle. "Why again are you asking all these questions?" he asked.

"Sir, I'm trying to learn. That's all. I apologize if my question isn't acceptable."

Pausing, he suddenly appeared older. "Yes," he reacted with a long pause. "That is a problem. But you have this in America, no?"

"True. But if I may just ask about the legalities here in Morocco."

"The secular courts are reluctant to charge the husband so strongly for taking his wife. I know of a case in the north in which a man was convicted of serious violence—so it was called—because according to the court the man did sex within wedlock."

"All marital rape is within wedlock." I spoke in tamped up frustration.

"We are working on it." Jamal had a look on his face like he wanted to end the conversation, so I took his cue.

"Jamal," I said, typing my last few notes. "I've taken enough of your time."

"Welcome. I am more than happy to be of help." His facial expression readapted a gentle poise. "Can I call you a taxi?

"No. Actually, I think I'll walk a little. Is there a café nearby?"

"Yes, turn left when you exit the building, and it is two blocks on the other side of the rue. Just be careful please."

"I'll certainly try."

We stood and he placed his arm all the way across my shoulders just below the scuff of my neck and, walking me out, said, "Don't worry. All is fine in Morocco."

We reached the big, green door and he opened it for me. I stopped and said, "May I ask please? How is that a lawyer is willing to talk with a total stranger—an America no less—about such things? You know nothing about me."

"What makes you think I know nothing about you?" His face was a clear revelation that he had done his homework on me. Interesting, I thought, as I turned and continued to descend the L-shaped stairs.

Nabil was still sitting where he was before playing his video game. "So why aren't you out doing things on such a nice day?" I asked.

"My dad wanted me to stay here."

"Why is that?"

"To watch for police. You've had eyes on you, you know." My mouth agape now, I swept the area in one, surreptitious glance. Nabil stood and said, "Don't worry. You're okay."

Chapter 10

Less than a full block from where Nabil was sitting, I caught a chiral image of myself in the windowpane of a store. My face appeared older to me that morning, and I speculated if others saw me the way as I saw myself.

The past days were struggling for someone to bring them into the world of meaning. And I thought how easily the strong take advantage of the weak. My right hand cupping my brow, I looked up into the canopy of fathomless blue and ruminated how the sun was soon to cross overhead. King of its realm, in equanimity to all, it didn't take, but it gave, a behavior much different from the world living in its warmth and light from day to day. Spreading wings, gravid by design, laden in the hearts of palms. One with the sand cats and jirds, the birds didn't vie for honor or shame, and I was happy to join them if by so doing I too could live free. A poultry trophy it would be, were I to gain the regard of others by disfiguring their spirits. For a man to build himself up by pulling others down, I thought, would not be a prize except to one of such incalculable self-loathing that, though a crowd erupt before him in cheers and applause, he would be in their hearts a little less followed than the smallest of the small.

I was tired. In the inner parts. A scritch idea just to forget my cares and see Marrakech without a trace of concern was working its way just below the surface of my skin. Yes. Just take the day, I said to myself.

I found the café Jamal had suggested. The place was a million places. Shadowed faces sitting around small tables, smoking and nattering. Regardless where I sat, the AC pushed the vinegary aftersmoke of cigarettes towards me. Does anyone not smoke in Morocco? I wondered. Two men sat alone, each stirring an espresso-sized cup of coffee and glistening cubes of sugar lined the mini-saucers. The half-drunk bottle of water I brought in with me was quickly taken by the waitress who didn't want me drinking from it. She held the bottle over a counter and shook its contents and said, "It'll be up—" Then she sat it down to let me know that's where it would be.

Her chin tucked in, she looked me over in proofreading detail, and her glasses hung low on her nose. Then she pulled down her tight, red and white striped shirt to cover the white sides of her midsection, and asked, "Youwa toowist?"

"Oui," I replied. She stood expressionless just starting at me, chewing gum. "Un espresso, no, um, un americano, merci."

The waitress brought the coffee and wanted me to pay on the spot. She didn't give me a bill, and I knew she was trying to overcharge me. I asked for a bill and she walked away without a word. Then she jerked herself up onto a tall stool at the front of the café and, lounging her back against the wall, smoked a cigarette and chatted it up with the guys; big-boned men, their faces hard and talking loudly.

A young, single woman sat at another table with three men. Whenever I saw a lone woman in a Moroccan café, she always moved through the room with sinister silkiness. And if it was a restaurant, a single woman was always surrounded by a group of fenestra men and a big bucket of iced beer sat to the side, a sure sign she was a prostitute. But a lone woman in a bar didn't necessarily mean she was a prostitute. Foreign women could go to a bar, and if their ethnicity was obvious, they weren't considered prostitutes. But they were nevertheless likely to draw the unwanted attention of young men looking for a quick date.

Sunlight through the big rear pane in the back had shifted and my gaze was attracted to its light like a moth. The entrancing mixture of refracted light through the cage in front of the window, darkened shadows in the room, and cigarette smoke coiling upward in helix formations, provided a sfumato canvass on which dust particles jumped and twirled like little ballerinas. I have my own Rembrandt, I said to myself in amazed reaction. Nothing was clear in the image, but the lack of precision made it all the more entrancing.

Trained on the admixture in hypnotic slowness, a little island of light came to me. Maybe the lives of the prostitutes roaming the cafés and brasseries were as imprecise as my masterpiece. Maybe they were just like Sanaa at the riad—women whose misfortune had been that they had married good-for-nothings and were doing anything to keep their children. Why were the women to blame but not the men who drove them to this point and took advantage of their services?

Rather than give the extra money for the coffee to the waitress, I added a little and gave it to the woman bargaining at the table with the men. She looked up at me. Wrapping my hand around hers, I tightened my grip, and said, "Pour vos enfants." Her expression remained unchanged, and I felt her eyes as I left.

Less than a block from the café, I heard a voice. "Hey man!" I turned and saw the woman whom I had suspected of being a prostitute. A sudden rush of instincts battling to make sense of the vision encumbered me.

The woman said, "You American?" Her tone was ominous and authoritative.

"I am," I replied somewhat nervously

"I am police. Let me see your passport." A sudden tightness deep inside my ribcage heeled me strong to one side but was counterbalanced by my lungs filling up like a giant sail.

"Can I please see some proof you are police?" I tacked my eyes on her and refused to move them.

"Just let me see your passport." She appeared bewildered that I wouldn't move my eyes.

"Show me proof," I insisted, speaking with my eyes also.

Keeping each other in the bullseye of our optical fields, like we were locked in some eternal struggle, she reached for her ID, held it up to my face, and repeated, "Now show me your passport, sir." I pulled my passport out of my black bag, all the while, keeping my focus dartled on the bridge of her nose.

"You look for some trouble, maybe, huh?" she said. Right then, another woman walked up and began talking to the officer in Arabic, and I just knew she was police too.

"No ma'am," I responded, and a voice inside me said to stand my ground. But I was nervous and couldn't stop shifting my weight from one foot to the other.

Pointing to my mini-travel bag, she verbalized sharply, "What inside that?"

"I am more than happy to show you if you want." I spoke respectfully. She returned my passport and said nothing more about my bag.

"Why did you give me money?"

"I only wanted to help you; that's all." I was speaking dejectedly now.

"Why you in Morocco?"

I told her as much as was necessary to get out of there. She seemed satisfied. The mood relaxed and I asked, "Why did you stop me?" Undercover police officers like her, she said, were working to slow illegal prostitution in the Red City. Nocturnal sex workers were the main target, and she had made many arrests of women of the night and their johns.

I was ready to walk away when, pulling up the sagging left strap of her off-the-shoulder crop top, she warned, "You are American. Be careful to help even the women in Morocco." Too late, I thought to myself.

After what seemed like a one-hundred-year-long morning of much mental exposure, an overabundance of airborne tracers from secondhand cigarette smoke, and the unbolting of my masculinity on a Marrakech road, my confidence was escalloped. Cars parked on the uneven olive-colored sidewalks, and people walking in the streets, I opted for the sidewalk where just a few people squirmed and wriggled past each other and the shop owners wreathed their entrances.

The jagged sidewalk squares turned my ankle a couple of times and added to the growing magnitude of vertigo. Without warning, I threw up right where I stood. The feeling of cutaneous veins pushing toward the surface of my face met my curdled embarrassment.

I glanced left just enough to notice a woman's foot in a babouche. "Moslim?" she asked.

Then, I heard a man's voice and felt a hand on my back. "Sir, you okay?"

"Yeah, it's been a crazy morning."

"Can I help you please?"

"Thanks. Say, what did the woman say?"

"She said, 'Moslim.' That means, "are you alright?""

"Guess I drew bit of a crowd."

"People are friendly here, sir."

As I stood erect, the temple of my sunglasses, draped over the top button of my shirt, slipped out, and I watched as they hit the pavement. Thankfully they didn't break. The man, average height, his hair slicked straight back and black as night, picked up my sunglasses and handed them to me. "I get you some water," he said.

He walked into a store, and I saw a little girl look at me through the store window, and she had innocent eyes. She waved at me through the glass, and in all my uncomely and broken unsightliness, I saw in me a rose.

"Here, sir. Water." He brought me an average-sized bottle and some *serviettes*. "You don't want cold right now. This good with you?" I nodded, my throat desert dry, and I drank quickly.

"Oh, be careful to drink so fast."

A gulp did go down a little hard, but settled quickly. "I'm fine. Thank you. I think I'll be okay. You're so kind."

"It's all good," he said. I couldn't believe it.

"Who's the little girl in the window?"

"Oh, my daughter, Sabrina." She was still looking at me and so I waved back at her.

"I am Hamza." A shop owner, Hamza ran a little store full of knick-knacks, trifles, and drinks. In the summer he served ice cream.

"I'm Jack. Thanks again."

"Very welcome," he said with zeal.

"You been here long?" I pointed to the store and sipped my water.

"We come from Sidi Ghanem where I had nice store."

"Is that a city?"

"No. Is place; now stores; shops."

"You had a shop there?"

"Yes."

"What happened?"

"I leave. My wife did cancer. Use money for doctor; hospital."

"Oh. I'm sorry. Your wife is okay?"

"Me and my daughter now," he said, wordlessly shuffling his feet on the pavement.

"I'm very sorry."

"One time, I heard a man say in radio. I remember. Always. 'God uses our defeats as an ingredient towards our victories.'"

Hamza's words echoed in the emptied parts of me. "That's great."

"Sidi Ghanem," Hamza said. "Many shops. Very good. You like very much."

Goring the space between the open top button of my shirt with the temple of my sunglasses, and then palming them gently, I said on a dime, "How do I find this place?" It was just up the same road where I had met Robin at the restaurant, and realizing I knew where to go, the feeling of ratio kick-started my internal compass. I waved at Sabrina one last time, said goodbye to Hamza, and looked for a taxi.

~ ~ ~

I stood waiting. Taxi driver after taxi driver breezed by me like I was the invisible man. No fares that I could see. Either they pretended like I didn't exist or looked at me as if I were a street hawker. Either way, they turned their heads in Pecksniffian indifference. Maybe I should move to the other side of the road. I imagined that I might have better luck. All of a sudden, I saw the same giant of a driver who brought me to Jamal's. He stopped without me even waving him down. I got in and said, "Oh man, thanks so much."

His sequoia frame was still bent like a silly straw to fit in the hole behind the wheel. I said, "Sidi Ghanem please," but he looked at me like he didn't want to go. He said something, so I folded my praying hands and added, "S'il vous plaît." We agreed on a price and were after the arrow and my head went back.

Banking hard left, hard right, one pothole after another, I abandoned my efforts to read about the shops and, using my elbow on the armrest, hoisted myself up from the seat so the impacts from the potholes weren't quite so hard on me. The road flattened and after a while we made a turn and entered an industrial-looking zone. I did a doubletake. But I trusted the driver. The sparing steeliness of the area, full of many of the city's factories and ateliers, was the exact opposite of the medina. I had never seen the loft spaces of New York's SOHO district. But once inside the high-roofed building at Sidi Ghanem, I guessed I had made up for lost time.

The open, concrete spaces invited me to explore. The high and ascending ceilings, the reaching walls, and especially the clarity of the artisans' cubbies, inspired me. I felt renewed. I had spent my life in entwined nature, so perhaps that's the reason the simple symmetry of less is more spoke to me. There were contrasts within the spaces also. Discordant sets of craft art depicting values old and new, as in the case of one shop displaying Art Deco motifs while, immediately next door, traditional designs vaulting back through time set the tone.

The juxtaposition inspirited a metaphor. The old and the new, I had thought, is the picture of Morocco in tension. But rather than rest comfortably aside each other, modernization and established rituals were vexing.

Dear, old Mr. Rollins had explained something similar to us kids when he taught us the parable of the wineskins. The parable posed the possibility of putting new wine in old wineskins which were already stretched to the limit and had become brittle. The addition of new wine expanded the skins even farther to the point that the skins broke and their contents poured out. Moroccan culture is like this, I thought. Politicians, religious leaders, and NGOs, could press for reforms where women were concerned. But unless the old ways were adaptable to change, the new ways would deplete, and no one would be served.

The sound of crying caught my attention. I inched around a corner toward it. A little girl, not more than five, with tears running down her pink cheeks and onto her light shawl, was wandering the wide places. Upon seeing me, her movements suspended, and I moved toward her ever so carefully so as not to scare her.

Where was this little girl's mother? I crouched before her and, looking into her eyes, intoned the question, "Mama?" Even though she didn't seem to understand me, our eyes fixed, and I felt as though we were communicating on a different level.

She stopped crying. And her eyes, diademed in blue sparkles, shined at me. I believed she was aware of my care for her safety.

A woman then came rushing up suddenly, appearing mentally flossed. She grabbed the girl's hand and rushed her away. I stayed crouched for just a few seconds, watching the two of them walk down the prosaic corridor. The girl then looked back at me, her face sheened calm and pure as if to say, thank-you for trying.

An apparition of sorts then combed my mind. In the little rounded face of the girl, but somehow in the distance, I envisioned every woman, and every woman stood for the little girl. Even though my mood became a shade darker, I wasn't startled. Dipped beneath the projection, the hushed room in my head heard an interpretation. To behold one woman is to behold all, and to behold all women is to behold one. A ghostly flash of light discharged in my field of vision, and the little girl vanished into its corona.

The ellipticity between what might have been, and reality, grew wider apart the more my true surroundings outwitted my daydream. I snapped out of it, scolding myself for permitting my mind to cast adrift like an unmanned boat in a sea-fog. But one thing remained unchanged. Commitment to my journey. In the hope that the knowledge I was gaining was somehow serving a higher purpose for both men and women. For I had come to realize. There is something that stitches all of us together.

I returned to peruse the workshops of designers and craftsmen interestedly for over an hour until a large group of Dutch-speaking, slow-strollers dammed me up between two tables in towels and bedding, and I realized how very tired I was. The dyke broke and I walked out of the store and saw a little chic-looking, French spot across the way, and poked my head in to scope the place for the taint of cigarette smoke—my taste buds still lacquered from the café earlier that morning. To my utter alarm, no smoke. Was I in Morocco? I entered and a well-dressed, young woman greeted me.

"For one?" she said.

"Now how did you know I speak English?"

"You walk like an American?"

"Walk?" I though in amazement. She smiled wide and gummy and when she turned to take me to a table, her head tilted back and her long, brunette hair swung.

"So," I said, "I have that John Wayne swagger, do I?"

"Yes. John Wayne. You are John Wayne." She answered with a big laugh.

Then, to my surprise, I heard my name from a distance. "Jack! Jack! Over here."

I looked. "Oh, my word," I said out loud. "Eric Killebrew." My old friend from High School. I remembered him. Originally from Georgia, he had a way about him as big as the sky.

"Jack," he yelled again. He rolled up on me with that kind of real look you get from people with which you have chemistry you don't need to work at.

"Eric!" I said, still shocked. "Well—hell man. How long's it been. What in the world—"

"Jack," he interrupted. "Aren't you a sight for sore eyes! Whatcha doin' in Morocco, man?"

"Work, you know."

"Hush your mouth. I forgot. You went into agriculture, right?" He spoke loud enough to turn some heads. Even in High School he had a manspreading style and I liked the guy. He wasn't cosmetic.

"Forestry. Eric. Forestry."

"Oh. I knew it was somethin' like that."

"Eric, what on earth brings you to Morocco?"

"You won't believe it. But my daughter, oh, I don't think you knew I got married and we have two daughters. Well, the oldest—pretty as a peach that one—she met a young, Moroccan fella, and they're fixin' to get married. But because the young man can't come to America until they're married, and we want to make sure our girl isn't marryin' the wrong kinda guy, we got an extended visa for six months."

The wrong kind of guy? I thought, bobbing my head in feigned agreement. Didn't I just hear something like that this morning? "Eric, that's incredible." I spoke in forced tones.

"Yeah, we call him Adam. His name is somthin' else. But Adam is easier and the Mrs. likes callin' him that."

"Alright then. So, Eric, why are you here at this restaurant?"

"Adam and me—we were planning to meet some expats Adam met on the Internet. I think a cuppl'a young women from the Middle East. It was really

Adam's idea. But he's not here yet. Jack, look, you wanna join us? Oh, ya gotta stay less ya got sumthin' else ta do?"

"Well, I—"

"That's great."

Eric put one hand on my shoulder and with his other he pointed to a table. We sat and Eric's relaxed 6'4" frame bowed like a question mark and his knee hit mine. "Oh, excuse me, Jack. I was always a little long in the britches."

"No problem."

"Oh," he said, looking over my shoulder. "Yup. That's them. And Adam's not here yet."

My internal batteries drained—a get-together was the last thing on my mind. But Eric was already on his feet, shaking the women's hands. I wanted to stand also. But one of the young women was standing so close to me, there wasn't room enough for me to get up.

Eric made the appropriate introductions. Hamia, from Lebanon, was short and petite and wore a dark, floral lace dress and had braces which didn't intimidate her welcoming smile. Amira, from Egypt, was tall and wore a dark, ruffle trim dress. And I never did quite understand why either woman was in Morocco.

Amira looked at the table as if she were sizing it up, and asked if we could move to the lounge and laze around a small table with chairs and a couch. Eric gathered the air with words of southern wisdom and the space slanted in his direction like a seesaw struck to the ground. He made apologies for Adam's tardiness and filled in the time interviewing the women who interacted easily and undisguised. Never one to be good at chit-chat, I sat like the old man in American Gothic. Amira kept glancing over at me and a sudden fear hit me that my prosaic stiltedness was being felt at the table every bit as much as Eric's self-assured style. But how does one interact normally when one doesn't feel normal?

Then the thought passed my mind. Should I? Eric was oblivious to what I was really doing in Marrakech, and to introduce the subject of the abuse of women without warning, I thought, could come across like calling one the ladies, babe. But two young Arab women were sitting right in front of me.

In anticipation of how the others might respond were I to turn the discussion, my head rocked back and forth between Eric and the women like I was watching a tennis match. A twinkling of pure inspiration then broke through my imagination and reminded me of my new purpose. The words of Sartre then came to me. I was condemned to freedom.

Courage dilating within me, it just came out. "Do you mind if I ask a question!" I said it so loud that everyone suddenly stopped talking and appeared flummoxed.

"Sure, Jack," Eric said, as if to dulcify me. The women shifted on the couch and stared at me curiously.

Clearing my throat, I said, "Since you ladies know something about North Africa and the Middle East, can I please ask something about the treatment of women?"

To my great surprise, Amira became aggressive. "Why do you want to ask about the women? You're a man. Just focus on the men and leave the women alone."

Instantly, the ambience became awkward, and I was sure that avulsing so delicate an issue without warning had been wrong. But then I thought that Amira may have assumed that I was ready to take the side of the men and to duplicate the same power dynamics between the sexes in Morocco at our table.

Widening my eyes, and keeping my composure, I decided to respond. "I ask because I'm interested in the men as well."

"Oh, that's different," Amira said.

"Really. Why is that so different?"

"Son, Eric chortled, "you could start an argument in an empty house."

Replying to me as if Eric was in another room, Amira said, "We're always to blame. And I thought you were going there."

"No, no, no," I pressed. "Not at all."

"Men say we have breasts," Amira said, and so it's our fault. She placed the palms of her hands underneath her breasts to illustrate her point, and Eric's face bulged.

I could see Eric about to say something, so I seized the stage. "Let me ask a pointed question. Let's imagine a young Moroccan woman is assaulted by a husband or boyfriend. Why would she not stand up to him?"

"It's because of pressures from the society," Amira answered. "We're made to feel like we have to accept abuse or the skies will fall on us."

"The peddlers in the streets, boys, men, they all harass us," Hamia added.

"What do you do?" I asked.

Hamia sat with a dash of sadness, twirling her straw. "We are used to it."

"Not me, insisted Amira. I let men know right away I won't put up with it."

Hamia put her hands together and stared at Amira and her eyes were urgent. "His question. I think we're off his question."

"She loves him," Amira said forcefully. "That's how I was. I put up with a lot from a man because I loved him. But a time came when I had to make a decision. And I made it. You need to know. Men who abuse women rarely ever change."

Walking barefoot on sharp rocks at the seashore could have produced in me less squinting inner pain than Amira's answer.

Hamia became increasingly engaged in the conversation. "I just read something about these things. I think it said that almost 59 percent of Moroccan women in the cities are the targets of violence from men, compared to about, I think, 15 percent of women in America. And most of the Moroccan women are in their 20s."

"They're mostly young, then," I injected.

"But that's not necessarily from husbands or boyfriends," Amira said.

As an academic, I was curious about her source. "Where did you read this?"

"Online," said Hamia. Of course, that didn't tell me a lot.

"Why did you read it?" Amira asked Hamia.

"A friend—her boyfriend pulled her hair and slapped her. She said I was a safe person to talk with. That made me interested."

"There's too much of this." Amira looked at me, her brows iron tight.

"True," Hamia said. "Let me think. Oh yes. I also read that over one half of fiancées and a little less than one half of married women have been victims of violence in Morocco."

"That's incredible," I responded. "You would think that a fiancée who's been attacked would have better sense not to marry the guy."

"Well, not all of them marry the guy," Hamia retorted.

"But many do," said Amira. "Pressure from family, friends—so much pressure. And what perpetuates the violence is women not speaking out."

Hamia said, "And Jack, did you know that until 2014, a Moroccan man who committed rape could escape prosecution by marrying the victim?"

"I don't doubt it." I reacted in disgust.

"Yet," Hamia added, "something like 60 percent of men and almost 50 percent of women continue to support the idea that a woman who is raped should marry her attacker."

"Well, I declare," Eric split open. "I think I need to have a chat with the wife." Eric's face was blood-dispelled.

"Yeah, those are incredible stats," I said. "In fact, I met with a lawyer early this morning about legalities affecting women here and he didn't tell me that."

"Maybe me and the Mrs. need to have a talk with Adam," Eric said. He tapped the leather sides of his chair in unconventional bats with his knitted knuckles.

To both women, I asked, "Okay. But what if I said we have the same kinds of problems everywhere."

"Welcome to the center of everywhere," said Amira.

Her incisive response staggered me. A moment of impromptu tranquility coned the area until I broke the silence. "One last question, please. If there's one bit of advice you have for women suffering abuse, what would it be?"

Hamia said, "Make the love in you stronger than the abuse that comes to you." Her reflection had such a delicious taste, I just wanted to savor it. It had a sapient flavor.

"Yes," Amira concurred.

"Ain't that something," said Eric. Glad we got that one fixed up."

On the periphery of my vision, a shadow appeared on the wall and I was drawn to its arc growing larger through the air and in my imagination. A young man then appeared and pressed his hands down on Eric's shoulders, gave one a slap, and said, "Hello. Very sorry I am late."

"Jack, everyone, this is Adam, my son-in-law." The young man was tall like Eric.

"My name is really Abdel," he said to me, extending his hand, and I thought that his name was no harder to remember than Adam.

Standing, I said to Abdel, "Look. Please take my seat. It's time for me to move on. Ladies, thank-you so much."

"Very good to meet you," Amira said.

"Jack," Eric said. "Are you sure?"

"I'm sure. I should get going."

"Well, Jack. I reckon I never thought I'd see you today."

"Boy, that's for sure. Let's not wait another thirty years."

"You got it, partner."

Just as I waved goodbye to the group, Hamia reached for my attention. "Jack."

"Yes."

"You saw something. I can see it in your face. Just let me say once last thing."

"Sure."

"You need to let this go."

There's a little box in my heart where my lies are kept. I pulled one out just for Hamia and said, "I will. Right away."

Chapter 11

Not many taxis were around. So, I used an app to call one. Twenty minutes passed and a taxi arrived and a woman wearing a nude-colored hijab was behind the wheel. A female driver in Morocco, I thought? I was so shocked that I almost tensed up like one of those Myotonic goats—the ones that appear to faint at being stunned or elated.

Her face was full of life, out of accord with the ashen-faced male drivers I had seen scuttled in boredom behind a wheel. I started to get into the front, but her henna-designed hand motioned me to get in the back. I was reluctant to follow her command because I didn't want my butt and back sitting directly over the rear axle, and I could just see myself squinting over every slit, cut, and chink. Grudgingly, I capitulated. She adjusted the rearview mirror and her slantwise glance revealed her deep-set eyes, sparkly pools of hazel framed with thick lashes, the kind that don't need to be fused with.

"You speak English?" I asked.

"Good enough. Where we go?"

I told her the name of the riad, and the modular-looking midget car bit the pavement with a sudden acceleration and I grabbed the window handle. Then the car's front wheel caught itself in a long, fissuring crack, so I sat jockey-style: leaning forward and hiking up just a scooch to relieve any direct impacts to my lower spine should the car veer hard. The wheel let go and so did I.

Tired and needing a nap, I rubbed my eyes using the heels of my palms and thought to ask her how a female taxi driver was laboring in the dominion of men. "Are there many woman taxi drivers in Morocco?" I was really hoping my question wouldn't insult her.

She began with what sounded like a rehearsed presentation due to the fact, I had guessed, of having been asked the same question so many times. "I wanted to be one of first woman taxi driver. The first woman to drive taxi was in 2008 in Fez. I want to be big example for women. We can do things. Like men."

"You have children?" I asked, grabbing my phone to take notes.

"My name is Oumayma. I have thirty-three years and two children. I have degree in Environment and Sustainable Development." I was intrigued by the fact that she had a college degree in sustainability, not only because of my profession, but also due to the disconnect with being a taxi driver.

"Why are you a taxi driver?" Vacuous seconds followed my question, and I had thought that the rehearsed part of Oumayma's speech had ended and she had nothing more to say.

I was adjusting myself on the seat when she unshrouded in a whirlwind. "When my husband takes another wife and he not tell me, he gives money to judge so he can keep number two wife and I find the divorce. My husband keep house, and he make me and children leave. No haqq. No justice."

The word "justice" stirred my thoughts in the same way "standard" did at Nitta's, "light" did at the café with Nour, and "freedom" did at Jamal's office. Is justice something changeless? Or is justice a social construct, perhaps the bequeathed language of trampled classes of people?

"Wait," I said, stammering. "Your husband married another woman and you did not know?"

"He say, 'You go. You I not need.' So, I take children." My skull grieved in pain as if I were biting on a spoon really hard. Our eyes then met in the rearview mirror, and I could see her waiting for my next question.

A difficult question was erupting in me and I had to ask. "Oumayma, have you had any problems in the taxi with men?"

She split open. "Men say, 'You woman. Do things in home. They say you run from the duty given you by God.' But I not run. My husband violates our marriage." The heat from Oumayma's voice rose steadily as she spoke, and I could only imagine her difficult position in Moroccan culture. "My family not want. My father say, 'You in danger. Why you do this? Taxi for men, not women. Why you do this?'"

I sat riveted, trying to make sense of it all. Then I looked out my window. An early moon was buoying in the late afternoon. And its dour beauty, exuding through the Tuareg-veiled atmosphere, said everything that needed to be said about Arab women.

"Thank you," I said. "But that was not my exact question."

"I know question," she replied. My tongue pinned to the roof of my mouth and my jaws clamped in advance of her answer.

"Problems. Many problems. I listen to Quran here; look." She pointed to the old-style, tape player in the car. Quran play here. I listen always. I pray nothing happen to me. And I drive man and woman; not men alone."

"You pick up only couples? But you picked me up?"

"You look okay. Tourist. And I not go for people in bad places."

I saw in Oumayma a woman on the edge of losing her children. How could she feed three mouths as a taxi driver who drives days only? Still, on the forefront of my mind was the question of whether or not men had abused her during her working hours. I was preparing to press the question when she intercepted me. "I harassed in beginning. Always. The men think I drive to do sex. They think, why alone woman drive taxi; only she want to be with men." She caught a tear about to fall from her chin and wiped it.

All of a sudden, a picture appeared to me of the headless body of a man hollowed out in the middle where his heart should be. Taking two puffs of my asthma inhaler, I said, "It's okay. You don't need to say more."

Then she went to the core of my question. "A man took knife and put against my neck." She illustrated with her hand to her neck. Then she looked back at me through the rearview mirror and asked, "Neck or throat?" Her forehead was drawn tight to the elbow.

"Throat." I replied calmly, but my whole body was on edge.

"He make me drive to small place and he want rape me. He tell me to get out. But I not go. He walk away to my window to pull me, to pull me out window. But I drive and I hit him. I not look. I decide no more alone Morocco man. Just couple or group. But I cry. I cry a lot."

We arrived at the riad just then. She wept and little pieces of my own insanity drowned out her sobbing. Stars were poking through to join the moon. Gazing up at them, I rolled down the window all the way and pointed to the heavens, and said, "Look at the stars. The skies are full of miracles."

To see, she elongated her neck between the wheel and the roof and looked up through the windshield. "Beautiful," she said." I lay with children on handira. We look at stars. We think blessings."

"You are a blessing" I said. I paid the fare and watched with utter admiration as Oumayma rode away with a burning candle of hope for her children.

I wanted something to eat. Anything that sat comfortably in my hand, and not another tuna pizza with olives. A large food market was nearby. A little reluctant at first, I decided to walk through to see what I could find.

As soon as I entered, eyes satellited all around my pasty white American face dabbed with island-patches of sunburn. A ring of self-consciousness followed me wherever I walked, though I tried hard to blend in. A survey of the place was in order, so I walked each aisle checking out everything. When I got to hair products, a short, Asian-looking woman was bent over trying to read the label on a bottle of hair conditioner. She popped up and with a pre-thank-you gesture, asked, "You can read this? Fruit good for hair." Unable to read it myself, I played slide trombone with my glasses until I gave up and handed it back to her.

The last aisle was electronics-cleaning-supplies-bathroom accessories-fans. Moroccans, I had learned, confuse fans with air-conditioners. Fragrances discharging pine and cedar, cleaning products musking xylene and ketone, overcame me like I had walked into a morgue full of decaying corpses with a whiff of sweaty socks thrown in.

At the end of the next aisle, a man in a black shirt and black jeans and dirty from head to toe, and a woman with a brilliant body wearing a red djellaba and scarf were arguing heatedly. So that they wouldn't see me, I stood back and periscoped my head surreptitiously around the corner.

Two women, one older-looking than the other, rounded the corner from the opposite end of the same aisle and were all ears to the fracas. The woman in red was yelling something in Arabic at the dingy man while trying to get away from him. But the tall and skinny ghost of a guy followed her up the aisle, and he looked like the shadow of death. The two other women walked up to me and the three of us watched as the mess spilled over at the cash registers.

On the chance that one of the women spoke English, I asked the young-looking one, "What's happening?"

"He harassed her. She's saying that he touched her butt. And he's really insulting her now. But she really told him."

"What did she say to him?"

"I don't know if I should repeat it. She said, 'You f—ing asshole. You have a dirty mind and you should go to jail.'"

"Oh my," I exclaimed.

"Now he's saying, 'Want more? I know you want more.'"

The aggressor was looking into the woman's eyes, and as the harassment went unabated, I started to feel anger rise up within me and a fast river of epinephrine surged through my body and was accelerating. In the hope of slowing my emotions, I asked the young lady her name. "Chaima," she said, and she had the most incredible smile. A counter clerk started to dial, and I was hoping to the police.

Another man then walked up to the woman in red and spoke to her. Chaima said, "He's saying, 'I will go with you.' He's offering to walk her out the door away from the guy. But the lady is refusing his help. She's saying, 'I can go myself.' Now she's telling the bad guy, 'You'll see.' She means she's turning down the other man's help to show the bad guy she's not afraid of him."

Then the degenerate started yelling again. "What's he saying?" I asked.

Chaima answered, "He's saying, 'You see. You see. You talk to him. But not with me.'" The woman's face, blood-filled by the heat of her anger and her legs cocked rigid, had me wondering if it wasn't the harasser who was about to need protection.

The Asian woman at hair conditioners had even bent down and, from what I could tell, was praying in latria to God. I told her, "It's not his time yet."

A police officer arrived and Chaima said that he told everyone just to go home or about their business. To my shock, he didn't arrest the aggressor.

The victim was enraged and started yelling. "What's she saying now?" I asked.

Chaima interpreted. "I am married and have two children. You can't pull me down from my dreaming cloud. I'm a woman. I own the street." Chaima said she had "soul-confidence." The woman left all her groceries at the check-out counter and walked out.

The debauched guy then exited the market and walked down the rue in the opposite direction from the women. And I was thrilled to see him go because, against the implausibility, I had just witnessed a Moroccan woman stand up for herself in the face of sexual harassment. In public, no less.

"Chaima," I said. "Thanks for explaining all of this to me today."

"My pleasure, mister."

Feeling threadbare, I left the store for the riad and was surprised to see Chaima walking beside me. "Where are you going?" she said with a joyful snap.

"I'm staying close by at a riad."

"Oh, I am too. Which one?"

"I don't really know the name. There was a large group of young people there when I came yesterday."

"That's where I'm staying. Hey!"

She walked so close to my side that she bumped my shoulder twice. So, when I replied, I was almost able to look straight down into her eyes. "Yeah," I responded. "Remarkable things happen."

"For. Sure!"

"So, you're with that group?"

"Yeah. We just stayed last night. We're leaving pretty soon."

I could have soaked her up all day. Her manner of speaking was like a partita piccola. Each word and syllable she spoke was full of fun and adventure. Something else was interesting to me about her manner of speech, and I asked her about it. "Chaima, has anyone ever told you that you speak with a British accent?"

"Ha! That's like so funny." Her voice was electrifying now. "My God, I can't believe it. No, I don't do any British stuff. At all. Oh, I find that, like, so funny." She had me laughing and my face pitched forward and my upper lip must have jumped up because she added, "Oh, look mister. You've got lines by your eyes," and she reached her hand to my face and drew little imaginary lines to match my crow's feet, which made me laugh all the more.

"Chaima," I said, trying to bring myself under control. "I think the place is right up here. Oh—wait."

"What?"

"I never did get anything to eat at the store."

"This is the place you're staying?" She pointed at the riad.

"Yeah. That's it."

"Well, I'm definitely here too. And they have absolutely; I mean, such good, wonderful, things for you to eat. Oh, so good."

"That's fine. Yeah, I'll find something to eat. No problem."

Then my gray matter inspired a thought and I raised a pointed question. "Chaima, can I ask something please?"

"Sure. About?"

"You're Moroccan, right?"

"Absolutely."

We approached the entrance of the riad and walked through the happy jam of young people alchemizing in little pockets out front and some were inside the lobby.

"Let me just walk to the office a minute," I said to her. "Then I'll ask my question."

"Sure," she said with a long glissando between each letter.

Impervious to my litany of "excuse me," I pressed through the young bodies, keeping my hands in the air until I reached the office to ask for my key.

"Mr. Jack," said Yassine. "You stay tonight?"

"Oh, I completely forgot to pay."

"Mr. Jack. Can I say, please? When I first saw you, you look like businessman. Now you look defeated."

"I'm fine, Yassine. I just need to lay down a bit. Say, is Sanaa here?"

"No," he said with a woeful face. He didn't elaborate and I didn't want to ask what might have happened to her.

As I moved backward to walk away, I bumped right into Chaima standing immediately behind me.

"Oh, sorry mister." She giggled as she spoke.

"No problem. And please call me Jack."

She laughed and bent over a little, and with one hand on her stomach, and another hand over her mouth, she tried and tried to stop herself from tittering on.

"What's so funny?"

She said, "Oh, I just love that name. Jack. It sounds so, like, sharp, and—to the point. Jack!" When she said my name the second time, her voice cracked hard and loud like walnuts sound when their shattered by a nutcracker. I just loved her. She cared for life.

"You've sure got a lot more energy than me right now," I said.

"Being energetic has its own pure, unique, touch to view the world from that new magical keyhole." All I could do was smile. I had no idea what she meant.

"Chaima, what are your friends talking about?"

"Lots of things. Mostly life."

"Life?"

"Yeah. And beauty."

With a touch of sarcasm, I said, "I've been in Morocco for some time now and I think there's room for the women of Morocco to experience some of that beauty."

"What do you mean?"

"I am investigating disrespect of women in Morocco; how so many Arab women live fearfully and are under the foot of men. One woman I met even said to me, 'I'll give you everything I have if you just get me out of this place.'"

Suddenly, her demeanor became very serious as did her words. "That's not how I see it. I know what you mean. I hear many friends who say, 'I want America. Everything is good in America.' But I say, 'You were born here.' Mister, I am Moroccan. I love Morocco. I love malhun music. I love zellij tile. I love amariya at a wedding." My concerns lowered now as I heard her viewpoint, and she had me thinking that the things that oppress us are not entirely external, but internal.

"I guess I hadn't thought of things quite that way before."

"We are different—you and I."

"Hmm. Interesting," I replied, searching hard into the invisibility inside me for that same freedom. Before I could say another word, she took my hand and walked me over to a small mosaic, wooden table.

"Look," she said. "Here is a napkin," and she held it up to me. "It has a Moroccan design on both sides, see? Now I can see just a napkin or I can see the beautiful designs. When I get up, I can complain or I can look up and say what a wonderful day I have to live."

Taking the napkin from her hand, I realized that I would never have noticed the simple, blue and white, geometric design conveying indigenous realities had it not been for her insight. But then the napkin was being crushed in my hand under the weight of what seemed to me a paradoxical question. Are we to tell women repressed by men and societies to be satisfied with peace within? Or shouldn't we, and they, also work to change the contiguous cultures of oppression where they are?

I asked her, "But don't you fear abuse as a woman?"

"No, because I learned how to soak up knowledge to shape my reality, to enjoy the incredible journey of life. It is true that a single cell had developed into a full baby, but that decision we make can let the life appear like a movement forward, so of course I had that idea but then I was aware of that jazz, ha! and I took a decision not to fear."

Having no idea what she had meant again, I could only say, "That's incredible. But don't you think something should be done to stand up to harassment and cruelty?"

"Only the fearless win."

"Got it. Hey, I'll see you around, I hope. I'm beat. Going up to my room."

"You're welcome—Jack!"

The gay cadence in her voice and her stream-of-consciousness style of speaking had delighted me. But something of far greater significance had caught my attention. She possessed a meaningful worldview; a message of hope yet realized, and I had wanted so much for her to be a prescient marker of the future of Morocco. She touched me in my God-part.

Chapter 12

Near my second-floor room, images of the bow and scrape of the women desperate to build castles on feathers beset me hard this time. The tip of the key at my lock, I turned to see a tall woman dressed in a burqa with her face showing fully. Our eyes met. As if she were putting on a show just for me, she walked up the hall sighing heavily and, slumping both of her shoulders from the neck down, her attractive, olive-toned face appeared exhausted. But there was a gentle humor in her gestures which intrigued me. Because I intuited her desire for me to notice her, I said, "Got hotter this afternoon." No reply. Her eyes locked on me and she moved toward her door immediately next to mine, the Orchid room, and her attention felt encumbering.

I opened my door and walked right into the bathroom a mere foot away from the door. But I failed to close the door. In the cocked mirror, I saw her watching me, her left hand on the door to her room, and her right hand trying the lock blindly. A stark discomfort ran through my body and I moved to close the door slowly; gentlemanly, so as not to convey a sense of her turpitude.

My arms spread like a heraldic eagle and I fell backwards onto the bed and it sprung tight as money. The sound of rustling in the Orchid room attracted my attention. More so than if I hadn't seen her staring at me indiscreetly. Then a series of frictive halts sounded from her room, and I could only imagine the woman in black dragging a chair. That was followed by the sound a drinking glass makes against a wall and a part of me crawled into my secret panic room.

My phone rang.

"Hey," my wife said. "How are you doing? I haven't heard anything." I knew Beth well enough to know that she was waiting for me to say I had decided to come home.

"Hey. Sorry. I guess I've been really busy." I was trying to talk with one ear focused on the conversation, the other focused on the wall.

"Are you there?" she said.

"Yeah. I'm here."

"You going back to work? Or what?"

"No. I don't think so." Attention to my wife was growing sclerotic in my fear of all the variant sounds on the other side of the wall.

"Well don't you think maybe it's time to come home?"

"Sweetie, I will. But I don't think I'm done here yet."

"Jack, what are you trying to find?"

Her question closeted my emotions and a mere consonant emerged in the breath escaping from the narrow opening in my throat. "Um."

"Jack, somewhere you took a left turn. I'm really worried about you. You realize I'm the only one who calls. You never call me to say you're okay." Her voice was fluid and pitch unenhanced, neither alarming, nor elative, like a Mona Lisa smile.

"I've emailed you," I said, one ear still on Beth, the other on the wall.

"That's not the same."

"I'm okay. Really, I am."

Dead air.

"Sweetie," I went on, "you know me. My ADD makes it hard for me to concentrate on more than one thing. I'm sorry I haven't been in touch. I'll do better. Really I will." I was trying hard not to match the form of my words to the color of my erratic inner emotions.

"Well, do you think you're making any progress?"

"I think so. I've learned so many things about women in this part of the world. Just incredible."

"Jack, I never thought I'd hear something like that from you. I told the kids about your change of plans and they don't get it. They're a little worried about you too."

"Tell them I'm fine." I was doing my best to remain calm but little by little was coming apart at the looming opposite the wall.

"Okay, I'll wait to hear. Now call me, okay?"

"I will. Trust me."

I threw the phone on the bed and laid back again on the bed. My hands on my forehead were locked at the fingers, palms up, and I wondered if she bought it.

The subtle sounds on the other side of the wall looped aimlessly and shot daggers into the hidden parts of my heart, and my skin wept sweat.

I paced the room.

The titular sands of the hourglass appeared to me. Will I die here? My legs gave way and I sat on the floor with my back against the wall adjacent the din. My elbows on my knees and hands on the top of my head, I pulled my chin to my chest and the specter of all four walls altered, closing in on me. And an image of that night of dazed-up trembles and of glassed winters came down, and it was hard to stand the chill.

I had to resolve the question or die. Was I the objective student of culture I had been claiming to be? Or was I the standard-bearer of an earthly battle of my own making? People wanted to know what I was after, and why it mattered. The cold war of emotions inside me had boiled over and demanded to be reconciled. To the bars and blocks the ghosted questions came and hung themselves in loose alignment above a blue lantern. But unable to materialize, they fell back behind my fears.

Wait, I said to myself. Jan, the night man, a young, handsome fellow who had come from Germany to study Arabic, opened the door during the wee hours. He would know who occupied the Orchid room. I was sure of that.

Immediately, I pushed myself up along the stucco wall and onto my feet and bolted from my room.

Over the railing outside my room, I glimpsed downstairs and the central area was abuzz with young energies. On the steep stairs, a blank fenestration of young faces, one completely mottled, pressed past me. To let them pass, I pressed my back against the wall and inched down the stairs like a crab, one foot after the other. As soon as my feet hit the bottom floor, I saw only backs and tails escaping into the ground level rooms, and there was a sudden bottomlessness to the moment.

The large, open doors to Jan's room invited me to inch up slowly. I peered into the room so as not to surprise him. Suffused in soft shadows and in hard shadows, Jan's room seemed vacant. Riveting me, a redness dilated glowingly in the soft shadows and a crackle split the wordless space. A shaft of moonbeam speared an open window and a figure, reclining beneath, came into view. And clouds billowed and plumed ghostly white and played hypnotically within the halo.

"Jan?" I said timidly, trying to look through the darkness.

"Oh, excuse me," he said, sitting up. His figure revealed in the light of the moon. And he sacrificed his cigarette.

"Oh, you didn't need to do that for me."

"Oh, Dr. Jack." No problem sir. Can I help you?"

"Yes, it's me, Say, I wonder if I can ask a question."

"Yes, of course."

"I don't mean to be nosy, but can I please ask about the woman in the room next to me?"

"I don't believe we have a guest next to you."

"But I saw her. In fact, I can hear her."

"That room isn't occupied right now. Are you sure you heard someone?"

"Yes, I just said. I saw her." Confusion filed me.

"I'm only here at night. Maybe someone was there today. But according to the guest list, the Orchid room is unoccupied."

"That's impossible. She's wearing a burka. I saw her. I spoke to her less than an hour ago," I was becoming more unnerved by the moment. Jan checked the front door and we went up, my glare dogged. He knocked on the door of the Orchid room, softly. No answer.

"I don't think anyone's there, Dr. Jack."

Jan was preparing to walk away. "Wait, can you knock again, please? Maybe a little louder."

His knuckles rapped hard. "Hello. Management." No answer.

"Dr. Jack, I can assure you. No one is staying in there now."

Dejected and confused, I responded, "No—No, I guess not. Thank-you. I'm sorry to have bothered you."

"Not at all, sir. If you happen to need anything else this evening, please don't hesitate. You know where to find me." He walked away and I, in a spiritless trance, asked myself what had just happened.

Inside my room, I fell on my bed again and found myself enmeshed in a crisis. If the room next to mine was empty, I thought, then maybe my wife was right. I wasn't acting myself. And my path to be some sort of light for the women had been shown to be nothing else than the animations of my mind. Undisguised vanity.

The dimmer switch on my energies dropping, the light bulb on the wall above my bed started flickering, and the effect nettled me to the bone. The bed wobbled as I wangled my way to its center and, reaching up, the hot bulb bit my hand and I snatched it away in a reflex arc. I had neither the strength nor the will to try again. I dropped onto the bed, diagonal this time, the variations of blackbody radiation starring me in the face. And the umbra resided deep inside me.

Then my conscience spoke to me in the form of my wife. Leave now Jack. Come home. Slowly. Dismally. I gathered my things. "It's over," I said out loud this time. The chimera on the other side of the wall had served as a metaphor for the unreality I had projected from within.

I called a taxi to take me directly to the airport. A flight left for New York at 11:19 p.m. I would call my wife at the airport. Jan let me out.

"Dr. Jack, you sure you need to leave us? Is there a problem?"

"No. No problem. It's just that I need to go now. Thank-you for everything." I said it all with a plastic smile. Beyond that, I couldn't say more.

Twin beams of light through wavy shades of nocturnal black portended the cab and its advent triggered both feelings of hope and disappointment. The rear passenger door opened quietly and not hearing the shrill, little squeak of the old rag, overcast me in memories I had to forget now.

About to sit, an image on the external boundary of my attention drew me. Instinctively, I scanned left, my right eyelid already half-closed from the lung-staining exhaust pouring out the taxi's defective muffler system. "What?" I said silently. I strained to see. "Yes. Yes, it is," I said loudly now. "It's her! Why—she's getting into a car. The women in black. I wasn't imagining!" I watched as the unidentified SUV pulled away, its windows tinted solid, and felt certain that the woman and her driver had seen me.

A cataract of numbing tentacles streamed down and over my face and shoulders. Nabil, I was sure, had been correct. Eyes were on me. "Come?" said the cabby impatiently. I watched as the mystery SUV drove farther away. "Come?" he said louder. I needed time. "Je suis désolé," I said to the cab driver and he drove off in a huff.

I stood. I waited.

Just then, a stillness came. Occlusive of every thought, voice, and experience, to the lip of that moment, it surrounded me; pinioned me, like the wings of a great, white dove, and I could hear the voice of her saying, "I'm here, Jack, as long as you need me." Without want of human opinion or fear of what people could do to me, I yielded; listened. The outer layers of my fascia tingled supra clean like a crystal-clear stream when the light of the sun hits it dead on. The sensation lasted several seconds. Just as fast as the stillness came, it left. And yet, I knew it would never be far from me. I knew what to do now. Something was waiting for me.

I decided to return to the riad. From the dank, shaded mouth of the alley, I saw two young boys; dirty-faced sprogs, icing their bodies like gargoyles on the steps leading into the riad. One young face mired hoary beyond its years, the other burnished proud and lined with protuberant hills of meandering acne, smirked at me in unison. A late-night breeze ruffled my long-sleeved shirt and the way shadows crept up the walls blanketed me in niggles about the boy's intentions. But the preceding minutes had endowed me a gift of power, and with a gentle center and untossed confidence, it waited for me to act.

I looked back at the boys with a grin azured calm and commanding. And the rapscallions transformed into young men and parted for me like the waters of the Nile. Rather than pass between them, I looked straight into the hazel eyes of the proud-looking boy, and when I did, a touch of moonlight let in the lightening, and his face beamed. He stood. His eyes remaining on me, he took his hand the size of a catcher's mitt and slid it along the door until he had found the handle. He pulled it. But the handle refused to move.

"It's locked son," I said.

"Sawwy Missa."

"No problem. Thanks for your help."

Just as I reached in my pocket to give both boys a little something, the front door opened. "Someone out here?" Jan said inspectingly. "Oh, Dr. Jack. You are back?" Jan was surprised and elated to see me.

"Yes. I changed my mind. Is my room still available?"

"Of course, it is. You've only been gone a few minutes. Please come in."

Before entering, I looked back to wish the boys well, but they had already disappeared into the night, just like that. "Let me get your key," Jan said. "I think I put it with the others. Please, come in. I'll be right back."

Jan flipped on a light. And the youthful faces I had seen earlier in the atrium were still playfully alive like bundles of candles. The zellij tiles appeared distinctly amplified as if to welcome me back and the hairs on the back of my neck felt relaxed. Peaceful and poised, I couldn't have been more surprised when a conviction sworded me to pivot my travels in the morning to another city in Morocco.

"Here, I found your key," Jan said, racing up. "Sorry it took me so long. I found it on my desk instead of with the others."

"Not a problem. Rattling the key inside my half-closed fist, I said, "Jan, I don't want you to think; just give me the first answer that comes to mind."

"What do you mean?"

"Just give me the first thing that hits you."

"Okay."

"Name a city, big or small, you like in Morocco."

"Fez."

"Fez?"

"Yes. I love Fez. Very traditional; not so modernized as Marrakech."

My heart rate synchronized with his answer, and in the time that it took a few seconds to float, I said "Fez it is", and my manner remained placid and expression sure.

My beautiful room was as before. The creases on the bedsheets were still intact and at the bottom were folded forward into themselves. The soft cushions of the tips of my fingers ran back and forth over the uneven and rippling sequences of the wall facing the exterior world, and I imagined the stars outside. Somehow, the stars were as real to me as if I had been standing outside looking up. The impression resonated with me and I had hoped always to see through the hardness to the light and life above.

Resting my head on the pillow, my mood turned pensive—it could do that as quick as the pinion on the end of an eagle's wing. And I questioned my constancy to see to the life above. Really, I questioned if there is such a thing.

Then, in the borderlands between wakefulness and sleep, a memory of Indela washed ashore, carrying me off to the counsel I gave her at Taroudant, when we walked the grand sidewalk.

"You look concerned," I said. "Something wrong?"

"I don't have a peace."

"Peace about what?"

"Things going on in my family."

"Like what, if I can ask?"

"I'm speaking to you like a father right now and so please don't say anything."

"That's fine."

"I graduate school soon and I want to do more study, maybe abroad. In Europe. But my family insists I stay here and get married. They've even picked someone."

"Picked someone? You mean someone other than Mansour?"

"Yeah. Someone else. And I barely know him."

"But what about Mansour?"

"That's part of the problem too. I love him and respect his opinion in every-thing. But. I don't know. It's like—" She appeared confused.

"It's okay. You don't need to say more. If I can offer some advice?"

"Yes, please."

"You have to listen to your heart."

"What do you mean?"

"Well, I'm not an expert. But one thing I've seen over the years is that we have a way of convincing ourselves of certain things we want. In relation-ships, for example, we can see things in people that act as warning signals. But because we want that relationship so much, we suppress the signals, or we tell ourselves that somehow it will all work out. I've learned that those seeds of concern never go away but only grow over time and become major problems later on."

"I think that's what I'm feeling. I do have concerns and they worry me."

"That's your heart speaking."

"How can I hear it clearly?"

"Without courage to listen to your heart, you will forever live in fear of who you really are."

"Courage. You mean not to make excuses?"

"Don't think better or worse of a situation or of yourself than what is real."

"And my heart can guide me?"

"Yes. But also, be careful. Our hearts can deceive us."

"Really? Now I'm confused. Then how can I know if what I'm feeling is right?"

"I recall something my grandmother taught me when I was just a boy. We were sitting on the porch of her home; she was in her favorite rocker, and she pointed to the grass and noted that each blade has a spine running down the center. On each side of the spine are the leaf parts. When its dry out the little leaves fold inward and close tight. She said 'They're praying for rain.' Then she said, when the rain comes, the little pieces of grass open up to receive the blessings from above. I'll never forget that picture. She said, 'Jackie.' She called me Jackie. 'When our lives are dry and we are confused, we need to fold our hands like the grass.' Indela maybe you just need to be alone, to fold your hands and meditate."

"Jack. You know me better than anyone."

Rolling over to sleep, the memory comforted me. But it also unsettled me. Why, I thought, am I able to give advice, but have such trouble taking it?

The early morning jumped at me. I rose with a jolt of energy only to realize I hadn't a clue how to get to Fez and had forgotten to ask Jan. My mind began to clear, and the night's dream came to mind, saddening me. I didn't have time to be sad. Jan was just leaving his night shift downstairs and I managed to catch him.

"Jan," I said, "I'm so glad to see you."

"You had a good night, Dr. Jack?"

"I slept as long as Rapunzel's hair."

"Ah. Good one. I'm German so I get it."

"I knew you would. Say, I decided to take your advice and go to Fez."

"Really. What's in Fez for you?"

"I'm not sure. But I won't know if I don't go."

"Well, you're free to go where you want."

"That's what freedom is." Jan looked at me like someone pulled the switch.

"Is it far to drive? What's the best route?"

"It's a long drive. I think five hours or more."

"Oh."

"But there are flights. Most take a long time with stopovers. But if you're very interested, I know one that is short. One hour."

Not knowing the local language, I asked him to call for me. The flight was to leave in less than two hours. Jan looked at me with the airlines' representative on hold. "You want it. Dr. Jack?"

Indecision numbed me for a second and my mouth hinged half open like the door of a metal mailbox when it's not quite closed. Then a gust of charged certainty filled me and I said, "Grab it!"

Perfect, I thought, and started to run and was halfway up the stairs when I realized I wouldn't see Jan again. Starting back down, I saw him standing at the bottom of the stairs. "Keep going, Dr. Jack. We will meet again. I'm leaving now. Yassine has come."

"Jan, you take good care of yourself."

I scampered up the remaining stairs, my thoughts a billowing mindscape of new adventures to come. My morning hassles, dog-eared in my implicit memory, took longer to do than I had wanted. But I was out the door in time for the taxi to take me to the airport.

≈ ≈ ≈

Near the airport a pine tree with no bark stood among a clump of palms. That was a bad sign for the pine tree, I thought, because the thin roots of most palms stretch away from the trunk in their search for moisture and nutrients and can become entangled in the thick, heavy balls of the root systems of other trees and die off. Into departures I went and the image of death was still on my mind, and I didn't know why. The arabesque of busy comings and goings distracted my thought, especially how the intricate pattern of moving bodies was not much different than the world outside.

Behind brown eyes, she sat in the aisle seat next to me, a woman about my age from what I could tell. About to put my phone on airplane mode, a story in my newsfeed stabbed me in the eye. "Oh, my word," I gasped in vocal tremors long and loud. The woman took notice and I fathomed that my voice had been too intense like an incoming wave hitting and washing over the rocks when people don't expect. "Oh. Sorry," I said with my head lowered and voice hushed.

"It is okay," she said.

"My name is Jack."

"I am Nesrine."

"You are Moroccan?"

"No, Algerian."

"What brings you to Morocco, if I may ask?"

"I was here to lecture at the University Cadi Ayyad University in Marrakech. Now I go to Fez to see a friend."

"Wonderful. You're the second academic I've met in Morocco."

"What are you reading? Please pardon if my English is not very good."

"It's the account of an honor killing that just happened in the Middle East." I waited for a look of exclamation from the newly minted Ph.D. But instead, Nesrine's pupils remained unexpanded, so I continued. "The reason for the murder, it says here, is that a young woman had posted a video on social media of her boyfriend proposing to her. And even though the family had approved of the proposal, they hadn't granted formal permission to the engagement. And so, her father ordered her older brother to kill her." I glanced again at Nesrine and said, "Can you imagine?" But she didn't answer and her countenance blanched stoic.

I continued reading. "It says the attempt failed due to the fact that the young woman had jumped from the balcony, and she broke her spine." I looked yet again at Nesrine for some response but nothing. "Okay, well, it says she was rushed to the hospital and recorded some messages on social media of confidence to carry on. But it was there; get this, in the hospital, that her brother found her, and finished what he had started. He killed her right in the hospital. Where in the world were the hospital workers? Isn't that incredible?"

Her mouth set oddly broad, she peered down through her professorly bifocaled glasses at my phone as if her impress me button had yet to be pushed. Challenged by her lack of incredulity, I boosted up the drama like a Shakespearean actor working the audience. "Now get this," and I embellished with my index finger waving in the air. "The nurse on call had, and I can't imagine why there weren't more people on the floor, recorded the bloodletting screams by leaving her cellphone on record and then hid herself."

Nesrine began scratching through her purse for something.

"Did you catch that part?" I asked.

"Yes. Is that everything?" She continued riffling through her purse and my entire being anesthetized painfully at her rest and digest attitude.

"If I may," I said, my brain feeling like the string raveled in a yo-yo. "It goes on to describe the families' sick rationale for killing her."

"Okay."

"It says here that because dating is often viewed as a synonym for sex in the more conservative sections of Morocco, a couple's going out together, or courting for marriage, could be viewed as improper and as a cause of shame to the whole family. You know, Nesrine, I met an anthropologist; her name is Robin, and she told me roughly the same thing."

"Excuse me a minute," she said. Nesrine started to get up, and I had assumed to the bathroom, but the seatbelt light was on and the attendant asked her to remain seated.

The second Nesrine buckled herself back in, I asked, "Nesrine, were you aware of this story?"

"Yes. I heard."

"I wonder. Are Algerian woman talking about it?"

"Why should Algerians be interested in a story from the Middle East? These things happen frequently all around the world." All my mental capacities were stymied momentarily.

"I must have misunderstood you," I replied.

"No. I don't think you did. There are several issues that happen nowadays, and I don't see people talking about all of them. Why not, for example, talk about U.S. relations with Syria?" Little jets of confusion fired choppily in me. What? I thought. We can't be horrified over an honor killing because we're not discussing Syria? I was sure that anyone looking at me would have seen blood streaking across my eyes like a subconjunctival hemorrhage. I wanted to crawl into my own nothingness.

The abyss of vileness from which the burdened women cry queued my imagination again and I wrote my thoughts:

> She comes with a need and believes he will love her. She belongs up there. She knows she belongs there. In his arms, central, up front, she has no doubts that she doesn't have a right to be loved. No one has told her otherwise. Then he enters the room and says, I can love you. Then the words begin to slide; he's good at that; he's practiced. My plan, he says, is to love you, but love is for you to define. Or another can love you. It makes no sense, she thinks. Her heart begins to race. Another can fulfill my needs? I came to you in need. I came to you when I didn't have the resources to get to the other person, and even if I go there, they will tell me the same. They also have my name and information

and if they look, they will see I'm a woman. So, to tell me to go somewhere else to find love is an empty gesture. And you know that. But you're good at that, aren't you? You know how to sound right; look right, but you've learned to suppress who you really are. And if I expose you, you'll hurt me in love.

I looked through my window and took a deep breath. Gentle streaks of sunlit grace kissed the wing, and where the veil met unfathomed space, a misty edge divided the tints. The horizon, I thought to myself. Its point of reference to judge the scale and distance of objects in relation to us provides perspective.

That's it, I thought. Maybe Nesrine has been so overexposed to the idea of violence against women that her perspective is different from mine. But what if Nesrine's daughter had been brutally attacked? The horror would have grabbed her by the hair. But that's the way of it. The closer a tragedy hits home, the greater its impact. The farther away it happens, the less its effect upon us.

Gazing out my window, I continued to thread my own perspective mentally. Women, pain, freedom, brutality, had meant little to me in my life in America. The forces were like Byzantine mosaics: unreal figures; mere abstractions on flat-surfaced walls representing real people but without progression, reality, or life. Once I witnessed the attack on Indela, figures frozen in time foreshortened providing breadth. But with nothing else to go by, I couldn't have known the scope of the problem women in Morocco, and its contiguous countries, faced. One can't measure the size of a bird against a deep, blue sky without trees near it, or buildings to judge its speed. By hearing other women's voices, my mosaic passed to a new form of understanding, one with enlarged perspective, and the severity and scope of the dilemma had become clearer to me.

Assuming I had come to understand Nesrine's dulled reaction, I turned to her, and said, "I guess I had expected a little more solidarity from an Algerian woman, even though this murder happened in the Middle East. But

I understand your point. We can't speak to every issue at the same time and not all of them affect us equally."

"True. No one has killed me."

My head ticked and brow tightened. Her added remark now struck me as bordering on unsympathetic. Now my opinion of her position was only as the line of placid sky drowsily touching the delft blue beyond my window. But then a flash razored the wing and split my eye to another possible explanation. Was Nesrine in denial because she didn't wish to face the long tenure of the subjugation of women in her lands? Not to grapple heavily with the killing is one thing. But complete moral and intellectual blackout is never justified by lack of firsthand experience with evil. No one had killed Nesrine. But death comes to us in different ways.

Chapter 13

Nic. Scream. Bounce hard. The brakes grabbed tight and overhead compartments jiggled and wracked and backs held tight against the seats and the compartment above me opened and some light luggage of mine fell out, brushed an older gentlemen's leg, and hit the floor. "Are you alright?" I asked across the aisle with concern. A wave of his hand said all was fine. But I wasn't sure.

A light Autumn shower glanced the airfield at the Fez-Saiss Airport just as we existed the clam-shell style door and several big globules hit the tarmac in diamond-shaped smatterings. Inside the terminal, an ebony tassel swished quickly in little oval circles as the same sophisticated-looking man, whom my carry-on had hit, bent to pick up his fallen passport with unrushed deportment. A young, rawboned man, walking fast and with a pronounced limp, bumped the gentleman from behind just as he stood and knocked the passport from his hand and it fell to the floor again. The old man stood and looked at the young man, his demeanor calm, as though he had been through it all before.

"Please, let me get this for you sir," I offered.

"Thank-you, sir."

"You're the man my luggage hit when we landed. I trust you're okay."

"I'm fine, sir," he said jauntily. His headdress, the Fez, was sodden where the rain had hit; of pure reddish chains, and his gray mustache had not yet soaked the rain.

"You are here on business, Mr.—?" he asked.

"My name is Jack. Well, I was here on business, but my plans changed."

"Pleasure to meet you. My name is Omar Belkacem. I assume you are—?"

"American."

"Ah. I thought so. May I ask what brings you to Fez?"

"Actually, I was south of the mountains, doing scientific research. But some things happened and, as life would have it, I spent some days in Marrakech, and now I'm in Fez."

"Welcome. Now my daughter is picking me up. Do you have a ride?"

"No. But that's not necessary. Thank-you. Maybe I can take can taxi."

"Nonsense. You waste your money on taxis. It will be my honor. You are a guest in my country. And besides, you helped an old man today and I want to return the kindness."

"I'll take you up on your offer. And it will be my honor. Thank-you."

"Is this all you have?"

"I travel light."

"Then we can go. My daughter said to meet her outside."

We walked toward the airport exit, and when I saw it, a stick was gouged in the old scabs. And my anticipation that had been eager to see, to explore, to learn—suspended there, and so did I.

"Everything okay with you, Jack?" Omar asked caringly. "You look lost in thought. Did you forget something perhaps?"

"Yes. I mean. No. Sorry. Why don't we go?" We exited and I caught myself licking my lips, a sure sign of my typical nervousness.

"My daughter said she can meet us outside. She doesn't like to park, but wants to drive in circles until I come out."

"You know, I met a young, Moroccan woman whom I could have sworn speaks English with a British accent. But she said I was wrong. Do I detect a British accent in you also?"

"Ha! Yes. I was educated many years ago in London, from my youth."

"Well, this time I'm right."

"I think so."

"Say, may I ask the name of your beautiful, red hat."

"It is a Fez."

"Oh, like the city." I reacted the way people do when they see the stars align.

"Yes, exactly. The hat is rather politically incorrect in these days. But I like to wear it when I travel."

We stood for minutes without saying a word. And a light rain rimmed the distance, before which a rainbow showed full, and the air was forgiving. Then a newish, black sedan pulled up, its trunk popped, and a woman got out and greeted Omar. I stood motionless as the two sorted things out.

"Jack, please come," said Omar. "Meet my daughter. Nadia, may I introduce, Jack."

"Welcome to Morocco." She extended a hand of greeting.

"Pleasure is mine." We shook hands and her handshake was weak. Strange to me because her strong, rectangular jawline, which figured more prominently than did the fine embroidery of her neckline, implied canyons of stamina. She put our luggage in the trunk just as the sun nudged through the clouds, showing the few streaks of her white hair, and I thought she was on cusp of middle age. And her blue kaftan blew gently in the breeze.

"I now passed through a little rain," she said.

"Yes, the rain's over there." I pointed to the rain, and then popped my things in the trunk. "You should have seen the beautiful rainbow."

"I offered Jack a ride," Omar explained to Nadia. He has been in Morocco for some days." Nadia listened attentively to her father as though she were evaluating his every word when a sudden hoot and blare of an impatient driver wanting our space made us get underway.

"So, Omar, may I ask your line of work? Or, are you retired?" Nadia laughed at my question. The leather seats of the spotless sedan rumpled and creaked as Omar scooched forward and the leather still had that new smell.

"Don't worry about my daughter's laugh," Omar said. "She laughs a little because she knows her father should be retired. But he likes to—how you say in America—?"

"Poke his nose," Nadia injected with a laugh. She looked at me sidelong with a squint of her eyes, and the natural position of her frowned, half-crescent mouth turned way up into a blustery freedom.

"Jack," Omar said. "Perhaps you do not know, but Fez is home to some of the more famous tanneries in the world. Our family has owned and operated one in our city. Do you know of the tanneries?"

"I'm afraid I'm not familiar with the tanneries. Isn't that where—the leather—?"

"Yes, exactly," Omar said. "After we take you—oh, where are we taking you?"

"To be honest, I came to Fez on a bit of a whim. I thought I'd find a place; riad, hotel, whatever, and just stay a while."

He was eager for a guest; a friend. "No, you will stay with us. We have a big place in the medina and hospitality is very important in our culture."

"In the medina?" I reacted with a happy expectation because I had so wanted to visit it.

He must have sensed my receptive mood, because he reacted exuberantly. "Yes. Yes. You will like it."

"Oh, I don't want to be a burden."

"Now you will disappoint an old man and you don't want to do that." I felt his hand on my shoulder.

It was really an easy decision. "Then yes. And I can't thank-you enough." Everything: meeting Omar, the stylish ride, and the generosity when, without a clue how I would maneuver the days, vivified the magical providence in which I was walking and comforted me. Kaleidoscope impressions narrowed along the Route d'Imouzzer, from new to old, and the thought hit me to call Beth like I had promised. But I didn't want to appear rude.

Thinking I should reach out to her, I asked, "Omar. Do you mind if I make a call?"

"Not at all."

"Hey," my wife answered.

"Hey."

"Where are you?"

"I'm in Fez now. It's the cultural capital of Morocco."

"What are you doing there?"

"Ahh—Not sure. Guess I'm still searching." A slight suspension in time followed, and I knew that meant she still wanted me home.

To change the subject, I said, "Beth, I met this really kind man at the airport and he offered to let me stay with him."

"Who is he?"

"His name's Omar. Met him at the Fez airport."

"You sure he's okay?" Not wanting to speak about Omar openly, especially with a question mark over his head, I replied, "I'm driving with him now. And his daughter." I smiled over my shoulder at Omar, but he was looking at his phone.

"Oh, okay," she said.

Ill at ease, thinking Beth might want to start a conversation about my home coming, internal pressure built in me to wrap the call. "Um. Look. How about I call later? We can talk more then. I just wanted to check in like I said I would."

"Okay," she said, her voice rabbity. Call me again. Promise?"

"I will. Promise."

"Thanks for calling. Oh, wait, Jack you there?"

"I'm here."

"I love you."

"Love you too."

"That was my wife," I said to Omar and Nadia, fumbling with the phone, trying to switch it off.

"I guessed as much," said Omar. "How long have you been married?"

"Almost thirty years."

"Is that right. You look younger." He stared at me momentarily as if he were trying to size me up.

"Well, I feel older, so it balances out."

"Ha! Very good."

Empty time passed and I said, "Omar, I see a wall. Is that the medina?"

"Yes. Fez el Bali is the old part of our city. We started here as far back as the eighth century. And an ancient legend says that the city was started when a golden axe divided the River Fez in two parts. In fact, by the—oh Nadia help me."

"Twelfth century," she said vacantly.

"Yes," Omar confirmed. "By the twelfth century, Fez was the largest city in all the world." His voice effused pride.

"Really." I spoke a long "really" in total surprise. "The largest city in the world?"

"Yes."

"And where does the name Fez come from?"

"Fez means axe. I told you."

"Oh. The golden axe that divided the river." I stated it as if I had asked a question.

"Yes," Omar verified. "Now you have it."

I looked over at Nadia and leaves of faded brown befell her façade and I knew she had heard it all before like myths of dungeons and knights. She turned the wheel and I didn't see a ring; instead, a train of thought, those missing car keys, that one sock, the forgotten umbrella, and words that should have been spoken.

"We have our place to park outside," Omar said. "Cars are not allowed in the medina. But the walk is short."

We entered the medina and the style and the labor, the people grazing the souks, and time fortified against modernity, brought couplets of thoughts to mind.

> Lips and alleys not unusual then—
> Narrow streets, but narrow to who?
> To those, these silken archways climbed when—
> A few penetrating steps; bright lemons; steamed snails
> The city spoke and I said to myself
> A severed camel head hooked on a chain?
> Still, the values in the myriad of medersas and minarets—
> Be lost amidst entrancing the present in vain.

"Welcome Jack," Omar said, as we entered his home. The modest front door and flat, bland frontage hadn't prepared me for the aesthetic contradiction into the ambrosial yet restrained opulence of the interior. My eyes wanted to look out at first, but were drawn downward by lanes of gold crests crisscrossing the creamy white sea of zellij, and whispers of light blue feathered the tiles. The lines drew my eye to an antique alabaster fountain, and twin birds fluttered near the emerald water surrounded by palms. The scent of native citrus trees and jasmine linked sight to smell.

"I will take some tea in the setwan. Will you join me?" said Omar.

"Of course," I said. I had no idea what a setwan was.

"Do you mind leaving your shoes?"

"Oh. Not at all."

As we walked slowly, Omar motioned to the fountain. "I do not know how informed you are about our homes. But this is the courtyard. It is set around the sahrîdj, a fountain or basin."

"Oh, that's what it's called," I said. "I stayed overnight at a beautiful riad in Essaouira. But your fountain is even more beautiful."

"The sahrîdj is valued highly among us. Water is viewed in our culture as a vital life force; as you know, water is needed in the desert. The fountains are also how we cool the interior courtyards when it's hot. As you move around Fez you will see many fountains. Please come."

Angled away from the open-sky courtyard, Omar led me to a room apportioned with divans and plumped silken cushions.

"I wish I had a beautiful place like this," I said with a hint of sarcasm.

"Someday you might." Omar smiled at me, and his front tooth flashed gold.

"I love the walls of this room."

"It is tadelakt, intricately painted stucco. Lime-based material is rubbed in and is then polished by hand with various treatments and olive oil."

"I saw this type of wall also in Essaouira. So, the olive oil gives it that shine?"

"Yes. The walls are quite common in our riads and dars. Please sit."

"Thank-you. Now you said you own a tannery?"

"Yes. I inherited the business from my father and he from his father. But old ways of doing business are not as acceptable in these days."

"Why is that?"

"The chromium, the chemicals, and the process we use. We are under some pressure from foreign influences to change what we do. Environmentalists. You know."

"Yes, I work in forestry and have worked closely with environmentalists."

"Interesting. Then you know."

"Yes. And I'd love to see your tannery."

"We can take you. You can see firsthand."

"But obviously you have a good life."

"If you mean the house, my father owned it." A cheerlessness enfolded his expression and it said more than words about the contrast between making a living and living. A desolate, few seconds passed between us and I struggled to know what to say next. I wanted to move into him, to learn, and to feel what he was feeling in that moment.

"You sound a little down," I said in a reserved way. "Some personal challenges. Perhaps."

"The hardest part of being rich was having been poor."

"Life was simpler?"

"I enjoyed the days of my youth. At seventy-two, I've lost my objectives." His head and shoulders slouched, and his knuckles broadened white as he pulled himself straight using the arms of his chair, and I imagined his invisible struggle—that the lion still alive in him hated the torpor of weather-beaten days.

"Let me change our talk," he said. "I do not want to pry." I knew where he was going and my thoughts began darting around for a place to land. "I am curious why you are with us in Fez."

I was about to speak, but a young woman entered the setwan. Her brunette hair was sleek, like the transparency of a glassy mirror, and tied up. And her necklaced lines connected her dimpled chin to her beauty bones. Her beauty was almost make-believe it was so real. She poured the sweet, aromatic tea, and my eyes were captivated once more by the grace of the long cascade.

"You are watching her pour," Omar said.

"Yes, and that was high. She poured from at least eighteen inches."

"The pour is done high to make—how you say?—foam. The tea is not ready without the foam."

Omar spoke to the server in Arabic and she left hurriedly, her head down. As she turned to walk away, I caught the fulness of her face. A scar extending from just below her right eye to the bottom of her jaw surprised me, but not in an offensive way. She was a beautiful work of art. Not a perfect canvass. She was a woman.

"Oh, that's the reason," I marveled. "To create air. So, the exhibition is practical after all."

"Yes," Omar concurred.

We took a sip of tea and the laggard interlude allowed me to consider how to annotate my path up to that point to a man of the culture without impugning the majority religion. That was the furthest thing from my mind.

"Now, you were telling me what brought you to Fez," he added, placing his tea on the table.

Halfway into my story, the server returned and I stopped talking again. "Please continue, Jack," Omar said. "Would you take Mlouwza?" The woman held out a stainless-steel tray of delicacies for my inspection.

Not so much confused, but curious, I asked, "What exactly is a—"

"Mlouwza," Omar jumped ahead. "It's a cookie with an almond."

The calluses and broken capillaries of the server's hands caught my eye and my hand hovered aimlessly over the cookie tray, and I felt that hers had been a life lived hard. Two cookies were in my hand and she placed the tray on the table next to the tea. When she turned to walk away our eyes met this time and I was pulled through her docile glooms and into her luminous élan. Recognizing that I had seen in her an epic humanity, populated by her own drives and expectations, I was sure she wasn't ready to trade her dreams.

It hit me. "Wait," I said. "Is Mlouwza the same as Ghriba?"

"I think it is," Omar said, and there was a curiosity about him. "How might you know that?"

"A young, Moroccan woman told me." I answered disconsolately, for obvious reasons, and took a long, sumptuous bite.

I finished my story, and Omar soaked it all up sharp-eared. By the second glass of tea, I had to pass on the Kaab el Ghazal.

"You've had some unfortunate experiences in our country," Omar said, "and you've heard some regrettable stories. I apologize for the brutish way our men often act. I was educated at the University of London and so I know the West and I know our lands. I am Muslim. But I like to think my views of the world are cosmopolitan."

"Then you're a good person to ask."

"What is that?"

"I had a conversation with a Moroccan woman on the plane; an educated woman, about an honor killing in the Middle East."

"Yes, I heard also."

"What surprised me is how uninterested she was when I raised the issue."

"You asked an Arab woman her opinion of honor killings? Nature is not so kind to all of us." He spoke now in a redolent tone, and my apparent naiveté hit me like a jackhammer.

My confidence feeling suddenly weak-kneed, I asked, "What should I have known?"

"Jack," I need to go to the tannery for a brief time. Will you join me? I take a short way through the shops of friends."

"I'd be most happy to." I struggled to understand what the tannery had to do with my question.

Chapter 14

We exited Omar's palatial home through a keyhole-shaped back door laden with locks, bolts, and a chain, and into a compressed space between buildings woven tightly. The yellow sunlight was just in position to hit my neck. At the edge of the shade, we entered the back end of a shop and walked through a world of chestnut inventions. At the front of the store men sat on wooden stools banging pots and producing miniature lightning bolts with each strike. Some people stopped to watch while others whooshed past with one eye looking at the craftsmen. When the artisans saw Omar, they paused their battering just long enough so they could greet him. I could tell he was important. A pall of sheesha from a nearby café mixed the air and the air was thirsty. My allergies reacted and my breathing became hard. Then a butcher, his arms a river of veins, thwacked and ripped the carcass hard and squidgers of bone flickered high. Sprigs of mint and coriander leaves hung at the base of the meats and the coriander tops were feathering. Women in djellabas wrestled for the meats and flies were after the sticky treats.

"I always wondered why the meat is left outside," I said, looking ahead to Omar just in front of me as we walked.

"Moroccans don't like frozen meat," he said over his shoulder.

A smell, not as bad as I had expected, but interacting morosely with my allergies, met us on the stairs leading to Omar's old office. "Follow me, Jack. Just up the stairs." The office was now occupied by a younger man. The space was compressed with items I could have spent all day asking about. Omar spoke briefly to the man at the desk and the man left us. Omar handed me a business card from the desk. "Thank-you," I said to him.

Standing at a window, I looked out and saw men hard at work in honey-combed pits. Between the varied colors and varied smells in the dense, aerial spaces on the way from Omar's home, and the new smells now wafting into the office from the pits, the temperature of my skin heated and my eyes turned inward to the droplets of perspiration on my face.

"Omar, I think I need to sit."

"Sit here, Jack. Let me get water for you and give you a sprig of mint to put under your nose."

"No thank-you. No more smells. Just the water. Please."

"We receive many tourists, and some are offended by the cow urine and pigeon poop that makes ammonia to soften the hides for leather, but—"

"Please, Omar. You don't need to say more." I took a large sip. "I think it's all the smells and I have an asthma problem. Just let me sip this for a bit."

"Jack. I brought you here, in part, to help you understand why the woman on the plane acted as she did."

"This place?" I stood and walked to the window and the great, colorful tannery was in motion and men were dipping the hides and curious tourists were watching from terraces.

Omar joined me. "You see the men down there working in the sun? Leather has been prepared much the same way in Morocco for hundreds of years. It's done by hand and we have not changed the basics of the process. Can you think of anything that has been done the same way for so long?"

"No."

"Jack, I'm sure you know that nations of the Western world are called law-based societies, and our countries are called honor-shame. There's an important difference. If all you do is tell people what is right and wrong under the threat of punishment, then many people will respect the law, but only outwardly. But if you lead people with honor, then you instill virtue and people will develop a deep sense of right and wrong."

"I'm following."

"Now, what is virtue without serving people, what we call 'the companions of the right hand?' That is why our nations are considered collectivist. Since your European Reformation, the individual has come to play a dominant role. That has permitted capitalism to overrun family-operated and time-proven production."

"I'm afraid I'm not an economist."

"I am. Remember, I studied in England."

"I'll take your word."

"What I'm saying, Jack, is that everything we do considers the horizontal effects on other people. And so, families, tradition, rites, and religion, govern our attitudes and even our modes of production. Many westerners think of shame as a bad thing. But what if shame and guilt were a check and balance on social virtue?"

"That's certainly a different perspective."

"Jack. Do you know of Hshuma?"

"No. I don't think so."

"In Morocco, Hshuma means shame or losing face. Shame can result from doing many socially unacceptable things that disrespect others. Failing to introduce someone, lack of respect towards parents, swearing in public, blowing your nose very loud in a restaurant, or talking with your mouth full, even telling dinner guests you're going to the restroom."

"I didn't know any of this." And all I could think of was how many cultural blunders I had committed on my trip, especially my bad eating habit.

"Jack, have you had a meal with a Moroccan family?"

"No, I don't think I have."

"You will this evening. Moroccan families eat together from the same plate and share food because we consider ourselves as one. So, not simply because it is hygienic, but out of respect we wash our hands before saying Bismilah and then eating. And many families use Lmeghsel, a small copper, wash basin, to wash their hands."

"You're saying that failure to do these things is a sin against God?"

"No. Haram is a sin in the eyes of God. Hshuma is a sin in the eyes of other people."

"I understand." I was growing increasingly interested in how what he was saying would connect up with my question about the woman on the plane.

"Hshuma can also be passed on to a child," he said.

"What?"

"Yes, if a child is illegitimate, especially, woman have abandoned a child in the hospital and walked right out."

"You're kidding."

"I would not joke about such a thing."

"Who is a mother honoring by abandoning her daughter?"

"Her family."

"Her family? Unreal."

"Yes, but that happens far less in our day. But it has happened. My point is to make an observation about the woman on the plane."

"I'm listening."

"Hshuma also refers to taboo subjects that can cause embarrassment. Jack, how would you feel if a total stranger, a woman, asked you your opinion about male sex drive on a plane from Boston to Philadelphia?"

"I get it. I didn't consider her when I asked my question—the horizontal effect, as you say, of my question."

"Exactly."

"Now, allow me to take you down to show you the process if you think you are okay."

"I think I'm up for it."

Another set of stairs took us to a private balcony below where I saw a man stomp and grind hides in vats of brew that could melt the carbuncle on a witches' nose.

Omar said, "The vats as you can see, contain different colors depending on the dye, and the dyes depend on the plants used."

"You use plants?"

"Yes. Orange is from henna. Red from poppy. Green from mint. Yellow from saffron. Brown from cedar wood. Blue from indigo." The color palette and the unremittingly gnarly smell joined and a dry heave caught my esophagus and all I needed was for Omar to start eating a tuna fish sandwich.

"Jack, you look green. Let's get you back."

"Green. I think that's—mint."

"You are a funny man," Omar said with his hand around my wrist.

"Guess I'm not feeling quite as good as I had thought."

We exited through a different passageway and back out into the mare's nest. And my eyes, which had been fading, considered Omar's hold still on my wrist, and I had hoped never to lose his friendship. Then I recalled having expressed that same concern to one now gone.

My strength returning, I said, "Omar, I think I'm okay now."

"Are you certain?"

"Yes, I think so." He let go of my arm and I was warmed by his kindness.

We stopped where two alleys intersect, and Omar pulled me aside and away from the human traffic. His hand still on my arm he said, "Jack, permit me to offer an idea we can do if you are feeling better. I know a young woman. Her father worked for us, but unfortunately, he died from cancer last year. I can see if she is available. She studies law at the university that is just at the end of the medina; a close walk. She is a strong believer and can give you many ideas on women, and from the perspective of our faith. I can see if she is available if you want."

I hesitated. Then, I said, "Sure, I would more than happy to see her." But was I?

Omar dialed his friend. To think, I walked the length of his shadow. My indecisiveness had forced me into a sudden vortex of doubts about my overall honesty. That Omar's friend was an ardent believer virtually guaranteed hearing a different defense of women from what I had heard up to that point. Was I willing to hear both sides speak? Or, had I figured out the research before the research had been conducted? The previous evening had relieved my confusion about why questioning the women had mattered so much to me. What I had not considered was whether or not I had projected my emotional state straight out of a nightmare onto the answers. The large muscle bundle at the back of my head tensed in the troubled air.

Then a man walked towards me through the narrow passage. When I backed up for him to pass, he stopped right where I was standing. His face was brash. With one eye he looked at me and his other eye was solid smoke. His shirt was black and arms brown and muscular. His hair was curly and dark like a poodle's. Wrapped in his arm was an antique, handwoven wool rug. "They are magical," he said. "I give you happy price." His words were as prosaic as crisscrossing, gypsum crystal. And the more I tried to wave him off, the more dire life for his children became. Then he saw Omar behind me and took to the air, a whirling dervish to behold.

"My friend, who was that?" Omar said, having finished his call.

"He was trying to sell me a rug. I think maybe he's a shop owner."

"Shop owners do not permit selling like that in the medina." Omar's tone was one of warning.

"He said he was needful for his two sons."

"Yes, many needs here. Now Jack, she is available. In fact, she is near the library now; not far. She can meet us at the library café. We can go now if you wish."

"Let's do it. And thank-you so much for your interest, Omar."

We walked not more than a minute and I felt the clamor coming before I saw it. From the near distance, the cry of little voices had spiked misery into the air and above the hubbub of shoppers. I turned my head to see the man who had come up to me with the rug now sitting outside the entrance to a souk, and two, little boys were begging his attention in tears, great pools of impatience. Mild tightness gripped my chest in the realization of my black and white judgements of people and I wondered why it is, I tend to suspect the worst in others when I expect them to think the best of me. We are a strange lot, we humans. Could I have facilitated a little food for his children had I listened rather than preclude? The path to Omar's friend had just become a little shorter.

"Jack, you coming?" Omar said.

"I'm with you, and I can't wait to meet your friend."

The medina was all disordered order. They've done it all before: young men selling special and junk items. "Sir, you like this for your wife?" If I passed without looking, "sir" shot over my shoulder as if I had dropped my wallet and needed to look back. I was on to them. A cat asleep on another cat. Each time I ducked my head to pass under leather handbags, or some other items, my shoulder was bumped. The tunnel narrowed often and I stopped to let others pass, but Omar knew how to keep going. Old shop keepers waved and bowed to him, but the young ones didn't pay much attention. Some of the young ones were neat, deftly pushy, their smiles broad and eyes aggressive; others silent, but I suspected they were watching me for the chink in my armor. Shy steps, walking gently against a strong current like a salmon swimming upstream. "Follow close behind me Jack," Omar said twice. I tried hard.

Into the light. Unguarded day bathed me full on, the sky a shade darker than the sea and without a tinge of nebulous lace.

"Wow, what a difference in the sun," I remarked.

"I do not see her yet," Omar said.

"But she's coming?" I said it more as a statement.

"Yes. She should be here soon. Now Jack, the mosque is right over there and we can walk around outside."

"We can't go in?"

"No, only Muslims are permitted inside. But we can enter the university library. It was restored. Would you like to see it?"

"Yes, of course," I said with an eager tone. "And are those the university buildings over there?"

"I think those are the old buildings. Yes, I failed to say that the university was moved to another area of Fez some years ago. Jack, do you know of the University of al-Qarawiyyin?"

"No, not really," I replied.

"al-Qarawiyyin is the oldest university in the world. And this will interest you—"

"Wait, excuse me. You said the oldest university in the world?"

"The Tunisians think they have the oldest. But we think here." He smiled big.

"Absolutely mind-blowing. Now, please continue. You had something more to say about the university."

"Yes. What would interest you is that the school was started by a woman, Fatima al-Fihri, in the year 859."

My gaze beamed incredulity. "Seriously? That is great."

"I thought you would appreciate that. And you want to know that the Kairaouine Mosque has the oldest, active library in the world."

"That's amazing." My surprise mechanism was almost out of energy. "I really had no idea."

"If you're ready to see the library now, follow me."

We entered the library reading room. The high-ceiling hall, filled with highly polished, wooden desks and chairs, and centered above by a spectacular chandelier, made me wonder if anything was common in Morocco. Intricate reliefs on the columns were breathtaking as were the updated mosaics, all of which safeguarded the library's original beauty. A museum recounted the history of al-Qarawiyyin.

"Those chairs wouldn't work for my bad back, though," I said. "Too straight. No lumbar support."

Omar glanced at me with a shade of concern. "The chairs at the café will be better for you. I am sure of that. We can sit outside. Let us wait for her there."

The café was perfect. Nothing like the oxygen-deprived, rest homes of grayed despair.

"Jack," Omar said. "You can sit under the umbrellas to hide from the sun."

"Oh, look." My eyes pointed. "There's even a misting station."

No sooner had we sat, then I heard, "Kouya!" fissuring the air joyously. I twirled my head to see Omar greet a tall, slender, woman wearing a light, yellow djellaba, a button-down kaftan, and a black headscarf over perfect skin. Omar was a vision of great care in her eyes, and I could see how much they meant to one another. They spoke together in Arabic for some minutes, laughing and smiling, and I thought they were catching up.

"Rihab," Omar said. "This is my new friend, Jack, from America."

"Welcome to Fez," she said. "My pleasure to meet you." Her eyes were penetrating, and when she shook my hand, I saw how her upper-mid face tapered towards her chin perfectly.

"We met on the flight from Marrakech," Omar elucidated.

"Very good," she said to Omar.

"You enjoy your time with us?" she asked me. She fluttered her outfit a little and I had thought she had walked far.

"Oh yes. Omar is taking good care of me. He took me to the tannery. And please call me Jack."

"Thank-you. I will."

She had a particular sensitivity to the sun. And she wanted to sit where the sun wasn't hitting, where the canopy cut in blocking the sun. I wanted to sit there too, but she sat wide for a slim woman.

She adjusted her headscarf. "Many visitors to the tanneries," she said as the three of us sat.

"Yes, I saw some tourists on the balcony," I said, "but I was a bit overwhelmed by the smells."

"Not everyone is affected by the smells." she said. "But it can be that way. I'm sorry."

Omar reentered the conversation. "I worked there many years. So, I am not a good judge."

"I think the older I get," I noted, "the more sensitive I am to smells." I waited for Rihab to tell me I don't look as old as I am. But she said nothing, and I hoped I wasn't developing a tendency toward self-flattery.

A man then walked past us wearing a gandora of similar color to the one the man wore walking down the stairs just before I confronted Mansour. And memories skulking beneath the day's adventures began to trundle forward and the conversation around me became mere sounds, and still were for several seconds.

"Let me see if I can get something for us," Rihab offered.

"Jack," Omar said. "I guess you can do some tea with honey? Good for your stomach."

Rihab looked around as if an answer would come to her. "I'm not sure that is here but we can see."

"Jack, what do you think?" Omar asked.

Memories still winding through the tender days, I snapped out of it, and said, "Oh yes. Sorry. You're always kind, Omar. Tea or coffee is fine."

We sipped our drinks and Rihab started in earnest. "Omar told me a little about why you are in Fez. You have interest in the place of women in our country?"

"Something like that. But it's a little more delicate."

"Please tell me." She appeared genuinely interested and that comforted me.

"I want to learn about attitudes toward women in Morocco, and hopefully across North Africa and the Middle East. And what women think about those attitudes."

Her face grew tense where her laugh lines would be and, leaning forward in her chair, said in a serious tone, "But why here? Why not Australia or South Africa, or even in your America?" Her spontaneous reaction was strong and I was worried she had taken offense at my purpose focused on her homeland, even though Omar had told her why I was there.

Feeling offset by her response, I bit my tongue on the corner just enough to snap myself out of my nervousness. Then I matched her energy and responded. "You are very right. I could ask about this issue in any country of the world. But I'll tell you why I'm asking here. I've learned there are particular undercurrents in your culture that do not exist in mine, and that some men use to justify their treatment of women."

"Good answer," she said with a mollified look. "Now, what do you plan to do with all of this information you're finding?"

"It's really for my personal use. But maybe I'll do some writing on it someday. Who knows?"

"If you do, I just ask one thing."

"What is that?"

"Be fair." Her expression was sharp and persuasive.

"I will. I'll certainly try."

Ideas must have met in her mind rapidly, because she spoke now like a runaway train, faster and faster, and I could barely keep up. Omar remained silent.

"Too many people think of Muslims as killing," she said, "but people are full of stereotypes. We have globalization, Facebook, Twitter, WhatsApp, the Internet, and Instagram. But we don't know each other. We must stop marginalizing each other and listen to the voices of others. It is pure ignorance not to listen and if we live in ignorance, we will continue not to trust one another. So again, I ask you to be fair in your assessments, Jack."

"Wait," I paused. "Let me take some notes. This is really good." As I looked for a place to write, I said, "Now, I met a woman; an Egyptian visiting Morocco, and she sees it differently. When I said to her that abuse is every-where, you wouldn't believe what she said."

"What?"

She said, 'Welcome to the center of everywhere.'"

Holding her gaze on me, she tidied her amazed look into determination. "She's responding from her personal experience. Just ask women what they want from their personal relationships. They want love, respect, under-standing, attention; to be appreciated. I find these things in my religion and maybe she doesn't find it in her own experience, and that is why she replied the way she did."

"That's certainly possible. Interesting, isn't it, how Arab women can react so differently."

"It's not that one reaction is right; the other wrong. It's that we can all learn from each other. I think I can learn from you, and obviously, you are learning from me now. What would happen if more of us did that?"

"There would be a lot more understanding."

"Yes. And I think the world is lacking that."

"I certainly agree on that. Now, let me change the direction here a little. Why do you think an Arab woman, a victim of male-instigated violence, would defend her attacker?"

"I can't speak to all Arab women. But there can be many reasons. First, some women may lack confidence. Second, they might need time to be away, to think, and to deal with things in their lives. Maybe she has had a rough life and all of this added attention may not have been good for her, in her opinion. Third, she could have experienced an assault early in life and the attack brought back memories and was too much for her. Forth, projection is another problem. Some women defend their attackers because they project hurts from the past onto their defenders, when in reality, their defenders were trying so hard to help."

"I don't get the connection on your last point."

"Any confrontation," she said, "even one in her favor, can be seen through the windows of earlier confrontations in her life, so even family or friends coming to her side after an attack can be placed in the worst light."

"I get it. I think it's called transference."

"Transference?"

"Yes. Transference is when someone transfers their feelings about someone else to yet another person. Something like that."

Her face lightened. "Yes, that's what I'm saying. And, beyond these reasons, there are religious and cultural pressures a man can use against his female victim in Morocco which you must appreciate and maybe you don't know about."

"Please tell me. I'm here to learn."

"Okay, for example, if a couple is seen kissing in public, that can be a problem."

"Really. Why?"

"Because if they broke up the boyfriend could use their affection together against her to keep her quiet about the abuse. He could talk about her in ways that could hurt her reputation in the community. Public affection is avoided because people can spread the word about what she did with her boyfriend, and the last thing a young woman, especially one with few options wants, is for her family to think her reputation is in question." Pale memories of Indela and Mansour whirred deep within me, and I couldn't stand the noise.

I focused and said, "There really is a community aspect to how women can respond to violence, one I don't think we have in America."

"The role of the community here is very prominent is controlling women's reactions to all forms of abuse."

"But why could rumors about something as innocent as kissing ruin a woman's reputation?"

"It's not the kissing alone. The community can assume very easily that if they're kissing, they're doing something more together, and sex outside marriage is illegal here."

"Oh, right. I heard this before and forgot. But thanks for clarifying that for me."

"Sure."

"Please continue."

"And there are different ways a man can manipulate a woman, especially a wife. She could be dependent on him, making it even harder for her to leave. And he can use that against her. That is why divorce is so complicated in our country. If a husband finds his wife isn't a virgin, the man has several options. He can divorce her. Or, if she's honest and tells him the truth, he can keep her. Or, he can use his knowledge of her past to manipulate her. Finally, he can just accept her and love her the way she is, but that's rare."

"You mean a man here can divorce his wife if he discovers she's not a virgin?"

"Yes. Moroccan women, and this is true across Arab lands, are expected to be virgin at marriage. And men want only virgins here. But if it turns out a wife is not a virgin, then the husband has legal grounds for divorce."

Omar spoke for the first time. "Yes, Jack, and that's the reason some women use special methods to hide the fact they're not virgins."

"It's called, White Magic," Rihab specified.

"White Magic?" Now my thoughts were a maze of disbelief. "That would have to be pretty powerful magic."

"There are ways a woman has to hide this." Rihab seemed quite confident.

I said, "A lawyer whom I met in Marrakech spoke to me about divorce. He was really interesting."

"You talked to a lawyer in Marrakech?" Rihab had a look of concern.

"Yes." I braced myself.

"You know this man?"

"I met him through a friend."

"And how well do you know this friend?"

"We met in the mountains. She's an American, and then I joined her and her group for dinner."

"But you didn't know her for a long time?"

"Not really."

"Jack, if I may say. Please be careful about who you are speaking with. Morocco is very safe for you as a visitor. But it's possible for you to attract attention also. Just be careful." I simply shook my head in agreement and scanned my memory nervously for all of the times my unfettered naturalness with people might have entangled me in a spider's web.

She then asked a question that surprised me. "Can I see your notes once more to make sure you have everything?" She reached her hand for my phone.

"Certainly." Now I was warmed by her helpfulness and desire for precision in my research.

On the table where our drink sat, she made a few last edits on my phone, and her help was priceless. She sat back in her chair and moved her arms out to her sides and then took a sip from her drink that had sat the whole time.

"But I'll need my phone back," I said.

"Oh, sorry. Here." She held out my phone for me and then pulled it back, and added, "Oh, you have anything else you want to ask? I can write it for you."

"Not really. I'm just super grateful for your help. And you made it so easy. You really understand these things. Of all the people I've spoken with, you've been the clearest and most helpful."

"Well, these are things I think about. Now if you do think of anything, anything at all, you can contact me through Omar. In the meantime, I wish you every good luck the rest of your journey."

The three of us made our way to the main street, and Rihab and Omar spoke again in Arabic, in tones tender and sweet—that made me think they knew they wouldn't see one another for some time. I walked to their side in careful deference to the moment. We watched her go. She vanished behind a shadow that looked like it had never moved.

"Jack," Omar said. "What do you wish to do now? Something to eat? Remember, I have guests this evening, and you are invited."

"Thank-you. But if you don't mind, I think I'd just like to return to your place, and pass on food for now. Hopefully, my appetite will return by this evening."

"And we'll see what the night has in store for us."

Rihab's studied responses centered my churned ideas. But rather than settle me, the bringing together incited reveries of the attack and the unexpected happened.

Little by little, the narrow medina passages constricted, my eyes grew drone-like, and my steps faster. Every moving person appeared to me as hollow-eyed, apple-cheeked mannequins. Faster still, I walked. Then like a cue-ball bouncing off the cushions, I bumped and rebounded off body after body. "Jack," Omar shouted. I heard him, but the denizen wasn't home. I knocked over a small table of babouches and pouffes and a shopkeeper blared like a sackbut. Omar yelled again, "Jack!" but I didn't know him. I started running. Now the chorused cries of alarm rang out, but I didn't care. I wanted to see how fast I could go. "Jack! Jack!" Omar yelled in long lances over heads jouncing and jostling. He yelled something to the people in Arabic. Then again to me, "Jack. Please stop!" It all stopped. People were all around me. I was on my face. A hand rolled me over and onto my back. "Jack, are you okay? What's wrong?" Omar asked. Now eyes and noses, all taking turn hovering.

THE TREES HAVE GOATS

A man approached Omar asked him something and he looked down at me too. "Just help me up," I said to Omar. The crowd began to split up and people resumed switching and swapping. And no one would have guessed anything had happened.

Omar helped me to my feet and leaned me up against a wall. "Jack, what happened to you?" Omar spoke with great concern in his voice.

"Omar, what did I do wrong?" I said, feeling helpless. "Why didn't I do something to help her? Why didn't I get off the couch?"

"Jack, I think we need to get you back. Can you walk?"

"I think so."

Omar guided me all the way back to my room and helped me lay down. He sat on the edge of the bed. "Feel better now?"

Mildly embarrassed, I said, "A little bit."

"Jack, can I call someone for you; your wife perhaps? Should I call a doctor?" His voice grew more urgent with each word.

"No, no, please. But thanks. I'm okay now. I don't know what happened."

"Well enough, then. Let me leave you and either I, or someone else, will check on you later."

"That's fine. Thanks." Omar put his hand on the wall and looked back under the weight of a question on his mind and drew it out in peaceful strokes, keeping any judgement of me clear of the conversation.

"Jack," he said as he walked back to the bed. "With all due respect, this young woman you told me. I must ask. Are you sure you don't love her? You act like you've lost a lover."

"I'm absolutely positive."

"How can you be sure?"

"I don't love her romantically. It's bigger than that."

Omar paused and his smile was understanding. "Fine, then. You lay here and we will call you later; see if you are able to attend."

He was about to go again, and I grabbed his arm. "Omar, what did I do wrong? I was trying to help her."

"My friend, this is not your world."

"But I want to understand."

"I can see that. And I'm trying to help you. But no matter how long or how hard you try to understand, ours is a different way. And perhaps it is best for you just to accept that." Feverish wheels spun in my head as he spoke and my hand dropped from his arm.

Two soft pats of my chest, and the verse of his voice was that of a father to me. "Please stop trying to think about this and rest." The lightness of his care was so heavy on my chest, it was all I could do but smile.

Chapter 15

I woke. In the immersion of sleep, an image of myself passed and a chain was breaking off my neck, and I did not recognize the chain. The vision did not last in my waking. How I wanted it to last, to see it fall off my neck over and over again.

I arose and, shy as I am, moved slowly to the dinner. Aware of myself. From the upstairs, I counted ten people. Upon seeing me appear downstairs, Omar greeted me warmly. "Jack, you made it. How wonderful. I was just about to send someone to check on you. Are you hungry, I hope?"

Not having something to eat for many hours, I replied in the simplest way. "I'm famished."

"Excellent. Come and let me introduce you."

Omar presented me as friends and family nibbled hors d'œuvres of seasoned olives and almonds. Omar's sister, Ranim, probed me in her best English as I munched the goat cheese and tomato jam on round crackers. "You like time Morocco?"

"Yes. Very much." She stood looking at me and then her pinky finger wiggled at the side of her lip; her neck extended back just a touch. I grabbed a napkin and wiped my mouth, wondering how many more times I would arouse the impersonator in others before I learned to eat better.

"Hello," Ranim said, and joined the others. Clearly, Ranim had mistaken hello for goodbye.

The mosaic blue tablecloth was thick and smooth. I leaned on it, hoping to find refuge in a nonchalant look. To my side, a woman in a pure white djellaba, white scarf, and white tennis shoes, approached me, and I stood half-looking at her timidly. Her sentinel eyes were on me each step she walked, and the closer she came, the more a flutteriness expanded from dead center in my gut to my arms. I was certain she had mistaken me for another man. But she extended her right hand straight out, palm down, as if I was to step up and kiss her hand. The cloth was slippery, and I pulled over the tall tray of kefta meatballs. She walked directly to the mess and reset the tray, and the tray was fussy.

"Ne t'inquiète pas," she said. "Je peux le faire." I knew what that meant. But never in the history of don't worry has don't worry ever worked.

"My French is not good enough," I replied. "Oh, wait, um. Anglaise?"

She transitioned to English. "I was pointing to the tray. It was falling over. You not see me?"

"Ah. Yes. Of course, I saw. Clumsy of me not to move faster. Thank you so much for your help."

"I am happy to help. I am Layla."

"Jack." I started for the three-cheek-kiss, but she extended her hand again, this time to shake it, and I felt stupid. Her handshake was boneless, and I couldn't grab it. Then she touched her right hand to her heart.

"Are you okay?"

"Yes. I am fine," she said, with a startled look. "Oh, you think I have pain. No, I do not have pain. You do not know our customs."

"I'm trying to learn, in fact."

"In Morocco, after shaking hands it is customary among many people to touch the right hand to the heart. We do so as a greeting or sign of respect before we shake hands also. We love to shake hands. But not hard." She laughed and that was the first time I understood why Moroccan handshakes were squashy.

Putting my hand to my heart, I asked, "My hand flat like this?"

"No, only touch there; right there." She showed me how again. I did as she wanted and she seemed rather satisfied, walking away without another word.

As I looked around the room people stood disarranged, the archipelago of salvers balanced perfectly in their hands. And the bright ladies and bright men, whether by sun, by moon, or by candlelight, taught me wonderful things a rhyme the seasons of life.

We gathered around the table with a beautiful beet salad paired with a frothy, creamy avocado puree and a sweet-savory pumpkin seed crumble. Omar was right that the Moroccan meal is a communal affair. Each person shared from the tagine of chicken chermoula with chickpeas, and each diner carved out his or her own triangle of the dish. I watched cautiously; helplessly, fork in hand. Then Omar raised a large slice of bread for me to see, and with the bread he soaked up some of the broth and scooped up some of the vegetables and meat. A sunshined inspiration hit me and off I went, digging my bread deep into the tagine just like the others. Omar's sister posted her steely looking-over-her-lorgnette look on me throughout the entire meal through to dessert—an orange blossom parfait with lime granita and a hazelnut tuile.

Festive hours dimmed, and ponytails of orange-red lashed beneath a starlit dome. Might be rain tomorrow, I thought. The sky is more urgent.

"Good night, Jack," said Omar.

"Already? Still rather early."

"Dinner guests can be draining. And I want to read."

"Yes. Entertaining is work. Have a pleasant night."

"Same to you, sir."

Halcyon shades of sleep brought me to where lacy imaginings wander, and I dreamt of my wife sitting outside a beach-front hotel on a summer's eve. Only a few hours later, a sudden jolt brought me to full consciousness, the room ringing with ear-piercing quiet, and I felt compelled to call her.

"Hey," she answered.

"Hey there." I replied in restrained enthusiasm.

"Why are you so quiet?"

"It's late and sound travels here. There's a fat carpet on the floor of my room, but outside virtually everything is tile."

"You're staying with that man?"

"Yeah. Omar. And what a place he has. Beautiful. And he took me to his tannery; he owns a tannery. But wow, what a smell."

Silence.

She said more in her silence than in her words. She had a way of communicating without communicating if she disapproved. I knew once more she wanted her husband to get himself home.

"Isn't it late there?" she asked, breaking the hush.

"Yeah. I can't sleep; only dosing."

"Sorry."

"What time is it there?"

8:45 p.m. Stillness followed. And then the ache deep inside me began moving up toward the surface through the gaps, the way I once saw water bubble up to the surface through the underground limestone mazes in Florida after a heavy rain.

"Honey, you okay?" she asked.

"I'm okay." But my voice broke just enough to allow her to say what was really on her mind.

"Jack, don't you think you've had enough?"

"I'll be home soon. Right now, I'm still focused on learning about the women."

"Jack, I'm sure the young couple is fine."

"Who do you mean?"

"The young woman. I forget her name. And her boyfriend."

"Look, I'm trying really hard not to be concerned with that now."

"I'm not so sure."

"Yeah. I'm just trying to understand what the women face here. And I've learned a lot already. A lot."

"Learned what?"

"Just all the ways women have to navigate this fine line."

"I don't get it—"

"Let me finish, please. The whole situation with Indela and Mansour really woke me to all the stuff happening in the culture."

"But why does it matter?" She spoke in long, emphatic strides of irritation. "I've lost friends. But I didn't spend days and weeks trying to figure out the culture."

"I know but—"

"Honey, listen. I just feel like you're after something else and I don't know what it is."

"What could it be?"

"I don't know. But something's wrong and I'm not sure finding out all about Moroccan women is going to help."

In a sitting position now, my despondent deafness looked for any way to escape her firm logic. "I guess I don't know either," I said. "Look, I'm going to try to go back to sleep. Okay? I just wanted to hear your voice."

"I'm glad you called. I love you. Be careful and come home soon, okay? Oh, and call me again."

"I will."

A knock outside my room kindled me to morning. To the door, my bare feet slid across the tile, and a young man handed me a note, walking away without looking up.

Mr. Jack. My apology for late time. Please, sir, if you are not busy, meet me
downstairs—Nadine.

My fingers scored speculations along the edge of my forehead. From the balcony, I looked into the atrium and only Nadine stood in the doorway to one of the large rooms, her hands clasped. Then she disappeared into the room, and I thought she wanted me to join her. I dressed fully and went down. She stood in the shadow's smile and inched forward into the irradiation as I entered the room.

"Sir," Nadine said. My father good man, and please, I ask you not say anything to him about our talk now." Her face was diluted and her words cobbled.

"Certainly," I said.

"I hear you speak to my father yesterday. You talk of the killing of the woman in Middle East. Sir, the woman that serve you, she is called Mey. I can arrange for you to speak to her today."

"You mean the woman who brought us tea and cookies?"

"Yes."

"Why would I want to meet her?"

"Sir, her father try to kill her."

"What? Why?"

"Her family arranged her marriage to a man, but she refuse. She go to Turkey. Her mother contact her that everything okay and come home. Mey have no money, so she go back, to family. When she came home, her father attack her. Again."

"Attack her? What did he do?"

"He use koummya."

"What? Sorry, I didn't quite understand."

"Koummya. Is knife. Big knife. He try and cut the throat. But she fight and he cut the face and arm," She pointed to her face as an example. "She run and her brother catch and hold her. Her father try to—" Nesrine couldn't think of the word and so she demonstrated a choke hold with her hands.

"He tried to strangle her?" I asked.

"Yes. Yes. But she escape. She strong."

Suddenly, it hit me. Nesrine had described an attempted honor killing. "This happened in Fez?" I asked.

"No. South. In Mountains. Tazalt."

"Nesrine, how do you know Mey?"

"I see her in streets. She sleep in front of building. She ask for help, and I bring her to my father."

"Your father knows her story?"

"No. He only know she need job. Please say nothing about any of the things I tell you. Please. To my father."

"Why do you want my help?"

"Mey think her brother come here."

"To Fez?"

"Yes. Mey think she see him in streets."

"What can I do?"

"Can you meet her?"

"Meet her? I don't know. You mean here? In the house?"

"No, today she will be with a friend."

"But she lives here?"

"Yes. But today she at apartment with friend."

"I need to know something. Do you want me to help her leave Morocco? I can't be involved in that."

"Please. Can you meet her?" I knew by the look in Nesrine's eyes that she wanted me to help Mey escape Morocco. That wasn't going to happen.

"Where is your father now?" I asked. "I haven't seen him this morning."

"He go to tannery."

"Why don't you tell him about Mey? Shouldn't he know?"

"No, no. Please, just us know. Please."

Looking at her with care and frustration, I said, "Nesrine. Listen. I cannot involve myself in some plan to help a woman escape the country. We'll all go to jail." She stepped closer and began to cry. And I could tell. From deep within sorrow's womb her tears confided a dream, and from her poverty her needs were few.

"Look. Please don't cry. I'll meet her." I paused, and thought to myself, oh no, what am I doing? Then I was quick to add, "But no promises. You understand me? No promises. I'll only meet her and try to encourage her. Okay?" I didn't know what was compelling me to meet with Mey, other than to be true to myself. "Nesrine. Why do you trust me?"

"My father say you help him in airport. People not help. You care. I see in you good."

"Where and when do we meet?"

"I come to you soon. Allah inwrak hyatk." She withdrew into the dark, on the morning's retiring tide.

Late morning put final touches of gray-white on the firmament and downy clouds above me lumbered like elephants. I sipped the dregs, and my mind was an underground anthill of thoughts; barren busyness, really. "Mr. Jack," I heard behind me and I turned to see. "You finish coffee? You come now?"

"I'm ready," I said. "Is it far; it is in the medina?"

"We walk. Yes, medina."

We left the riad and the correspondence between Mey's horrific experience and the threat of death made to Indela was stirring tempestuous waters deep inside me. Donkeys, mosques, carts, busy sellers, the vibrant city awake, and the royal tradition of technicolored dressers low balling for a handmade—all of it—fell away before my interests like someone had pushed over a propped up, main street façade at a theme park. Keep walking, one foot after the other, I muttered under my breath.

Slaty rays gleamed my sunglasses as we walked past divergent buildings. Sometimes light dappled rapidly through the buildings like a 1920s zoetrope movie watcher, flipping images in rapid sequence. The ocular impression reminded me how sunlight glanced and glimpsed through the holes in the slender clumps of trees as I sat in the backseat and my father drove us to grandfather's house in Ohio, and how those early experiences sparked my interest in trees. I climbed inside that memory as if it were my own safe place. It worked.

We turned and entered a narrow alley, cobblestoned as far as I could see. Before us, two boys played, one riding the back of another like a horse. They saw me and stopped to stare as if I had just landed from some distant planet. Cobwebs of misgiving began to overtake me until we crossed through the arc of a narrow place and a surge of hope ran through my heart, and I didn't know why.

A lazy curve laid just ahead. Past it, Mey waited for us, her thick, sleek hair tied back, and a green and yellow shawl with tassels swathed her upper body and arms. Penniless distress emasculated her beauty. Sympathy filled me.

The women spoke.

"Mey wants you to know she thank you to come," said Nesrine.

"My pleasure," I said, looking at Mey with a smile, and I thought she understood me.

"We can go up," Nesrine said, nodding her head in the direction of the building. Don't make any promises, I continued to say to myself.

"Which floor is she on?" I asked.

"She is at top."

"Top?" If travelers wanted to know if a six-floor walk-up existed in the medina, I had found it. The railings grabbed firm and I looked up and down through the hollow of the stairs and fibrous husks of questions hung in my mind like creatures trying to give birth. So dark was the staircase, I had to exchange my sunglasses for my clear glasses. Why was I here? I asked myself as I made the exchange. I still wasn't sure, only that conviction had drawn me. Sweat started to form and my hair felt moist in the cool, stagnant air. Mey opened the top door, which I expected to open into an apartment. Instead, we walked out onto the roof. The light blinding me, I worried that the three of us would fall into some bottomless pit; an irrational fear, but so real that my knees wobbled as I stepped out onto the roof.

"You okay, Mr. Jack?" Nesrine asked.

"I'm just fine." Really, I was a little confused. "Sorry. Where exactly are we?"

"Is here." She pointed, and I put my shades back on and saw an apartment unconnected on three sides. One side of the apartment shared a wall with an adjacent building, and the roof of the apartment was exactly even with the adjacent building. I was eager to see inside.

Mey led us through the thick, metal door. My legs like putty from walking up the stairwell, I sat in a chair, and the light beam through the paned glass behind me was hot and the paned glass was wavy at the corrugated wooden edges. The light evaporated like sluggish smoke into the dark spaces and hit a golden bow directly across the room, producing a creepy, greenish luminescence.

"Mister," Mey asked. "You want water?"

Stunned, I said, "Oh, you do speak some English."

"Little. Only little." She laughed, and when she did, folds formed near the scar on her face, a bequeath of her father's depravity, and in a sudden wave of self-awareness, she turned in shame to hide the scar with her hand. My hand reached and took the wrist on her other hand carefully and she stiffened. But I held her arm with reassuring eyes. She relented slowly and released her arm into mine and gave me her trust. "Dear, please," I said. "You are so beautiful." Her eyes appeared to think across my compliment the way a sailboat tacks into the wind, and I had little doubt she understood me, for in fact she started to cry and said some words in Arabic to Nesrine.

"What did she say?" I asked Nesrine.

"She said, 'No one has ever told me I'm beautiful.'" She was lovely in every way. But a world suffocating in perfection had turned away because it saw in her scar a reminder of its own ugliness.

"Nesrine," I said, "can you ask her to tell me her story in Arabic, and you interpret, please?"

"Yes."

"Mey, what do you want to say? I'm here to listen."

She sat in silence, in the inner citadel of green winters. Wringing her hands, her broken nails showed, and she bit the tops of her fingers. She tried to catch her breath, but only little sucks of air came in.

I moved next to her. "Dear, try to breathe."

To inhale, she released her hands flat onto the scruffy cushions of the couch and, squeezing hard, she drank the air. She released and tried again with determined eyes.

"I think she ready, Mr. Jack." Nesrine said.

Mey spoke through Nesrine. "My mom is sick. She is getting very weak. Her face has been changed. And she doesn't apply the doctor advice."

"You mean she doesn't take his advice?" I asked.

"Yes."

"And you know my father abused her too much. Imagine since ten years ago."

"How did he abuse her?"

"He married again with another woman."

"Was your father still married to your mother during this time?"

"Yes, he was. And Mom was very hopeless. And sad all the times. If he divorced her would be better. He doesn't visit us or take care of his family."

Then Nesrine interjected, "This shock you, Mr. Jack, but men here marry four times in our current law."

"I have learned that. Yes."

Mey continued through Nesrine. "When I saw mom broken and crying, I told him why you did that to her—by which right you do that? He said, with arrogance new wife is not the first and am not the last one. I will never forget how he abused us all."

"Mey, how did he abuse you?"

"Mom sacrificed her life and time and everything to take care of us. Me and my sister and brother were students. He didn't give us any cent. But he has enough of money to take care of ten families. My mom took the responsibility to take care of everything even until now. And he abused her too much by violent words. He say he is not the only one who got married again. He means that all men has right to get marry twice and three and four times. He was proud and very happy while my mom was drowning in tears. I remember every second of her sufferance. He brought his wife many times to my mom's house to break her heart many times. And I never forget my mom's tears."

"Wait, he brought his other wives to your mother's home?"

"Yes." When I heard that my heart thudded in my chest sporadically, the way shudders hit up against an old house in the wind. I took a drink of water and gathered myself.

"Mey, how old is your mother?"

"She is sixty. My big brother is thirty-seven."

"And father?"

"Sixty-two. This story started twenty-two years ago. And, what hurt mom more is the society and neighbors and close family."

"Why they hurt you?"

"They started bothering me and laughing while I was crying, and told me, 'What's wrong with you? Maybe he has a reason to leave you.' In our communities, woman without men has no value."

"So, family and friends blame you?" I had heard how society crushes women who fail to accept the status quo. But I had to hear again.

"Yes. And they started bothering us children also. We have no value also without a father."

"But why?"

"There is big contradiction between laws and practice. If they see a woman without a man, they start put their blames and judgments or her without thinking or seeking the truth. And the children are seen as illegitimate. Women are slaves in our communities. Worse than slaves." She was raining her heart and the rain burned my skin.

"You mean if a single woman does not have a father or husband, she is looked down on with suspicion?"

"Yes. They start accusing me of adultery and many bad things. But men also suggest directly to us, the children, to join them for adultery because they think without father to protect, they can abuse us. So, is a custom for a man to ask about his girlfriend's reputation again before he get marry her—if her neighbors or close friend say bad things about her, he will never stay with her."

"So why do young women in North Africa put 'single' on social media?"

"They escape from their environment to media to know a new people."

"Mey, you've told me about your family. Now what happened to you that you're here in Fez?"

"My father want me marry man I hate. He bad man like my father. He already have wife."

"Oh, that's why you're telling me about your father and family."

"Yes. He want me be marry to man like him. He have many women and he beat. I refuse to repeat what Mom go through. I have boyfriend. Good man. When I say I want marry him, and we plan to go Turkey, my father say you are prostitute. My mom not want me be so sad. We think best for I go away."

"You went to Turkey alone?"

"Yes. I have friends."

"But Nesrine said your mother told you to come home, that everything was okay."

"My brother do that. He use her email and say he is Mom."

"I understand."

"When I am home, my father and brother attack me. With knife. But I am strong. Father old man and sick. My brother hold me and my father try cut my throat. The knife here by my throat and I scream loud, loud. My mother try to help. My brother push her down. I scream so loud. I continue scream. Fight for life. I escape but knife cut me here. I run to friend; she help. She take me doctor and help my face. I hear from people my father and brother look for me. My father want to kill. He say his honor. Honor of family. But no honor."

Mey stopped to wipe her face, and ideas bent and rolled in my heart like tall grass blowing in the wind on a midwestern wheat field. No matter how many times I had heard these stories, the same questions assailed me. How can a person who says he loves act so treacherously? How can a father, a brother, dare to treat a daughter and a sister with such unbridled contempt? They are walking dead. Why won't the dead stay dead?

"I don't want to live like this," Mey added, "or live with a violent guy and put his muscles on a weak woman. This is not called masculinity and has nothing to do with masculinity. The man is known for his creativity and upbringing and tenderness and compassion for his wife and fear on her and his home and good heart and be her support and compensate for the tenderness of her father and the support of her brother and the love of her mother like what you respect and fear him and love him."

"Mey," I said. "Why didn't your mother warn you not to come home?"

"My father say he kill her."

"Okay, so how did you manage to come to Fez?"

"A man, friend of my cousin, take me in truck. I pay him everything I have."
She began to sob uncontrollably into her pain. Nesrine spoke up. "I think she
say enough."

I stood and paced, unable to focus as though I had been sungazing. My
pulse quickened. I knew that if I had come this far with Mey, I must be ready
to go the distance. But what more could I do for Mey? I rocked back and forth
between courage and guilt.

"Nesrine, can you ask her please? Mey, why are you telling me these
things?" She began to answer Nesrine, and a sudden interruption in the light
from the window behind my chair attracted my attention.

"What was that?" I asked in a speck of surprise. My neck stretched around
to see. Nesrine and Mey were looking through the window also.

Recognizing that both women had noticed the same thing, I said, "You saw
it too." On my feet, I looked out the window but didn't see a thing. "That's so
odd," I said. "There's nothing outside except the sky and the rest of the roof.
But both of you saw how the light disappeared for a moment."

"Yes, Mr. Jack," Nesrine said. "I saw."

"I wonder—um—is Mey expecting anyone?" Before Nesrine could relay
my question, a thump came from the other side of the apartment and all three
of us looked in its direction at the same time. Immediately, Mey got up and
started to walk toward her bedroom.

"Wait," I said with my hands motioning her. "Mey, attendez s'il vous plaît."
Again, a smallish, undecided sound, this time on a different side of the
apartment, and near the limits of my fears, made my blood fall, and a macabre
halo abstracted the air. What in the world was going on outside?

"Nesrine, please stay here with Mey." The two women bunched, and I
walked to one of the back bedrooms and, listening like a child shivering under
the covers, looked around. The air was quiet and unstirred. I reentered the hall,
and the women were holding hands. I looked left to the bathroom and kitchen
and without a word to the women, thought I saw something. A figure on the

roof. Not wanting to make noise, I rearranged the pots and pans around the sink carefully. Then I hoisted myself up and looked outside through a window. "It can't be!" I spoke loud enough that both women heard me.

"What," Nesrine spat, in a terrified voice.

"Wait, please," I signaled. But my revelation of alarm had been given, making the women even more nervous.

I turned my body away from the window and sat on the kitchen counter staring down at the floor. "It can't be," I said again, panic building in me.

"What is wrong?" Nesrine begged.

"I can't believe it. It's the guy I saw in the airport. The slender man who bumped into your father and knocked the passport from his hand."

"What?" Nesrine said, half yelling.

"Shhh." I put my index finger to my lips. "Quiet." My internal thermostat turned my spine to ice. I tried hard to pull myself together. Then I said to Nesrine, "We need to leave." But Mey ran to look out the kitchen window. By the time she did, the man had disappeared. Mey spoke to Nesrine, her voice on the edge of hysterics and her eyes jutting.

"She wants know if is her brother," Nesrine said to me. Streams of tears crisscrossed Mey's face in spidery meanders; hyperalert, pupils dilating, and breathing accelerating. Mey was losing it.

"No, tell her it's not her brother. We just need to go. Now!"

Mey unlocked the door and we bolted for the stairwell. "Wait, wait while I look," I said, motioning my hands for the women to hold on while I checked to see if anyone was on the other side of the door leading to the stairs. Neither seeing nor hearing anything, I motioned the women to follow me, and we made a dash down the stairs.

"Where we go, Mr. Jack?" Nesrine asked as we continued to move.

"To your father's place." The many fears inside the apartment were replaced now by the view of hard, gray steps, and it was just the exit we hoped for. Our legs moved down the stairs step by step. I watched my feet carefully and was eager for the world outside. To move. To run. Then, halfway down the stairs, we heard a sound. It was loud and vibrated up the stairs and up my spine and out the top of my head. We stopped in unison, dead in our tracks, and no one said a word.

We listened. Nesrine whispered. "Is him?" I shook my head in disbelief, and wondered how could he be on the ground floor so fast? We started again, but Mey grabbed my arm. Halting, I lost my balance briefly and, looking down, the stairs appeared to pull away as if I had been standing at the precipice of a great escarpment.

Then we heard it. Whish, whish—like grainy sandpaper sliding smooth and unvarying in its progression up the stairs. Someone was coming. Silence tightened around my neck like a noose and we listened stiffly. The women scrunched tight, and Mey mashed her body against the web-draped walls. Nesrine let out a wail, and I covered her mouth. The footsteps below us came to a sudden stop. Nesrine closed her eyes ringed with skeletons, and I put my hand over her mouth without touching it. She looked at me, her eyes just above the palm of my hand and we lingered there in the smell of terror.

Just at that moment, the sound of feet exploded on the stairs and looted our sanity. "Run!" I yelled. "Run." Nesrine fell, and I reached back to pick her up. She heaved cries of despair. Mey stopped to wait for us, but I yelled and motioned to her, "Go. Go." She dashed so fast that her feet barely touched the steps. The feet behind us were gaining, and Nesrine's face had turned corpse-like shades of death. I almost dragged her as she stumbled continually.

Mey was almost to the very top when the door leading to the roof opened suddenly and slammed against the interior wall and split the air like a hammer against an anvil, sending vibrating shockwaves ringing to the bottom of the well. Nesrine and I recoiled in terror on the landing between the fifth and sixth floors, mere feet from Mey. I looked to see who had opened the door. But only the shadow of a figure could be seen on the open door, cast there by the sun effulgent in the unobstructed sky.

The shadow moved. Became longer. And a man showed himself. "It's impossible," I gasped out loud. I was looking directly into the face of the slender man from the airport. The sight of him caused me to convulse mentally and I thought that if he was in front of us, then who was behind us coming up the stairs?

Mey emptied her lungs in one continuous scream. Fear stripped me bare, my controls unlatched. Cold sweat. I looked back, following the track of Mey's eyes, to a man standing on the landing below us, his shirt black and tightly fit around his well-toned body. The look of murder shrouded his face, and his face was lined with a black, chin-strap beard. And when he saw Mey, his face pierced in ferocity and his upper back thickened. He reached behind himself, and as his left elbow rose, a giant knife appeared and sparked death's lust at the edge of the subdued light.

"Jack!" Nesrine screamed. "Is Mey brother." I looked quickly at Mey and her face was an icy lake of terror, and I was certain the man was her brother.

Without warning, the slender man pulled out a pistol from underneath his tee-shirt. The midair became vile. My heart pushed blood, and my head pounded jackhammer throbs. He pointed the gun at the assassin and roared like a lion. But the killer lifted his brow against heaven, and unwilling to abdicate, stalked inch by inch up the stairs through lurking shadows and my dolorous imaginings saw bat-like wings pinned under his chin. The slender man yelled louder. The knife, rimmed with the presage of Mey's death mask enlarged, and my eyes must have rolled white as her brother stood just above me as I lain there on the steps.

Then, a shot rang out over my shoulder. The axle split, and nerve-ending pain paralyzed me. The ringing of the shot wouldn't stop. The killer faltered. The bullet had hit him in the throat, and his giant arms spread wide amidst grim gurgling in a fit of rage. But the dogs of death were tearing him to pieces and the knife dropped from his hand, jingling and clinking down the stairs. He fell to the landing below.

The slender man ran down the stairs and poked the assassin with his hot, metal gun. But the shayāṭīn had received their own. At the same time, Mey was asphyxiating in her tears, and Nesrine hurried to her side. "Yes. Is her brother, Mr. Jack," Nesrine said as her brother's blood dripped over the edge of the stairs.

"He's dead," said the slender man. Scarcely had his answer reached my ears than the bolting and screaming of voices and feet added to the bedlam and three more people appeared on the stairs and spoke anxiously with the slender man.

"Who are you?" I asked.

"Police," said the slender man, with a heavy-French-Arabic accent.

"Police?" I slumped in stunned disbelief. "You are police?"

"Yes. You need to go with these officers."

"What? What do you mean?" I was in utter shock. The policeman then spoke to the women in Arabic. Nesrine argued vehemently with them, and the argument lasted a long time.

Midway through the argument, one of the officers grabbed my arm and said to me, "Come. You must come."

"Come?" I shrieked. "Come where? Where are we going? What is going on?" I looked at Nesrine. "Nesrine what is going on?" The slender policeman yelled at Nesrine, and ordered all of us to accompany the other officers. Mey had to be carried downstairs.

"Mr. Jack," Nesrine said. "We must go with them." Her face was drawn in defeat.

"What is the problem?" I asked.

"They tell us at police station."

"We're going to a police station?" I was beyond incredulous, wondering if I really needed to go with them

"Sir," the slender policeman said to me loudly. "You come. Now!"

Chapter 16

We arrived at the police station and the officers spoke. Mey was taken away to a local hospital, so I had been told. Nesrine and I were split up. Just before she disappeared behind a wall, a tall woman emerged, took her by the arm, and looked at me with a dark stare. The sight of her stabbed my heart, and all reason abandoned me. It was the woman in the Orchid room.

Unable to speak, I stood in a breathless pool of thoughts. The officer spoke to me. And although my body was facing him with my arms resting on his desk, I continued to look back over my shoulder into the distance to where the women had taken Nesrine. Then an explosive sound rang through my body. "Hey buddy!" My head snapped around toward the officer and all seemed madness.

My passport and wallet were taken. And because my phone had a password, the officer insisted I open it. I refused at first, but thought that because I had nothing to hide, it would be better to cooperate. In fact, it might help me. "Can I make a phone call please?" No answer. He took my back medication and although I argued my necessity in italics, I may as well have been spitting in the wind. I decided to defer my need until later.

Flecks and smidgeons of dried blood lined the floor on the way to the holding cell and the sound of a man screaming caused a pernicious, psychological chain reaction in my beleaguered mind. I was kept in a tank for two nights. Five other men were in the cell with me the first night. The sound of yells came from down the hall and thrashed my ear. Food and water were scarce, and everyone seemed miserable in his own way. I paced around aimlessly in little circles, keeping one eye on the others, the other eye on my tumultuous morale. By now, my back was killing me, and I really needed my meds, but my pleas earned nothing but threats. A sharp-sour taste filled my mouth.

I called Beth. She cried. Not a cry so common as grief or of pain. But of a sound strangulated of hope. She said she wanted her husband home. But a plug had been pulled out, and the air and the light had rushed out of my center of gravity. And really, I didn't know when it had happened. But I had to find myself or else there wouldn't be a husband for Beth to hold, and I wanted her to have all of me.

The second evening, around midnight, two others were thrown in with us in the jail. Now there were seven. One fellow's shirt was halfway open, and his shirt collar hung over his right shoulder. His top buttons were missing, and I had presumed the poor guy had found himself at the short end of an officer's patience. The screams had ended but started again late, making me stay to myself in a busy loneliness.

The raven eye across the room distracted me from the sound of screams better than fear does. I saw a trap door open in my imagination, and I entered through it to a big, wide room, dark with pestilence and anxiety. Chains were attached to the bodies of those in the room. And when I asked, "Who are you?" they smiled big and one man looked upwards to the ceiling. I could see he wanted me to look up also. I saw the chains leading upwards through the ceiling, and each chain was attached to each man in the jail cell around me, and the chains were invisible to the men in the cell. Each man in the cell had a special friend in the deep parts below. And in time, I suspected, the weight of the chains would pull the men in the jail cell down to his special friend, to death. To the full realization of himself.

Just then, a gladsome-looking guy, his face fibrously matted from old scars and weathered lines, sat next to me against the wall and the scent of humanity broke the raven's spell. I touched his shoulder against mine just to feel human.

"Here," he said, handing me a piece of torn, dried meat, desiccated like the lives of the half-dead clustered before me; the outcasts, of an adagio growing dim.

"Thanks." I was so hungry I could have eaten dried leather.

"I'm Rachid," he said.

"I'm Jack."

"Sorry we meet in this place."

"Yeah," I said, ripping the leathery gift with my teeth.

"You are American?"

"Yes."

"I thought so."

"I guess I wear American well," I said with a mild laugh. Then I added, "Boy, this meat is tough." But so that he didn't think I wasn't appreciative, I was fast to add, "But good. Very good. Thanks again."

His head dipped closer to mine and I felt his breath on my ear. "You have a family?"

"Oh yeah. A wife and two grown children." I grabbed for my wallet to show him pictures then realized I didn't have it on me. "Oh, sorry. They have my—"

"Let me guess," he said with an idled smile. "A boy and a girl."

"That is right. Both grown."

"So, I guess you're about—" I could see him checking me for my age.

"Fifty-two."

"You look younger."

"I feel eighty-two, so it balances out."

He laughed and said, "You are a funny man."

"People say that." I thought of Omar.

"You like that little piece of meat?"

"Like a steak. Thanks."

"Jack, where are you?"

"I'm in jail. Like you. What are you talking about?"

"I mean, look around you. How did you get here?"

"It's a long story but—"

"No, I don't mean why the police brought you here."

"Then what do you mean?"

"Do you think you belong here?"

"Oh, because I don't look like the others? I look American?"

"No, Jack."

"Then what the hell do you mean?" I wasn't irritated just confused.

"I am asking, where are you? Think back. Where did it all begin? And where are you now?"

"Oh wait. You're some kind of spy sniffing around for information, aren't you? I saw the woman in the front. You're not fooling me."

"I am not a spy. And I'm asking, where are you?" I looked at him as if he knew me and the prison seemed far off as dreams of a distant place.

"Really, I don't know how I got here. I didn't expect to be here."

"Do you remember now?"

"Yes, yes, I remember now. A long time ago, I thought it would be different. But now, it's all so ambiguous, so—blurred."

"What do you mean, Jack?"

My hand with the meat in my lap, I stopped eating and, with a daydreamy look, said, "I don't know. It's just that when I was young, I had all these ideas, things I wanted to do."

"Like what?"

"Plans. Big plans. Things I wanted to accomplish. To be. I remember starting, but then it all started to slip away, and what's so strange is that the harder I tried to get back to where I was, things just slipped further and further away. You ask, where am I? I don't know where I am. It's like I got lost somewhere along the way, and I can't find my way back."

"You said you have a family."

"Yes."

"Do they love you?"

"I think so."

"What do you mean, you think so?" He asked in a sort of analytical niceness.

"I think so; I hope they do; I don't know."

"Jack what is wrong?"

"It's just that—oh man, I don't know, I just; I don't know, I just feel like I wasn't very good." Pools of tears began to form and sat like dead water on the mantles of my eye sockets.

"Go on," said Rachid.

"Funny, but it's like you're decoding me somehow." I looked again at him expecting to see someone I knew, but he hadn't changed.

"Please continue," he encouraged.

"I mean—I'm not sure what I mean. I don't know if I was all that great of a father, a husband, or a friend. I feel like—I don't know. Like somehow I failed."

"How did you fail, Jack?"

"Sometimes I think I was too hard on the kids, so—caught up in my man-world. I wasn't always sensitive to my wife."

"Is that what they would say?"

"I don't know."

"Jack, I would guess you're a man of many accomplishments."

"Well, that's just it. I teach at a respected university in America. I have a doctorate. I've written several books; published tons of articles. Travel all over. And it's funny but many people, my family—my daughter especially—look at me and think I've done a lot. They think I've done all these things. And it's all true. But for some reason, that's not what I'm talking about."

"Our great fear is not that we failed, but that we succeeded. And no one saw it."

"You think that's it? I don't even know. It's like something inside me, and I can't seem to—ah, I can't even explain it."

"Jack, it's okay."

"No, I want to try. It's like; I don't know, I can't find the words. It's like there's some unfinished puzzle in me that I wanted to put together. But time ran out. And there's not enough time left to put it back together."

"Don't you think everyone feels like that at a certain point in life?"

"I guess. I don't know. I'm not all people. I'm just me."

"Jack, what would it take to put the puzzle together?"

"I don't even know anymore."

"Jack, not long from now the doors of this jail will open and you will be released. But I fear you still won't be free."

"I know."

"Jack, I do not think it is too late."

"It's not? It sure feels like it is." It hit me hard that I really wanted to believe him, to be told these things over and over, like the beating of fists on my chest until my heart came alive again and nothing was left of the doubts of who I am, and what I am. I was tired of the way I'm sorry for being here and wanting so much to know that my life mattered.

"Who are you, Jack?" he said. "Maybe you should start there."

"I don't know what to say."

"Do not say anything. Do you know Les Mérinides?"

"No, what's that?" I wiped tears from my face and shirt.

"It is a place. Very important to Moroccans. It's in Fez. Go there. I think you will find the answer to the question?"

Rachid walked to the other side of the room into the shadowy place, and I didn't recall seeing him again. Maybe, I thought, I had fallen asleep or the officer let him go when night sleeps. I never knew. It was all so strange, beyond the measure of a man to comprehend. But he provoked me and the brackish waters in me would not settle again.

The hard bench, no blanket, little naps, and the feces and vomit mélange wafting through my nostrils throughout the nights, ended with a man coming for me early one morning. He brought me to a small room resembling a cell and a table and some chairs were around it. My three-second squint at the piss-hole in the floor, the metal bunkbed chained to the wall, and the little sink, made me think, I was getting an upgrade. The man pulled out a chair for me to sit, and the thought of finding myself lost helplessly and indeterminately in a foreign jail encased me in invisible panic.

Soon, in walked two men: the officer who checked me in, and a man whom I'd not seen before that moment, a very clean-cut man of medium build with no hair on top, but on the sides.

The second man said, "Dr. Lockhart. I am Mr. Talal. I am a police inspector. I apologize for the conditions, but it's what we have." His tone was polite and manner cultured, but I couldn't believe we were looking at the same stars.

I said, "It's what you have? I'm sorry. There's no bed. I've barely eaten anything. I'm an American. I have rights."

Talal remained standing and said, "I am very sorry," and pulled out his cigarettes and hit the pack hard against his hand. When a cigarette didn't pop out, he stuffed a finger inside the pack and dug probingly, and the pack crinkled loudly. He dug and dug so much that I leaned forward in the hope he'd snatch one and he did. He pulled it out and I felt relieved. But rather than put it in his mouth, he stared into the half-rumpled wrapper with an inspecting eye and said, "There's no more left. Do you smoke?" And he held up the lonely cigarette, offering it to me.

"No thank you. It's yours." He slid the cigarette in his mouth, and the end of the cigarette was gnarly. Without a trashcan in the room, he crushed the wrapper and shoved it in his shirt pocket. He held the match to the cigarette end a long time like he was charring a pipe.

Then he took his first drag. "I'm sure you had sleepless nights. I'm sorry about that." I couldn't imagine how a person could inhale and talk at the same time. Then on the exhale he said, "But a man is dead. And we have many questions about other things." The cigarette smoke swirled and shot around as he shook his match dead and threw it on the concrete floor, stepping on it.

"But no one has asked me any questions; no substantive ones," I said.

"We tend to do things differently than America, Dr. Lockhart."

"What has happened to Mey? You know?"

"Yes, yes. I know. She is fine, and we have spoken to her. We understand what happened with her brother. You sure you don't want a cigarette? We can get more."

"Now look, I haven't had much to eat." Now I was getting irritated. "Is there some coffee? I need some coffee."

"We can get you some coffee." Talal nodded a go-ahead to the other officer in the room, and he began to walk out. "Now Dr. Lockhart, do you understand—"

"Oh wait," I interrupted. "Please tell the man, and my medication for my back. I need that too." Another affirmative bob of Talal's head, and soon an Americano and croissant showed up, and the bottom of my Rx bottle hit the table hard with one of those bangs that send a message. The officer who put it there lingered and looked at me with contemptuous eyes that say to you, here buddy, now shut-up. I sipped the coffee, popped a couple pills, and my sensibilities started to touch the ground.

"Dr. Lockhart," said Talal. "Do you understand why you are here?"

"The man who attacked Mey?" I asked like I wasn't sure, but really, I knew. And I sipped some more.

"The attack is unfortunate. But we have other questions."

"About what?"

From that point, I fielded questions spread randomly across everything from my birthplace of New York City to my hobbies, to repetitive questions about why I had abandoned my studies to travel cross country. Why I had been in Marrakech seemed to be Talal's main interest.

Then the two men left the room and I laid on the floor and spread my legs and arms apart. And, looking up, I saw a single lightbulb suspended from a string. Minutes passed and the string broke and the light bulb fell oddly, swaying back and forth like a pendulum. The shadows moved in strange patterns against the walls. And I saw my death.

Still laying on the floor and looking up at the ceiling, I heard the door open. At the wrong angle to see him at first, I raised my head. Walking through the door with the same urbane officer was a familiar and welcoming face. When I saw it, I reacted all the way to the heavens and back. "Omar!" I said, jumping to my feet. "Omar! Am I ever glad to see you! What is going on here?" The officer motioned me wordlessly to retake my seat and not to embrace my friend.

Omar looked over at Talal for permission to sit, and Talal said something in Arabic to him. Even pulled a chair for him to sit. And I sat also. With grave concern written across his face, Omar asked, "Jack, first, are you okay?"

"I've certainly been better. How'd you know I'm here?"

"The police found a business card from the tannery I gave you at the office. The police called me, and I came here right away."

"Wow," I said with an incredulous voice. Omar spoke and his comfort so touched me in my deepest parts that I wanted to suck it through a straw and savor each part of it.

"Jack, your hand is scraped. Have you been mistreated?" Omar looked over at Talal with the look of a mother concerned for her child. Knowing I hadn't received good attention, I couldn't figure out where the scrape had come from and didn't want to complain until I had escaped the lake of ice.

"Jack, there is some trouble." Omar stretched his arms on the table and spread his fingers wide.

"Omar, they've been asking me all sort of questions, and I've answered all of them. I asked for my rights as an American, but my complaints have gone unanswered."

Omar took hold of my arms with both of his hands. "Jack, I have spoken with the police. Now I want to ask you some questions. And please be honest, because you can be here a very long time if you do not answer honestly."

"Alright." I held my breath and felt cadaverous from head to toe.

"Did you exchange money in Marrakech; at a currency exchange in Gueliz?"

"Give me a minute, please."

"Take your time, Jack." I thought hard. But the harder I thought, the more the thought slipped from my mind, the way a wet bar of soap slips the grip the harder one squeezes.

"Wait. Yes, yes, I did," I affirmed. "Just before meeting people at an Italian restaurant."

"In Marrakech?"

"Yes. Marrakech."

"Jack, one of the banknotes you used is false." I sat in the depravity of days; the strangest mixture of pain and numbness, and at least the paradox created a distraction.

"Jack, are you with me?"

"Yes. But what are you talking about?"

"It was a forgery. Jack, it was a ten-dollar note."

Trying hard to remain anchored, I replied in shock. "That's impossible. Where on earth would I get—oh wait."

"What is it?" Omar said. All the while Talal stood perched like a vulture waiting for the body to fall.

"Good grief." I spoke now with an exclamation.

"What?" Omar's entire body froze with concern.

"The bathroom."

"What do you mean?"

"The guy outside the bathroom. In Essaouira."

"Oh Jack. You didn't—"

"He offered to exchange money because I couldn't find a place. Wait." I closed my eyes and thought it all through, deeper this time than the recesses. I remembered being there, but not the bungling. Yet there it was, shining in my eye. "I can't believe it. I just can't believe it!" I said, opening my eyes, my soul lavished now in panic.

"Jack, please remain calm." I was trying to do so, but the sense of unreality had stymied me. Like a man who reaches up and presses his hands against a pure glass sky.

"We were in Essaouira," I said painstakingly. "And—I couldn't find a place to exchange money—and—I had to use the bathroom, and—I wanted—oh no, I feel sick."

Talal listened to everything intently. When he was ready, he intervened. "Dr. Lockhart. Please remain calm. I ask you to wait here please." He leaned over and said words to Omar and the two walked out. A long time passed, and I fell asleep on the hard floor; didn't fall asleep, so much as I passed out from the overload of it all.

"Dr. Lockhart. Dr. Lockhart," I awoke to a dangling light and it hurt my eyes. I reached up to the table and, being careful not to pull it over, picked myself up with Talal's help. My eyes skimmed the room for Omar, but I didn't see him, and became worried what was coming next.

"Dr. Lockhart," Talal said. "Please sit."

Rubbing the back of my head from the hardness of the concrete floor, I said, "Where's Omar?"

"You are released to our brother. You can collect your personal things at the front."

"But where's Omar?"

"He will attend to you outside the station. I am sorry for your long delay here."

Talal started for the door, but I stopped him. "I can go? Wait. What was all this about? The bad ten-dollar bill. Is that it?"

"That is only a small part of it," he explained. "A syndicate is operating in Morocco, passing bad checks and counterfeit banknotes. The Derb Omar area in Casablanca saw a big increase in restaurants. We think they are linked to an international group. But we are convinced you were a victim. You are free to go." Bundles of candles lit in me. I wanted to know more, but something said, get-the-hell-out-of-here.

The same officer who checked me in walked me to the exit and the day appeared to me like the aurora borealis. My eyes shut tight with my first step into the marathon rays of North Africa, and I exchanged my glasses for my sunglasses and breathed deeply.

Omar came running up. "Jack. You are free. Oh, I am so happy." He patted me on the back in his usual fatherly way, but my enthusiasm failed to rise up and grab his, leaving me mystified by my detachment. All I could muster was, "It was bad enough. And I never want to go through that again."

"It's understandable. And you look very tired. Let's get you to the car."

We walked toward Omar's car, but I stopped halfway, and as I did, Omar turned back toward me. "Something wrong, Jack?"

"Omar. I want to thank-you from the bottom of my heart for your hospitality and absolutely everything you've done to teach me and to help me. You are a true friend. And you always will be. But I think I just want to go back to your place and get my things and move on."

"Oh, I'm sorry to hear that." But his look of understanding said he wouldn't try to change my mind. "But Jack, where are you going?"

"Home. Obviously. I'm going to call my wife again and grab a flight. It's time."

We returned to Omar's home for me to collect my things, and he walked me to his door. As we stood at the door Omar said, "Jack, don't you want to call the airlines?"

"I will do that. But Omar, before you say anything more, I want to apologize."

"For what?"

"For causing all of this mess."

"Oh, no, no, Jack. You didn't cause anything. Mey's brother is responsible for his actions."

"Yes, I know. But I should have told you I was going with Nesrine to talk with Mey. She asked me not to say anything."

Omar stood in front of me and placed both of his hands on my shoulder. "Jack. Don't worry. You were only trying to help. And you had no idea about the forgery ring." A warmness filled me.

"Well, that's very understanding of you."

He opened the door for me, and I looked back at him. "Omar, please tell Nesrine I'll always think of her, and her care for Mey."

"Jack, my friend, next time you're in Morocco."

"Ha! Well, hopefully they let me back in."

"I'm sure."

Chapter 17

Walking, the day was already half gone. Tinges of happiness began to form in me at the thought of calling Beth to say I'm on my way. But a thought reached up and grabbed me. Rachid. He had flayed me like a fish. What was it about that guy? Cold shivers hit me. He had shown me things about myself. Or was it that he had just asked the right questions?

He said to go to some place, I thought. But where? My short-term memory was a come-and-go affliction and it had gone once more. The heavy traffic—some preferring the wide sidewalk to the slummish via—and one old Mercedes, pumping the equivalent of the black smoke of an old iron horse into my lungs, edged me away to stand on some steps leading into a building. I stood there and thought harder. Where did he say? Ah. Les Mérinides, I said, hitting the second word forcefully over my little success.

But wait, I thought, what is Les Mérinides? A young man dressed in jeans and a pure white T-shirt and wearing a Boston Red Socks baseball cap walked by, and I said, "English?"

"Yes sir," he said, coming to a sudden halt. His smiled wide.

"Do you know what Les Mérinides is?"

"Yes." As if his smile couldn't get any bigger, it did. I just knew that meant the answer to my questions was obvious. "It's a hotel," he added. "Not far from here. Take any taxi."

"Thanks."

No way I could just hop on a plane right now anyway, I reasoned. I could sure use a place for the night. But I was unconvinced, so I sat and thought some more. But I was so tired of thinking, of trying to think, thinking through everything, as if thinking hard is the answer to everything. The days of plight were having their way with me now. I felt it. I stared into space with unplugged eyes and a dim image of atrophy was cutting the threads of what remained of me. Then the air draped me weirdly and a greater sense of myself met the air. Struggling to reach forward one last time, some indefinite energy rose within me and above the battlement and I blurted out, "Fly Jack! Just fly." And I was in a taxi to the place Rachid said to go.

Outside the pristine hotel entrance, I caught my frowzy self in the reflection of the glass and felt uneasy about walking in. But I slicked my fingers through my hair, tucked my shirt, and entered the lobby. My self-preening didn't help. The man behind the counter, a young couple walking in front of me, and an old man dressed to the T in a white suit and a red, suit pocket handkerchief reading a newspaper, craned their necks, and I felt totally insecure.

A tall man in a uniform drew near. "Reservation?" His eyes were kind, and he seemed genuinely interested in me.

"No, but I'm hoping for a single."

"Please come. See the gentleman at the desk." He pointed to the front desk.

The hotel was a pleasure to the senses like so many places I had seen. Nearby the front desk, a spacious area of orange-red chairs and mustard-colored couches, led to an elevated sitting area with a fireplace. A spectacular dining area with a retractable roof to the limitless blue housed eighteen Moorish columns glazed in mosaic tiles and lights burnished the lower spaces winter hazel. The tables were full of little festive party props and decorations, as if some celebration was soon to take place. Outside, an inviting pool of turquoise serenity rimmed by white tables and white chairs, overlooked the medina. Perfect.

No matter how deftly I tried the keycard to my room, the green light was stuck-up. Near fatigued delirium, I didn't have the strength to go back down to the front for help. Then a maid noticed me blundering. She replaced some towels on her cart and walked towards me with a look of reassurance written across her face. She stretched out her hand to take the key from me, but my hackles were up, and I insisted to keep trying. Once, twice. "You see, what's wrong with it?" I asked angrily. She gazed up at me, and only when I released the key into her hand, did she take it from me. The unlatching sound. The green light.

"Merci."

"Vous êtes les bienvenus."

I had just been cloddish and wondered what I would have been like had I been born more dexterous.

The undreamed-of view from my room subdued me. The lambent hills buffed soft: khaki patches, grassy lawns, training shrubs, and little groves of trees, evergreen in their perfect possession. Hints of winter topped a mountain far. Some sort of ruins in the distance charmed me.

Standing at the window, I thought about the woman who opened the door for me. In the background were the vast efforts of men hard at work to preserve the artifacts of maghrebi culture: in tile, in music, in art, in the environment, but who had made little effort to respect the gatekeepers of the culture. Be beautiful for us, the men say. But do not be beautiful to us.

Women had spoken to me of balancing, of living around the verges. But the objets d'art had no such struggle. I reasoned the ephemeral nature of guarding any culture should the men endanger the beau ideal: the mothers who opened this world to us. And I wondered if, after so long, the hurting of the women hurt less, or it just became more tolerable.

But then the image of Beth began to playact on the crown of my mind. Worried for her husband. How tolerable were things for her at home, knowing her husband was doing something for himself, wearing her concerns on the lapel of his consciousness.

At my window, flicks of soft radiance warmed my face, and a memory of that now starless friendship intertwined.

"Jack" Indela said, from the back seat.

"Yes."

"Tell me about your wife."

"Oh, she's pretty important to me. What do you want to know?"

"How did you meet her?" Excitement filled her voice.

"Well, I met her at an office party at the university. A friend, by the name of Karl, introduced us."

"How did you know she was the one?"

"I remember she was very funny, and I guess a woman needs a sense of humor to be around me."

"Oh, I don't think so." She tapped my shoulder gently as a sign of jest.

"When I told her I was a forester, she said she was really interested in conservation. I remember she said she hates it when forests are cleared for suburban sprawl, and the little animals have to run and are sometimes hurt by cars because they lost their homes."

"Yeah, I know something about conservation. Not as much as you. We studied environmental sociology in school. That's really why I wanted to come along. To learn."

"And I'm so glad you did."

She pulled farther forward in her seat. "Can I ask a personal question?"

"Sure."

"What is the one thing that really stood out your wife that convinced you to marry her?"

"I've asked myself a thousand times what attracted me to her. I couldn't think of a single thing that didn't. Everything about her just pulled me in."

My reality returned to me, and I breathed a lament on the windowpane and dipped my finger in the humid glaze before it faded, and wrote, J L loves B L.

Morning light woke me. No shower the night before. Still in my clothes. I must have fallen asleep through until morning, I reasoned, the dreamless night black as ink. But I didn't know the time. My watch died at 4:27 a.m. The clock on the bed stand wasn't working either. I made my way downstairs. The clock behind the front desk said 10:57 a.m. Good grief, I thought, I must have been tired. Pausing in the vestibule, I asked for the breakfast, but it was finished. The woman at the desk guided me to the breakfast area to see if something was left. But everything had been put away, and the staff was preparing lunch.

"Do you want coffee and croissant?" the woman asked me.

"Sure, that would be fine. Really, I'll take anything."

"Please sit and I will get something for you."

Moments later, a woman dressed in all white, her hair in a net and wearing a twill apron, entered the room and set more croissants before me than I could eat. She poured coffee and when I asked her to leave the canister, she looked me in the eye and time dallied. Wait, I know this woman, I said to myself. Then her rain-washed face turned hueful and turned away from me.

"Oh, I'm sorry. I didn't mean to stare. It's just that I think I know you. Oh, wait. Of course. The conference in Tunisia."

"Yes, how are you?"

"I'm sorry. I can't quite recall your name."

"Cyrine."

"Oh, yes. Cyrine."

"And sir, I forgot your name."

"Jack. Jack Lockhart."

"Yes, I recall now." Her lips peeked in a squinched up smile. "Jack. How are you?"

"I'm fine. So good to see you again." I recalled her warmly. A young Moroccan technologist whom I had met at a conference on environmental sciences in Tunisia years earlier. I remembered her bright personality and her broad shoulders like those a champion swimmer, and how her off the shoulder dress made her delts glisten in the sun. She was easygoing in ways that differentiated her from the stoic others, and the fact that we tended to sit together for meals, given her English, provided us ample time to chat.

"Why you here?" she asked.

"Long story. Maybe we can talk later. I'd like that."

"Me too."

The longer we talked, the more I became curious why she was working at the hotel. But I wasn't sure how to go about asking. "So—you still researching as a technologist?"

"Yes. But I am in transition time."

Stumped by whether that meant she was gainfully employed as a tech, I asked, "You still working for that company? I forget the name."

"The company let me go."

"Oh, I'm sorry. Can I ask what happened?"

"My boss treat me badly. And when I said 'No,' he make life hard for me, so now I am trying to find new placement somewhere. My father knows the owner of this hotel, and he give me this part-time job to help me."

"I'm sorry you lost your job." I speculated what saying no to her boss meant. But by now I had a pretty good idea. "Well, I hope you find something good," I said further. "You're talented. I remember."

"I must go now," she said. "I see you again. You can tell me why you are in Morocco."

"Okay. Take care."

I drank, but wasn't thirsty. I ate, but wasn't hungry. I wasn't feeling yet. I folded my napkin in half, then in quarters, and focused pensively on the chance meeting with Cyrine, my eyes glued to the black top of the garbage can on the far side of the room. After breakfast, I headed back toward the lobby through the long hallway, balancing a full, Styrofoam cup of coffee and looking inwardly for any justification to remain in Morocco. But each idea peeled back like an apple skin with each step I took. As well as the fact that I kept spilling. Damn! Why do I keep doing that? Alright. Gather yourself. What do you think, Jack? Ready to go home? I guess so. Calling the airlines.

I sat near the dormant fireplace off the lobby to make my reservation and call Beth. But something said, I was missing the reason I came here. The windows were large and showy, and I walked to one. Past the pool, I saw a city, but didn't recognize it at first. The man who had been reading the newspaper when I arrived was sitting in the same place and had made room for himself by throwing a couple of pillows on an adjacent chair.

Perplexed, I said, "Excuse me sir. Do you know these buildings out here?"

"That is medina, sir."

"Oh, of course. That was stupid. So stupid. Thank you." Then my fastened imagination released and, wondering if I could put my finger on Omar's place, I rushed back to the window and looked out again, and the same city I had seen not a moment earlier, now looked new to me, as if I had never seen it.

"You are a visitor to our city?" I heard behind me.

Stripping my gaze from the window slowly, I turned to the man. "Yes. Yes, I am." The man appeared to wait on me to say more as I looked for a place to sit.

"Please. Sit here, sir," he offered politely, pointing to the couch. The couch looked good for my back, and the bolster was long and thick. I tried it briefly but sitting immediately next to a stranger felt awkward.

"The chair is fine," I said. "I'll sit here. Thanks."

"I am Amal."

"Nice to meet you. My name is Jack. I'm from America."

"I thought so. Yes."

"I saw you when I arrived yesterday. You wore a white suit."

"I love white suits ever since I see Robert Redford in The Great Gatsby."

"Oh yes!" I boomed enthusiastically. "Of course. You are Gatsby."

"Ha! No. I only like the suit. I wear it for special occasion. Here. The hotel."

"And the suit matches your mustache and hair."

"Yes. What is left of it." He spoke with a chuckle as he smoothed his hand across the top of his baldness. "At seventy-five, little remains."

"What was the occasion for the suit?"

"A Fassi celebration. My granddaughter. She take her doctor degree from university. Many people, so we do here. Now I wait. My son come for me."

As he looked around for his ride, he struggled to straighten his newspaper and, slanting the paper down, he shook it hard to find the back, and with a mighty lunge of his hands in the air, the paper popped into its proper position, and he folded it backwards and read on. At some point in the middle of his machinations, I saw his red handkerchief hanging out of his shirt pocket.

"Say, I saw your handkerchief yesterday. It's beautiful; the red really stands out against the white."

"Thank-you. But is not red. Vermillion; little different." I could see he was a man of precision.

The handkerchief stung my awareness, and for some unknown reason, my mind sat up. "Do you mind if I look closer at your handkerchief?"

"Not at all. You want hold?"

"Please. If you don't mind."

He handed me the vermillion handkerchief. This reminds me of something, I thought. But what? No more than two minutes passed, and I looked up to see Amal nodding off on the couch just that fast. Thinking I could concentrate better outside, I looked at Amal, then walked to the pool area, looking back to make sure Amal hadn't noticed me leaving with his handkerchief.

In the shadows, I could feel the broad day even before I stepped into it. In the light, I held the handkerchief up, and its color was scarlet. Then the burning on my arms and the back of my neck was too much, and I walked back into the shadows. I waited for my eyes to adjust and looked again, and the handkerchief had appeared darker now, the color of crimson.

Something in the change of colors moved the sequestered memory forward onto the sill of my mind. My lungs held still. When I couldn't hold my breath any longer, I gulped oxygen and rubbed my fingers across the cramped lines of my forehead. Only when I threw my arms down at my side, resigned to defeat, did the memory shoot across my mind's eye, and I lit up. "That's it! Cyrine. Her red dress."

At the conference where I had first met Cyrine, she strolled slowly out by the pool in the full sun during breaks. She stood in the shade one day under the palms, the very day I had decided to join her. My eye had noted the light red in her dress in the shade. But the vividness was attenuated in the full sun, more like the washed-out brush of Fiorentino.

She had joined me for lunch later that same day wearing the red dress. She spoke the whole time, her voice rising and falling like a bouncing ball, and the only time she stopped talking was to take a bite. And then she would hold her left hand crooked at the wrist the way a waitress does carrying a tray of food. Then she said something that almost made me choke. A man had attacked her years earlier. She didn't go into detail, and I didn't feel at liberty to ask details. The terrible attack, she said, moved her to join an institute for human rights in Tunisia.

Is this why Rachid wanted me to come here? I wondered. To hear all of Cyrine's story? I had heard so many.

I went to look for her. Anxiety's hoofbeats pounded within my heart the closer I approached the hotel kitchen. A young man wearing the same style of apron I had seen on Cyrine exited the kitchen and was walking past me, but I stopped him. "Excuse me. Is Cyrine here?" He ran his hand through his quiff hair and motioned me to wait at the swinging doors, and he reentered the kitchen.

The same young guy and Cyrine emerged soon after, and when Cyrine saw me, her eyes widened in surprise. She rubbed her palms flat in downward strokes on her apron. "Jack. Hi. I was just working."

"Cyrine. I don't even know how to say this. But do you remember at the conference telling me that you joined a human rights group?"

"Um—yes." Her eyes were little slits now, like she had been trying hard to recall.

"Okay. Then do you also recall telling me about how that started?" My voice lowered to ask her in case she didn't want others to hear.

"Yes."

"Right. Cyrine, do you think it would be possible for you to tell me the rest of that story?"

"Why?" Her one-word answers were making me nervous.

"It's a long story. But I've been researching the way women are treated in your lands and I've spoken with many women, and I wonder if you would be willing to assist me by sharing at least some of your story."

"Can you help us, sir?" Her face was full of concern and hope, and I felt like I was holding some sort of mantle.

"I want to help."

"I agree," she said to my surprise. "Do you have questions?"

"Oh, that's great. Ah. Questions. I can write some. But really, I just want to listen to you. When can we talk?"

"I am finished now. I am happy to help you."

I looked around for a place to sit and, finding people milling here and there, didn't feel comfortable talking in case they heard us. "Say, why don't we walk out to the pool area?"

"Fine."

We found some comfortable chairs around a table with a view endless in its perfection.

"Cyrine," I said. "Why don't you just tell me what happened, and I will take some notes if you don't mind."

"That's fine."

"Go ahead."

"When I was young, I lived with my mom and her husband. His treatment with me was mostly cruel and I get beaten every day. My mother was cheating on him a lot, and I could see my mom with other men. On the day of days, they decided to divorce. I go with my mom to a neighborhood of popular neighborhoods. My mother was a cleaner at a school. I am studying in high school. One day my mother had no money to pay the housekeeper. We had a neighbor that everyone was afraid of. His name is Hassan, aged between forty and forty-five years. I'll never forget that face."

"What did he look like?"

"Brown, brown hair. White. Medium, sturdy body."

"Why won't you forget his face?"

"You'll know soon. He suggested we share his house with only two rooms. My mother liked the idea, but I didn't agree. After we moved with him, he approached my mother very much. Every night a party of alcohol and drugs. He impressed me and wanted to marry me, but I did not agree. And as usual, mom with him in everything. One night he brought some kind of medicine and gave it to my mother. When she took one, she slept three days."

"She took the medication?"

"Yes. Then on the first night he grabbed me by force and entered me into the second room. He started beating me. Take off my clothes. I tried to resist but he brought a knife and put it next to me. He said you would die tonight if you refused. My mom is asleep. Because of those narcotic pills."

"You mean he said you will die if you refuse?"

"Yes. If I refuse sex, I will die. Me or my mother. Every night I was severely beaten and every night forced me to sleep with him."

"Oh! This lasted a long time. How long?"

"That lasted eight months."

"You were held prisoner for eight months? Why didn't you go away?"

"I didn't know anyone who was sixteen years old."

"Wait, you were sixteen?"

"Yes. After that, my mother took advantage of his lack of attention and we ran away." My mind went blank for a moment as I imagined something like that happening to my own daughter. "Sir?"

"Um—so he raped you?"

"Yes. Yes."

"Did you tell your mother; police?"

"My mother, she agree."

"What do you mean, she agreed?"

"My mom was consenting to what he did to me." Such a thought had been too monstrous, and I couldn't find a place for it in my mind.

"What? You mother agreed?"

"Yes." She looked so sad now. But I felt I had to go on.

"Okay. If I may, please. This brings questions."

But before I could ask more, she jumped ahead with another thought. "But after months he changed with us."

"I'm sorry, I don't understand?"

"He said, he send men to my mother until you bring him money. We became afraid of him a lot."

"Oh, you mean he threatened to send men to hurt your mother unless you gave him money?"

"Yes. When I had money for him, he seemed happy, and when I didn't have money, the situation changed." Now I had come to understand why her mother had agreed to the arrangement. It was all under threat of violence.

"Okay, now big question," I said.

"He was a psychopath," she interposed once more.

"Yeah, I agree. Now, you suffered a terrible nightmare. But a few American women have suffered like you. Can you think of any reasons that distinguish your terrible experience?"

"People's beliefs play a big role in this. The beliefs in our culture specifically protects men very much."

"Okay, how did your culture protect this man?"

"They say a man always remains a man. He has right over woman. But shame only haunts me."

"What does that mean? He has right over woman?"

"We live by the values of the people because it is a man who can start a new life, but I will be a pariah. I learned this."

"You can be a pariah in the community. So, you are blamed?"

"Yes. He had a lot of knowledge of the government, so I was afraid of the police and I didn't go to them."

"He worked for the government?"

"No, he didn't work there, but he had a lot of friends from them. His threats continued even after we escaped, and he went after us."

"One woman I talked to said that women who have sex before marriage are not considered pure."

"I'm pure."

"I thought it was rape? No?"

"The rape took place in a background manner."

"You mean against your will? I do not understand 'background manner.' What is rape in background manner? I'm trying to understand why you are a pariah."

"He slept with me not in the right way. Sodomy."

"Oh," I said in embarrassment. "Okay, so why are you a pariah?"

"I would have been a pariah if I went to the law. It was going to be a big scandal."

"Ah, I got it."

"We are a people who do not care about the truth."

"Wow." I was amazed at her candor and insight.

"We believe what we hear."

"You mean that people will believe him, not you, if a scandal were to erupt?"

"Yes."

"We are a people who do not care about the truth," she said, again.

"Incredible statement. Can you expand?"

"One of the simplest things. I will forget about marriage. Who will accept me?"

"I understand."

"Others sympathize with you, but do not want me as a wife for their son."

"Yes, I heard something like this. Men in your lands only want virgins."

"But they have many women."

"True," I acknowledged in disgust. "Cyrine. I think you have said enough. Let me say, you did nothing wrong. You should not feel shame. But I understand your feelings."

"My advice to every girl who was subjected to violence and rape is to face the truth and take her right. If we will not defend ourselves, no one will defend us. I am a new person, and I do not feel ashamed of something that was against my will."

"I am so sorry, dear. You are a marvelous young woman."

"I am now stronger. I hope to return to those difficult days and face it with such strength."

"I'm sure you will."

"Mr. Jack. I must go now. My ride come."

We stood together. "Cyrine, I can't thank you enough for telling me these things. I hope the best for you."

"Thank you, Mr. Jack. My Lord keeps you."

She was leaving when I stopped her. "Cyrine."

"Yes."

"The greatest gift a person can find is to be wrapped in the strong arms of unconditional love. I hope that for you."

"And for you."

A light breeze picked up across the pool, and I was mad at it, the shelterless exposure interfering with my concentrated effort to understand the horror I had just heard. But there was no understanding because understanding is human, and what Cyrine suffered was not. Just as soon as the rushes came, they calmed.

I was alone now, staring into the concrete. As if a trapdoor in reality had opened, I felt myself fall through to the wasteland of forgetfulness. Neither did I think of Morocco, nor of abuse, nor of culture, nor of Indela, nor even of myself. Then faintly at first, seemingly from the cloudlessness, I heard the question again, just as I heard it in the jail.

"Who are you, Jack?"

I lifted my head and looked heavenward. It came again, sharper this time, and it pierced me. Anger mounted. I shouted out, "What? What do you want from me?"

In the blue sky and in the white sky, a small bird flew skillfully, and I could not take my eyes away. She dipped and slopped her wings and made a circle. And I watched as the bird flew to my left over by the ruins, and when I saw the ruins, the bird vanished from my sight. Against the spectral blue and orange scatterings in the lower parts of the sky, the old, ruddy places effused a golden nimbus, and I saw myself differently in its glow.

Drenched in anticipation that someone could tell me about the remains, I broke my fixation, and I ran back inside the lobby. Inside, a young man was helping Amal to his feet.

"Amal, looks like you fell asleep," I said.

"Yes, I did. This is my son, Nadim."

"Nice to meet you," I said.

Nadim was helping his father put on his light coat. "The pleasure is all mine," he said, looking up at me.

"Amal," I said. "Before you leave. Can I please ask? What are those ruins outside and halfway down the hill?"

Even though I had asked Amal, Nadim answered. "That is al-Qula. The Marinids conquered this area centuries ago and later built a palace and a mosque overlooking the heart of the old city. All that is left of the ancient necropolis are those old two arched tombs. Today it is called the Hill of the Marinids."

"The Marinids? You mean Les Mérinides?"

"Yes. It is the same."

I stood in stark alarm. "I can't believe it. That's it. Rachid didn't want me to come to the hotel. He wanted me to go to the tombs. I'm in the wrong place!"

"The wrong place?" said Amal.

Knowing I had to get there immediately, I asked, "Amal, how do I get to the tombs?"

Amal looked to his son as if for an answer. "I am not sure," Nadim said, "but the man at the desk, he can guide you."

"Amal, it's been a great pleasure meeting you. Nadim, you also." I spoke in a rush and was certain they were wondering what might be the matter. The front desk in front of me, I stopped running on a dime and turned back. "Oh, I forgot. And here's your handkerchief." I placed the handkerchief back in Amal's shirt pocket and waved a final farewell.

The man at the desk gave me directions to the tombs and said, "You should go before sunset. You can watch—"

"Thank you," I interrupted, and ran out of the hotel.

The upward path to the tombs was ahead of me now. The crispness of the air together with the brightness created a sensation of cold heat, and my skin had an itchy feel. Step after step, my hamstrings felt drugged. My chin to my chest, I yanked my thighs up and out before me, my arms swinging. But I lost my balance and fell to my hands and knees, exhausted. Unexpectedly, a man appeared to help me to my feet. He reached his hand and when our eyes met, I was taken aback. For it was then that I saw compassion's face, and the dolor of days suspended in his condolent eyes. I thanked him and walked several more yards. But when I turned back to find him, he had disappeared from sight.

The rough-hewed walls of ochre and brunneous grew tall as I approached the most preserved tomb. My hand rubbed the wall as I entered, and the dust-flow kicked up. The darkness scarfed my eyes in halos of peaceful white, and my breathing chafed in the musty air. I knelt, keeping my spine straight. Memories, voices, stories—in the end had only served to raise more questions. The pressure built, and with it, my anger. I lifted my voice, not caring who heard me.

I need to say it out loud. I need to say it once. I need to say it to you. Why? Why evil? My body stretched to the limits; I think I've found an atheism that works. It works because it answers everything. It's not an atheism birthed in arrogance, imagining it's too sophisticated for you. It's born out of sorrow for those stepped on by some cosmic bully. It is hard-won atheism forged on the field of love's grief out of the utter agony of irresolvable injustice.

I told Indela to pray like the thirsty grass. But prayers are rarely answered. They say God will intervene. But neither in their lifetimes nor in mine. How long can we sit in the silent waiting of affliction for the dawn? How long can we absolve horror in the thought that God has a plan? All we can do is ask, is there purpose in the universe? But how long can we pretend meaning when we can't even find the starting line?

And yet the why keeps finding us. Like a splinter stuck under the skin. Or an innate awareness of some inscrutable mystery. I keep asking why because the women are living in the margins. I ask why because, like some unseen outrage, evil assaults all of us. The furtive, fierce hug of a son around his mother's neck; an unexpected wave washing ashore on a summer's day that makes us laugh as we run from it; the endlessly funny ways of dogs, are as if they never were when evil knocks.

I always believed in fairness. But what is fair in the madness of suffering? I can't find a connectivity that brings good in the end. And I can't accept the quick and easy fallen world; that's only to grant our indifference a place in the world.

But am I any better? Evil is unintelligible. But there's also some dark presence in me that drives my own thoughts, my own words, my own actions. Evil is out there. But it's also in me. I feel it. Maybe the greatest absurdity, then, isn't that I'm offended by the actions of others. But that I've been so blind to my own.

Maybe that's it. Maybe you've given evil a place in your world long enough for me to find you. Because if you dealt with the evil out there, then you would be forced to bring an end to the evil in me. And that would be the end of me. But I haven't been ready for you. Maybe you're there after all. So here I am. What I am supposed to see?

Pale tints of orange bathed the hill faces and summoned the people for the gloaming. Tilting my weight forward on my knees, I removed my wallet. The light of twilight sidling just enough now so that I could see well, I removed some old photos crinkled around the edges, and they gladdened me. "There she is," I said out loud. "My wife of many years." And the tears rolled again; tears no more of sadness, but of joy. "And my daughter loves me more each day; she always shows it. And my son, oh, my son, he's everything I had ever hoped for. And my friends at the university; how much they all mean to me."

Then the great disk peered brilliantly beneath the brim of the tomb and light flooded the place of death. And when it did, my soul came alive, and I cried and laughed a great circular fit. I stood and walked to the entrance of the tomb. The vibrant city purring and humming. Calls to Maghrib prayers bounding around the city in choral unison. And I saw myself. In a tomb. It had all become clear now. Life before me. Death behind me. And I had a choice.

To this moment, my questions had been so intellectual. Standards for society, freedom, and justice, caused me to pause enquiringly along my journey. My driving question was, why the women suffer such evil. Looking out over the old city, all my uncertainties shadowed behind the one question I hadn't considered. Who? Is there someone greater than all of it and who alone makes sense of it? I understood now. For he met me there. And all things had become new for me. And I came to see. Evil isn't answered. It was overcome.

In courage, no more in fear or questioning, I stepped out of the sepulcher and called her.

"Hey," she answered.

"Beth?"

"Yes."

"I'm coming home." Air hooked in her throat, and in mine, and the momentary silence between us was filled with triumph.

"I'll leave the light on," she said.

The day washed clean. And I'll never forget how the hushing of mystic night blanketed the old city first, leaving the sepulcher mound in a burst of final daylight.

And I saw with my soul and not my eyes.

Made in the USA
Columbia, SC
17 September 2022

67486577R00143